The Convict's Wife

Libby Ashworth was born and raised in Lancashire, where she can trace her own family history back to the Middle Ages and many generations of which worked themselves in the Lancashire mills. It was while researching her family history that she realised there were so many stories about ordinary working people that she wanted to tell.

The Convict's Wife

LIBBY ASHWORTH

1C CANELO

First published in the United Kingdom in 2022 by

Canelo
Unit 9, 5th Floor
Cargo Works, 1–2 Hatfields
London, SE1 9PG
United Kingdom

A CIP catalogue record for this book is available from the British Library.

Print ISBN 978 1 80032 761 0
Ebook ISBN 978 1 80032 762 7

Look for more great books at www.canelo.co

Printed and bound in Great Britain by Clays Ltd, Elcograf S.p.A.

1

To all the wives who were left behind.

Chapter One

Bolton 1812

Molly heard the distant chime of the church clock. It was midnight now and she was worried. Thomas had been gone since just after tea, setting out with his father as dusk began to fall, to go to a weavers' meeting up on the moors. She'd expected them to be back long since, but none of the men had come home and Molly knew that something was very wrong.

She went to the window, where she'd left a candle burning on the sill. All the cottages that were clustered around the fold had candles burning too. No one had closed their curtains and hers wasn't the only face that was peering out into the dark, looking and listening for the return of their menfolk.

Her little daughter, Annie, was fed and settled in her crib, and although Molly was reluctant to disturb the sleeping baby, she couldn't sit alone for a moment longer. The silence was making her desperate.

Annie whimpered when Molly picked her up and tucked the blanket around her. It was the middle of April and the nights were still very cold. She would never have taken her out into the night air normally, but she didn't know what else to do. She knew that her mother-in-law, Ellen, would have come to her if she could, but she was in a lot of pain after wrenching her back and couldn't walk far without leaning on the stick that her husband had whittled for her. She must be anxious too, thought Molly as she took her shawl from the peg by the door and went out.

Ellen and John Holden lived at the far end of the fold. When Molly reached their house and pushed the door, it held fast and she waited as she heard Ellen come limping across the parlour and turn the key. She must be very frightened to have locked up, thought Molly as she shifted the weight of the baby in her arms and called, 'It's only me.'

'Come in, lass,' Ellen said. She didn't need to ask why Molly had come.

'Where are they?' asked Molly.

Ellen shook her head. 'I'm right worried,' she admitted. 'They should have been home by now.'

Molly could see that she was close to tears. She reached out and put a hand on the other woman's arm to comfort her, but she was in need of comfort herself. She'd hoped that Ellen might say something that would reassure her, but her distress only made things worse.

'I wish they'd never gone,' said Ellen.

'I thought it were safe enough,' Molly told her, wondering if she should have tried harder to persuade Thomas not to go. 'Jack Fisher said that him and Joseph Lomax had gone out walking on Deane Moor a couple of nights ago but hadn't seen any sign of a secret meeting. I thought all this talk about General Ludd was just a rumour. I thought they'd be back within an hour or so. But something's delayed them. I hope they've come to no harm.'

'Aye, me an' all.' Ellen went back to her chair by the hearth and sat down with a grimace.

'Shall I make us a cup of tea?' asked Molly. The kettle was already on the hob and she picked up a cloth to lift it by the metal handle to check how much water was in it.

'Aye, put a pot to brew,' said Ellen. 'They'll likely be back soon.'

Molly put the baby on her grandmother's lap, then spooned tea into the pot and poured boiling water over the leaves. She set it to brew as she fetched cups and milk.

As she put them on the table she heard footsteps and she and Ellen glanced hopefully at one another. The first set passed by and went down the fold but the second had a familiarity about them and sure enough, they stopped at the door and John Holden came in. He looked grim and he was alone.

'Where's Thomas?' Molly asked him.

'He's been arrested,' he said quietly.

'Arrested? What for?' Molly tried to make sense of what her father-in-law was telling her.

John pulled off his cap and came over to the fire to warm his hands. Molly stared at him. He seemed unable to speak. He sank onto his chair and stared at the flames for a moment before looking up.

'We went up past Sweet Green, towards the Rope Walk,' he told them as Molly poured the tea and handed him a cup. 'We met up with some others going the same way – Jack Fisher was one of them. When we got near to the field we could see that there were about fifty or sixty men gathered. Someone approached us. He had his face blackened so's no one would know him, but there were summat familiar about him and when he spoke I were left in no doubt. It were Isaac Crompton.'

Molly shuddered at the name.

'Crompton went on ahead to ask if we could be admitted to the meeting.' He paused to take a drink of his tea and put the cup down on the hearth with a trembling hand. 'Some other men came up behind us. They gave the password "Church Steeple" and were allowed through. Then Crompton came back to tell us we were admitted and we went in. This chap who seemed to be in charge – I didn't know him – said that all those who were new had to come forward, so we went and stood near him. He told us that we were to say nowt about the meetings because he would have no truck with babblers – folk who'd tell all to Colonel Fletcher for a couple of pounds in their hand. He said as he knew we'd come up from Hag End and Lever Lane and he hoped we weren't babblers, else the meetings would be jeopardised and we'd all end up being transported.'

The word struck Molly like a blow to the stomach. 'Transported,' she repeated. 'Not Thomas?' She could feel her heart pounding and she was shaking. Surely they wouldn't send Thomas away to the other side of the world? He'd done nothing wrong.

'I don't know, lass,' said John. 'It were exciting at first,' he admitted. 'There were such an atmosphere of hope and determination. The man told us that the meetings were being held to destroy the present wickedness that reigns in this country. And after that another man came forward with a scarf covering his face and he had a book – I don't know if it were a bible or not – and we were told to put a hand on it and swear an oath that we would reveal nothing about what we'd seen and heard.' He paused and seemed to shiver, shaking his head as he continued his story. 'We hadn't even had time to finish the words when a cry went up that the Rope Walk were afire. It took hold quickly with it being a thatched roof and after only a few minutes, the place was lit up bright and folk took fright and ran. Thomas and I began to make our way back to the path. We thought we were safe enough, but then we heard horsemen coming up. At first we thought they were going to put out the fire, but then we saw they were members of Fletcher's militia. We tried to dodge behind some gorse so they wouldn't see us, but the flames were lighting up the sky and they'd already caught sight of Thomas…' He pulled a rag from his pocket and blew his nose. 'I'm sorry,' he said. 'There were nowt I could do to stop 'em. They seized him by the arms and took him away.'

'Where to?' asked Molly, horrified by the story.

'To Bolton gaol, probably. But he'll be sent up to Lancaster for trial if Fletcher finds any evidence against him.'

'But there can't be any evidence!' protested Ellen. 'He's done nothing wrong. And tha said tha wasn't even at t' meeting when t' militia came.'

'Aye, that's right,' replied John. 'All we were doin' was walkin' home, mindin' our own business. But I doubt Fletcher'll see it like that.'

'Tha'll have to go to his house and make him see as our Thomas is innocent!' Ellen told him.

'Aye. I will,' agreed John. 'I'll go first thing in the morning. Catch him early before he goes to his work.'

'I'll come with thee,' said Molly. 'Will tha be able to mind Annie?' she asked Ellen, hoping her mother-in-law would be able to manage.

'Nay,' said her mother-in-law. 'Take t' child with thee. He has young childer of his own and 'appen it'll soften his heart if he sees thee with a little 'un.'

Ellen insisted that Molly stay the night with them rather than be on her own with the baby, and she was easily persuaded. They put Annie in a drawer, taken from the chest in the back bedroom, and Molly slept in the bed that had belonged to Thomas until they were wed. It helped her to feel closer to him as she lay awake, waiting for the dawn so that they could go to plead with Colonel Fletcher for his release.

Ellen tapped on her door early.

'I'm awake,' she called. 'I'm feeding Annie. I'll be down shortly.'

'I'll get the kettle on,' said Ellen and Molly heard her going down the stairs, one step at a time.

As soon as Annie stopped suckling she changed the baby's nappy and took her down the stairs. Ellen had some breakfast ready – oatmeal and a pot of tea. Her father-in-law was eating his, blowing on the porridge and treacle to cool each mouthful.

Molly quickly washed her face in cold water in the back kitchen and tidied her hair. She wished that there was time to go home and put on a clean apron, but it would make them late.

'Get summat inside thee and we'll be on our way,' said John and Molly ate a few hasty mouthfuls and took a gulp of the strong tea before they left.

John Holden walked quickly with his long stride when they got outside, but Molly didn't urge him to slow down. She trotted to catch him up every time she was left behind, little Annie jogging in her arms. She knew it was important to reach the Hollins early if they were to have any chance of speaking to Colonel Fletcher before he left for his colliery office.

The big house was on the main road. Its chimneys rose above the slate-tiled roof and billowed smoke into the morning air. They went in through the front wrought-iron gate and closed it behind them.

'Shouldn't we go around the back?' she asked as John marched up to the front door.

'Why should we?' he replied. 'I'm not a tradesman.'

Molly hung back a little as he stepped up to the porch and rang the bell. She was afraid that they would be sent away without Colonel Fletcher even agreeing to speak to them.

The door opened and a maid in a white cap stared at them.

'I've come to see Colonel Fletcher,' John told her.

'Do you have an appointment?'

'No, but it's on a matter of some urgency. Tell him that John Holden needs to speak with him.'

The maid looked dubious but asked them to wait whilst she went to enquire if the colonel was available. Molly wasn't hopeful and was surprised when the maid returned and asked them to step into the hall.

Annie, who'd been sleeping, chose that moment to wake and start to cry and Molly tried to hush her as the cries rang around. The maid frowned and Molly jogged the child on her shoulder, hoping that she wouldn't be sick over her. It wouldn't be an auspicious start to the interview.

She was glancing around at the closed oak doors that led off the hall when one opened and Colonel Fletcher came out, wiping his mouth on a napkin as if he'd been disturbed at his breakfast. He was a man a little past middle age, with a paunch and wavy white hair, brushed back from his whisker-clad face. He frowned at the sight and the sound of them.

'What do you want?' he asked.

'I'm John Holden,' said her father-in-law, holding out a hand which the colonel chose to ignore. 'I'm Thomas Holden's father. Some of your men arrested him yesterday as we were making our way home after a stroll on the moor. I've come to explain that he's done nowt wrong and to ask you to release him from wherever tha's holding him.'

Colonel Fletcher stared at him as if he couldn't believe what he was hearing. Then he turned to Molly. 'Can you not keep that child quiet?' he demanded.

'I'm sorry,' she told him. 'She's only a baby. I'm Thomas's wife and I'm right worried about him. He's a good man. He's done nowt wrong.'

'Well I have to beg to differ,' the colonel told them. 'I have a reliable witness who says that your husband took an illegal oath at a secret Luddite meeting. That's a very serious matter,' he told her. 'So you will find your husband in the prison at Lancaster where he was sent early this morning.'

'But that's not true!' said John. 'We were just walking home!'

'As I told you, I have a reliable witness who says otherwise. Now, I must ask you to leave my house. I've been gracious enough to speak to you and inform you of the whereabouts of your relative. There is nothing more to discuss. Good morning! Show them out, Betsie,' he said to the maid as he turned away to resume his breakfast in the morning room from where the aroma of fried bacon and eggs crept out through the door to taunt them.

'This way,' said the maid, holding open the front door.

8

Molly glanced at her father-in-law who shook his head and made his way out. She followed him down the steps onto the drive and the door thudded shut behind them.

'What do we do now?' she asked, feeling bewildered and helpless at the turn of events.

'I'll go to Lancaster,' John promised her. 'I'll make sure that he's released.'

'I'll come with thee!' said Molly, thinking that she must do everything she could to help Thomas. She couldn't bear to think of him confined in some dark, damp cellar, probably with only rats as bedfellows.

'Nay lass, it's too far for thee to walk with the baby. Stop here with Mother and I'll send word as soon as there's any news.'

When they got home, Ellen wept when they told her what Colonel Fletcher had said.

'Lancaster? Why send him so far away from home?' she asked.

'Fletcher's got it in for ordinary workin' men,' complained John. 'He's afraid we'll turn on him and there'll be a revolution like there was in France. He even said he has a witness that Thomas took an oath. But he's bluffing. I'm sure of it. They'll have to let Thomas go if there's no evidence against him.'

Feeling slightly more hopeful at John's words, Molly made up a package with oatcakes and a little cheese for him to eat on the journey that would take him all day. John changed into his best clothes and Ellen counted out some of the money that they had put by and bid him to be careful with it.

'God go with thee,' she told him as she kissed him. 'Bring our Thomas home safely.'

'I shall,' he promised. 'If it's within my power then I shall.'

Molly stood at the door to watch him go. She and Ellen waited until he turned the corner with a last wave and disappeared from their view. Tears welled in Molly's eyes as they went back inside. All she wanted was to see her husband again and tell him that she loved him.

Chapter Two

Thomas walked around and around the filthy yard at Lancaster Gaol. The walls were high, built from grey stone, made even greyer by the smoke from the chimneys, and so high that they almost prevented any daylight from falling into the space below. The yard was mostly in shadow, except for one corner where a small patch of afternoon sunlight was receding by the minute. In another half hour it would be totally gone. Thomas shivered. Although it was April, the weather was still cold and there was little promise of spring in the dank air.

His perambulations were interrupted by a turnkey who came to tell him that he had a visitor. He hurried eagerly inside. Part of him hoped that Molly had come. He was desperate to see her. But part of him hoped she hadn't. He didn't want her to see him in this place.

When the turnkey unlocked the door, Thomas saw his father waiting for him.

'Tom!' His father clutched him in a fierce embrace and Thomas began to cry. When he'd been a child he had always trusted him to make things right, but he wasn't sure that it was within his power to make this right.

'I'm sorry,' said his father. 'There was nothing I could do when they seized thee. If I'd chased after thee they'd have arrested me an' all. How's tha doin'?' he asked. 'Hast tha been fed?'

'Aye, but I've used up what money I had with me,' Thomas told him. 'They'll not give me any more until I can pay for it. And there'll be the gaol fees too. There's some in here as have been found innocent, but they'll not be released until they can pay the two pounds and fifteen shillings.'

'I've brought some money with me,' said his father, handing him five shillings. 'That should keep thee going for now. Don't fret,' he continued, gripping Thomas by the shoulders. 'I'll get more. The Friendly Society might help us out, or else I'll sell my loom.'

'No, don't do that,' protested Thomas. 'Sell mine if needs be, but don't put thyself out o' work on my account.'

'I feel it were my fault,' his father admitted. 'We shouldn't have gone. I'd never have gone myself, let alone taken thee with me, if I'd known it would come to this.'

'I'm not a child,' said Thomas, feeling more like a helpless child than he ever had. 'I took my own decision to go. I thought it were safe enough, but now that other folk have been found guilty I think it were a trap.'

His father hesitated and Thomas could see that he had bad news.

'What is it?' he asked.

'I went to see Colonel Fletcher. Molly came an' all, with the child, to plead thy case. He told us as there were a witness who swore he'd been there when tha took an oath.'

Thomas stared at him. It wasn't the news he'd been hoping for.

'Who?' he asked.

'He never said.'

'Who'd do that?' asked Thomas, but he already had the answer. 'Isaac Crompton,' he said, remembering how uncomfortable he'd felt when he saw him at the meeting.

'Fletcher never named him.'

'Who else could it be? I should have known when I saw him there that he were up to no good. I know he hates me. He swore he'd have his revenge, but I never thought he'd do owt like this.'

'Tha doesn't know it were him,' said his father. 'Fletcher might just be bluffing. And that trouble's all in t' past now.'

'Not that long in the past,' said Thomas, remembering the fight on the moor when he'd knocked Crompton to the ground.

'I doubt he'd do this. I've known him all his life and his father an' all. They're weavers like us. They'd not betray their own.'

Thomas wasn't so sure. There was a lot of bad feeling between him and Isaac. Isaac had been walking out with Molly and had been set on asking her to marry him when Molly had changed her mind and decided that she wanted to be with him instead. Isaac had accused him of stealing her and had challenged him to a fight, thinking that he was sure to win. Thomas had never been much of a one for his fists, but his blood had been up that day. He'd been determined to defend Molly's honour and the punch had been a lucky one that had struck Isaac square on the jaw and felled him. No one had been more surprised than Thomas. He'd walked away as Isaac lay there cursing him and after a few weeks he and Molly had had the banns read at the parish church. He'd thought it was all in the past. But now he wasn't so sure.

'Dost know when tha'll be brought to trial?' asked his father.

Thomas shook his head. 'They tell us nowt,' he replied. 'But I just want it to be over with. Will tha stay? In Lancaster?' he asked his father. 'I'd be glad to have thee near.'

'Aye. I'll stay if I can get some cheap lodgings,' he promised. 'And I'll get a letter written to thy mother and thy wife to let 'em know that tha's well. I'm sure it'll be a verdict of not guilty,' his father told him.

Thomas nodded. He thought he was only saying it to cheer him and keep his spirits up. Now that he suspected Isaac Crompton might give evidence against him he was not so hopeful that he would soon be on his way home. And he kept thinking about Molly and his little baby, Annie. How on earth would they manage if he was found guilty?

Chapter Three

Molly woke and reached out a hand for Thomas. He wasn't there. His half of the bed was cold and empty and she felt the tears brim in her eyes again as she remembered that he was still in the gaol at Lancaster. All she wanted was to hear him come whistling down the lane and call her name as he came up the steps to the door, but the heavy feeling in the pit of her stomach taunted her with the idea that it might be a very long time before that happened.

She heard Annie begin to whimper and she unlaced her cotton nightgown, settling the baby to her breast as she leaned back on the bolster. Through a gap in the curtains she could see the sun shining. It was almost the end of May and it looked as if the summer had finally decided to put in an appearance. It would normally have filled her with happiness, but she felt that nothing would ever make her happy again until Thomas was safely home.

Molly looked down at the baby. Her little cap had come off and her dark hair grew in a circular whorl around her head. Thomas had been so thrilled with her when she was born. He doted on her; nothing was too good for his little Annie and it was because he was determined to provide for them that he'd gone to that meeting. He was just curious, he'd told her. He wanted to find out what could be done to improve trade and increase the price he was paid for the quilts he wove. He didn't want trouble.

He just wanted to work hard and put food on the table for his family. Surely it wasn't too much to ask?

When she was washed and dressed she took Annie up to Ellen's house. It was six weeks since John had gone to Lancaster and in all that time they'd had only one letter to say that Thomas was well and awaiting his trial. Every day since then, Molly had left the baby with her mother-in-law and walked down to Bolton to see if another letter had come for them and every day she'd trudged sadly home with no news.

Ellen looked tired, thought Molly when she went in. Her mother-in-law was still in pain, but refused to waste money on the doctor, saying that it must be saved for Thomas. They'd sent more when John had written but there'd been no word that it had been received and Molly hoped it hadn't gone missing or been stolen.

'Will tha be all right?' she asked, as she settled Annie into the drawer. 'She's been fed and changed, so she should sleep until I get back.'

'Aye, get along,' said Ellen, 'and let's hope as there's some good news waiting for us today.'

Molly nodded. She could see how sad Ellen was. Thomas was her only living child and Molly knew that she thought the world of him.

Molly walked the familiar route down the road towards the outskirts of Bolton. She prayed that a letter would be waiting for her, but she dreaded to consider what tidings it might bring. She knew that the gentry were determined to stamp out any trace of the Luddites and she was frightened that her husband might be found guilty if Isaac

Crompton gave evidence against him. She shivered again at the thought of him. She hated him.

She hadn't always felt like that about Isaac. Once, she'd thought that she was in love with him; she'd even considered marrying him. But that was before she'd met Thomas, and before she'd seen a different side to Isaac's character.

She couldn't recall the first time she'd met Isaac Crompton. They hadn't been childhood friends, or sweethearts, or anything like that. Isaac was about eight or nine years older and so he'd always seemed a grown-up to her. Sometimes she'd gone with her sister, Nancy, to watch the local lads play football and Isaac had always been the goalkeeper. He was tall and had filled the goal with a menacing presence, defying any of the opposition strikers to even try to get the ball past him.

Molly had thought he was wonderful, but looking back now she could see that it had only been a young lass's fancy. She'd not known what he was really like.

It must have been then that he'd first noticed her, because he'd approached them one Sunday afternoon when the game was over and asked them their names. Nancy had come over all shy and tongue-tied. Being older, she'd thought that Isaac was interested in her, but it soon became clear that it was Molly he found attractive.

At first Isaac had been very kind to her, especially when her widowed mother fell ill and died. He'd helped her and Nancy to make the arrangements for the funeral and burial, telling them not to concern themselves, that he would deal with everything. Molly had been grateful. She'd needed the support, but little by little Isaac's care had turned into something else. He didn't like her seeing friends and said that he loved her so much that he wanted her to be with him all the time. But Molly had found it too restricting. She liked her freedom and she needed to spend time with Nancy, who had taken their mother's death very hard. But if Isaac came around to the house and she wasn't there he would be angry and say that she mustn't go off without telling him because he needed to know where she was. When she asked him why, he said it was because he was worried about her and concerned for her safety, but Molly grew tired of it and decided to tell him that she didn't want to walk out with him any more.

'What dost tha mean?' he'd asked when she'd gathered the courage to break it off with him. She'd been dreading how he would react and had purposely chosen a time when Nancy was at home to tell him.

'I don't want to see thee any more,' she'd said, hoping that he wasn't going to be too angry.

'Hast tha got another chap?' he'd demanded.

'No.' She'd shaken her head, but it had been a lie and he'd seen through it.

'Who is it?' he'd demanded, and when she hadn't replied, he'd rounded on Nancy. 'Who is it?' he'd shouted at her, making her flinch in the chair where she sat with her sewing in her hands – as if a small sharp needle would offer her protection from him.

'Thomas Holden has asked me to go to the Wakes festival with him,' Molly had said. There'd been no reason for her not to be truthful. Even though she'd sometimes thought Isaac was going to raise the matter of marriage, he never had. She'd promised him nothing.

'What dost tha want to be keepin' company with 'im for?' Isaac had growled.

'I can go with who I choose,' she'd told him. 'Tha's no hold over me. It's not like we're promised or owt.'

'Tha's an ungrateful lass,' he'd said. 'And after everything I've done for thee – for both of thee. Tha should be ashamed to treat me like this. And tha'll be sorry,' he'd warned, pointing his finger at them both. But then he'd gone out and slammed the door behind him, and Molly had let out a breath and sunk down onto the chair, trembling. She'd just hoped that they'd seen the last of him.

The next day Thomas had called at the house and they'd gone to the Wakes together, following the cart piled high with fresh rushes to cover the cold stone church floor. Thomas was her own age. He was a quiet and serious sort of lad who hadn't had much to do with lasses before, but Molly liked him because he was so different from Isaac. He didn't have the same charming ways, but she'd had enough of the sweet-talking because she'd learned that it was meaningless. She wanted someone who would treat her with some respect.

As they'd reached the brow of the hill, hot and laughing from helping to push the cart up the last steep slope, she'd been dismayed to see Isaac Crompton making his way towards them with a face that meant he'd probably had more than one beer and was set on making trouble.

'Oy!' he'd shouted, approaching them unsteadily. 'I'm talkin' to thee, Thomas Holden! That's my lass. Thee stay away from her!'

Although Molly had half-expected Thomas to turn and flee, she'd been impressed by the way he'd stood his ground.

'She doesn't belong to thee,' he'd told Isaac.

'I'm tellin thee she does! And I'm tellin' thee to stop away from her, unless tha wants my fist in thy face!' Isaac had raised his arms in a challenge. 'Come on then,' he'd taunted. 'If tha wants her, then fight me for her, tha soft lad!'

'Don't.' Molly had put her hand on Thomas's arm to pull him away. She hadn't wanted him to get hurt, not because of her. But Thomas had shrugged her off and taken a step nearer to Isaac. Without a word, he'd swung a clenched fist that took his opponent by surprise as it connected directly with his jaw. Isaac had staggered backwards, then fallen to the ground to the accompaniment of gasps of appreciation from the gathered crowd who'd formed a circle to watch the fight. Some even clapped their hands.

Thomas had stood for a moment, staring down at Isaac. He'd seemed more surprised than anyone at his victory.

'Let's go,' Molly had said. The day had been spoiled and she'd no interest is staying any longer. Besides, she'd been afraid that Isaac would get to his feet and give Thomas a pasting. But he'd stayed on the ground, looking stunned, until he'd begun to call after them.

'Don't think that's the end of it! Best keep tha wits about thee because I'll pay thee back one of these days!'

Molly had been afraid at the time, but Isaac had stayed away from her. Nancy had said she'd seen him and he had a shiner of a black eye, and although Molly had loved Thomas for his gentle ways she couldn't help feeling a moment of pride when she recalled how he'd felled the bully.

A few weeks later, she'd agreed to marry Thomas. They'd been wed at the parish church in Bolton and taken the cottage at Hag End Fold, across from his parents' home. Molly had spun and Thomas had woven his quilts and soon she'd been able to tell him that she was expecting a baby. He'd been thrilled, and although life had become hard with the price of food increasing, they'd managed and they'd been happy – until now.

She quickened her pace as she approached the Golden Lion on Churchgate and pushed open the door to be met by the now familiar scent of the fresh sawdust on the floor. It was quiet at this time of the morning, with only a handful of men sitting around the scrubbed wooden tables with tankards of beer in front of them. The landlord was her husband's uncle and he greeted her with an excited smile.

'For Molly Holden!' he said as he handed the letter to her. 'From Lancaster!'

Molly gave him the sixpence for the postage and sat down to read it. She couldn't wait a moment longer, even though she dreaded what the letter might tell her.

Lancaster, May 27th 1812

Dear Wives, We take this opportunity of writing a few lines to let you know that nothing is done as yet concerning Thomas. The Assizes did not begin until Tuesday morning and the Westhoughton factory trial lasted all day. Today some of the Bolton folk were tried and found guilty. But we do not know what their fate will be as sentence is not passed on any of them. Dear Wives, these lines leave us in good health and hope they will find you in the same. No more at present. From your dear husbands, John and Thomas Holden.

To be left at the Golden Lion, Churchgate, Bolton, for Molly Holden, Hag End, near Bolton-le-Moors.

Molly read the letter out to Ellen, when she got back to Hag End Fold.

'It doesn't sound good,' she said. 'Not if others were found guilty.'

'Perhaps they were guilty,' said Ellen. 'But I'm sure they'll let Thomas go when they hear that he had nowt to do with it. John said they weren't even at t' meeting when he was taken.'

'I hope so,' said Molly. Hope was all she had to cling to, she thought, as she sat beside the hearth to feed her child. If she gave up hope then there would be nothing left.

Chapter Four

Thomas was in the exercise yard for his allotted hour outside the cell, standing in a patch of sunlight and feeling the comfort of its warmth on his face. It was almost the end of May and he'd been in the gaol for six weeks, most of the time confined with the other men in the cramped, fetid cell.

He wondered if he would be brought to trial the next day. Part of him dreaded it, but part of him just wanted to get it over with to know what his fate would be. Some of the other Bolton men who had been arrested the same night as him had already been found guilty. His friend, Jack Fisher, was one of them.

The rumours of babblers and spies must have been true, he thought as he trudged another circle. Fletcher's militia had known exactly where to find them on the moor that night, but who it was that had betrayed them Thomas was uncertain. The finger of blame was being pointed at anyone who'd been at the meeting but hadn't been arrested, even his own father – an accusation he had strenuously denied.

He'd known that he and his father were taking a risk by going to the meeting, but they'd done no harm – unlike the men who'd burned the factory at Westhoughton. They'd all been found guilty, along with some folk from Manchester who'd been involved in a food riot and taken some bread to feed their starving families. They would be sentenced soon and the prisoners were speaking gloomily of hangings.

–

They came for Thomas the next morning. The turnkey fastened irons around his legs and manacled his wrists with his hands in front of him. Then he was led from the cell and up the steep, narrow stone steps until they came to the heavy wooden door that led into the chamber where the trials were held. The sound of voices grew louder when the door opened and he was pushed through it and climbed the steps into the dock.

Thomas saw that the huge space was crowded with people. Below him, the men who were to bring the case against him sat at a circular oak table with their papers spread in front of them. Other clerks hovered around them, filling the well of the court. To his right, the benches were filled with onlookers and he caught sight of his father near the back. The gallery was packed with gentry, who had come with their wives and daughters to view the proceedings. But it was the sight of Colonel Ralph Fletcher taking his place with the other gentlemen of the jury that filled him with fear. He was afraid of what these people would find him guilty of.

Thomas was trembling and he clenched his teeth and balled his hands into fists to try to steady himself as the judge came in wearing crimson robes and a curled wig. He called for order and the voices quelled one by one.

'Thomas Holden,' boomed the judge, 'you stand accused of taking an illegal oath at Bolton on the fourteenth of April of this year. How do you plead?'

'Not guilty.' Thomas tried to speak clearly and with confidence. He didn't want to seem afraid, but his voice came out in a terrified squeak.

He felt the collective gaze of the courtroom on him as the judge looked to one of the men at the table below. 'Do you have a witness?' he asked.

'I do, my lord. Call Isaac Crompton!'

Thomas watched in horror as the man he'd once punched to the ground came forward and stood in the box where the witnesses were cross-examined.

Crompton smirked across the courtroom at him. He didn't need to remind him that he'd once vowed to get his own back on Thomas for taking Molly away from him. They both knew the real reason he was here.

After Crompton had sworn on the bible that he would tell the truth, the prosecutor began: 'You were at a meeting of Luddites near the Rope Walk in Bolton on the night of the fourteenth of April?'

'I was.'

'Can you tell us what you saw that night?'

'I saw this man, Thomas Holden, in the company of Jack Fisher, James Knowles, and others. They approached the meeting and asked to be admitted. They then came forward towards the man who was known as General Ludd, who was conducting the meeting, and he proceeded to twist them in.'

'Twist them in?' asked the judge.

'A turn of phrase used by the weavers to describe the administering of an illegal oath, my lord,' explained the prosecutor.

'I see. Thomas Holden, do you have anything to say in your own defence?'

'My lord, I only went out of curiosity,' said Thomas. 'I just went to see what was to be done about the rising price of food.'

'But you knew that it was an illegal gathering?'

'I didn't know owt until I got there,' protested Thomas as the prosecutor continued to question him.

'But when you got there you could see that it was met for an unlawful purpose. We have heard previously that a watchword was given. So there were none there who did not know the purpose of the meeting. And with the full knowledge you had of it, you did, without hesitation, take the oath which was required of you.'

Thomas had no answer. He knew that these clever men were determined to trick him with their words and phrases.

'They asked me to make a promise,' he admitted at last. 'I meant no harm.'

'Gentleman of the jury,' said the judge. 'Do you have a verdict?'

Thomas watched as the men conferred, their heads together, murmuring and nodding. It only took moments for them to come to a decision.

'Guilty, my lord.'

'Take him down. I will pass sentence on all the prisoners this afternoon.'

Thomas was led away before he had chance to protest further.

'Is that it?' he asked the turnkey. It had all been over with so quickly that he was still uncertain as to his fate. He wished he'd had time to acknowledge his father and wondered if he would get chance to speak to him again. The judge had said the sentences would be handed out that afternoon, so there wasn't long to wait.

He was put back in the dark cell. The turnkey left the irons on him and so he had to make himself comfortable as best he could whilst he held the bowl of cabbage soup that he'd bought with the last of the money his father had given him. Thomas struggled to eat it. He felt sick with worry. When he'd seen Isaac Crompton at the meeting, he'd never even thought that he'd use the opportunity to exact his revenge. But it had been clear from his face today that he'd delighted in giving evidence against him. Thomas wondered if he'd given evidence against the others too. It seemed that he was one of Colonel Fletcher's spies – one of the babblers they'd been warned about. Times were hard, very hard, it was true, but to betray your own for a few pounds was a despicable thing to do, thought Thomas.

It wasn't long before the key grated in the lock again and a little more light entered the cell as the heavy door swung open. Thomas found his eyes were watering as he was led up into the courtroom, chained between Jack Fisher and another man he didn't know. He wasn't sure if they were tears.

When all the prisoners had been crowded into the space around the dock, the judge frowned down at them, his heavy grey eyebrows obscuring his eyes. Then he called for silence and addressed them: 'The offence for which the prisoners at the bar have been found guilty is provided against by an Act passed eleven years ago and unhappily now called in to force. The wisdom of the Legislature has decreed, and the judgement of the Court is, that you be severally transported to some part beyond the seas for the term of seven years.'

Chapter Five

Molly had spent the days since the last letter from her father-in-law waiting desperately for news about whether Thomas had been brought to trial. There was no word on the Monday and on the Tuesday morning she went down to the Golden Lion early, hoping that a letter had come. Uncle Richard handed it to her with a grim face. It was clear that he thought it would contain bad news.

'Don't open it here,' he advised. 'Take it home.'

Molly ran all the way back to Hag End with the letter clutched in her hand. She dreaded what it might say but kept telling herself that until she knew the news was bad there was still hope that Thomas had been found not guilty. He might even be on his way home to her. But the memory of Uncle Richard's face warned her otherwise. It was clear he'd heard something that he'd been reluctant to tell her.

She arrived at Ellen's house flushed and breathless.

'Well?' asked Ellen who was at the door looking out for her.

'I haven't read it yet. Let's go inside.'

Molly closed the door behind her, glanced at Annie who was sleeping peacefully, then sat down at the table and slowly unfolded the paper.

At first she didn't seem able to focus on the words. She had to take a breath and try to calm herself before she could begin to read them out loud to Ellen who was perched on the edge of the chair beside her, staring at the writing and waiting impatiently to hear what it said.

> *Lancaster Castle. June 1st 1812*
>
> *Dear Wife,*
>
> *It is with sorrow that I have to acquaint you that I, this day, received my Trial and the hard sentence of Seven Years Transportation beyond the seas. I trust that my dear father will make all the effort he can to beg Colonel Fletcher to get my Transportation taken off. In prison I would try to content myself but to be sent from my Native Country, perhaps never to see it again, distresses me beyond comprehension. To part with my Dear Wife and Child and Parents and friends to be no more, cut off in the bloom of my youth without doing the least wrong to any person on earth. Oh my hard fate. May God have mercy on me. In Him will I trust. Adue, dear Wife. I will expect to hear from you shortly. Your Affectionate and Unfortunate husband till Death. Thos Holden.*

Molly's tears were falling onto the paper and blurring the ink. Ellen took the letter from her hand and put it safely on top of the chest of drawers then moved the kettle to the fire to boil it up for tea.

'Perhaps if John speaks to Colonel Fletcher again he'll help Thomas,' said her mother-in-law.

'But we don't know when John will be back,' Molly managed to say as she wiped her cheeks. 'I'll go myself, today,' she told Ellen, feeling the need to do something. 'I'll go and plead for Thomas.'

Molly had managed to calm herself a little and feed Annie before she set off for the Hollins, hoping that Colonel Fletcher would be there. She hadn't been able to eat anything, but she'd sipped some sweet tea and felt a little stronger. Surely Colonel Fletcher would help, she thought. He'd made his point now, and Thomas had learned his lesson. Surely he couldn't agree with such a severe sentence when all Thomas had done was go to a meeting.

As she walked towards the Hollins with Annie in her arms, Molly caught sight of a familiar figure and stopped on the track, unsure what to do. Should she continue and hope that he wouldn't see her, or should she turn and hurry back home? She'd almost reached the road where the big house stood and she was desperate to speak to Colonel Fletcher and beg him to help Thomas. But the last person on earth she wanted to be confronted by was Isaac Crompton.

She began to walk again, slowly, hoping that he would have gone on his way before she reached the road, but he seemed disinclined to move and as she approached him she saw that he had recognised her and was waiting to speak to her. Molly wished that she'd turned and gone back, but it would look so obvious now. Besides, why should she avoid him? She had a mind to tell him exactly what she thought of him and his lies.

'Molly,' he greeted her. His face held a smirk and he looked pleased with himself. Molly would have been tempted to spit in his face if she hadn't had the baby in her arms. 'On tha way to see Fletcher?' he asked. 'I don't suppose he'll be inclined to listen to owt tha has to say.'

'How would tha know?' she snapped. 'Or hast tha been in there spreadin' more lies about folk?'

She'd been determined to say nothing. She'd planned to walk straight past him without acknowledging him, but his words stung her and she couldn't hold her tongue.

He grinned. She could see that he was pleased at having provoked her.

'I've said nowt that's not true.'

'Did tha give witness against Thomas?' She cursed herself for asking him.

Isaac shrugged. 'He were at yon meeting.'

'He did nowt wrong.' She glared at him. 'Tha should be ashamed of thyself for tellin' lies like that, and in a court of law an' all.' She jogged Annie, who had woken at her raised voice and begun to cry. Isaac glanced at the child with distaste.

Molly tried to walk past him but he moved forward and blocked her way. She began to feel afraid rather than angry. It wouldn't have been so bad if she'd been alone, but she had the baby in her arms and she wasn't sure what he intended.

'Let me past,' she said.

'What's it worth?'

'What dost tha mean? Let me past,' she repeated.

'In a minute.' He put a hand on her arm and she was unable to shake him off. He couldn't harm her here, she reasoned. It was broad daylight, but still she glanced about to see if there was anyone who might help her. He laughed. 'Tha doesn't need to be affrighted o' me,' he said. 'Tha knows I'll take care of thee.'

'Tha hasn't cared for me by bearing false witness against my husband and having him sent off to t' other side of the world!' she said, trying to sound braver than she felt.

'Tha's well shut of 'im. He were never good enough for thee.'

Molly quailed at his words. Surely Isaac didn't think he had a chance with her again now that Thomas was in prison? Surely it wasn't why he'd testified in the court? She knew he'd vowed to pay Thomas back, but she'd never considered that he might try to exert his control over her again.

After a moment, he removed his hand. 'Tha'd best go in if tha wants to speak to Fletcher,' he said, moving slightly to allow her past. 'But if he can't help thee, then happen I can. Tha knows where to find me.'

With a smile, he turned and went on his way. Molly watched him for a moment as he strode off. Even from the back he looked well pleased with himself, and although she tried to picture him laid out on the ground after Thomas had struck him, the image flickered and changed to one of her husband chained in a prison cell. There was one thing for certain, she thought as she walked towards the door of the Hollins: she would rather starve than ask Isaac Crompton to help her.

She was trembling as she rang the bell. She wished that she didn't have to do this, but Thomas was depending on her, so she knew that she must be strong, that she must overcome her nerves and her reticence and try to speak coherently to the colonel. Surely he would show some sympathy?

The same maid answered her hesitant ring on the doorbell and allowed her to wait in the hallway whilst she went to enquire if Colonel Fletcher would see her. Molly felt so vulnerable as she stood there. It wasn't her world and she could barely imagine what it would it be like to live in a huge house like this with other people to answer the door and do your bidding.

After what seemed a long time, Colonel Fletcher came out into the hall, wiping his grey whiskers on a napkin. Molly was sorry that she had disturbed him at his meal again.

'Mrs Holden,' he said. 'I'm surprised to see you here again.'

'I'm sorry to take up your time,' she said, 'but I've come to ask if there's anything you can do for my husband. He's been sentenced to seven years transportation.' The last words came out as a sob and she fumbled in her pocket for a handkerchief.

'That is the rule of law,' replied the colonel. 'It's out of my hands.'

'But if he were found guilty on the word of Isaac Crompton then it were a lie,' she told him. The colonel frowned slightly when he heard the name. 'He's not truthful,' explained Molly. 'He hates Thomas. He would say anything to harm him.'

Colonel Fletcher threw the napkin down on a side table. 'I don't know if you are familiar with the court, Mrs Holden,' he said, 'but all witnesses are required to place their hand on the bible and swear that their evidence is the truth.'

'But he didn't tell the truth,' she insisted.

Colonel Fletcher frowned. Molly could see that he was impatient and irritated by her, but she was determined to plead as best she could for Thomas.

'I'm sure he did,' replied the colonel. 'Your husband was seen at a secret meeting of seditious men – men who are determined to overthrow the good and peaceful rule of this country and replace it with God alone knows what – something similar to the dreadful state of affairs under Bonaparte in France, I expect. They are dangerous men,

Mrs Holden, and cannot be allowed to foment trouble against the lawful government and the well-being of the citizens of this land.'

'Thomas isn't a dangerous man! He just wants to work and earn enough to feed his family. How am I to manage if my husband is sent away? Please, is there any way we can be shown some mercy?' She hated having to belittle herself in front of this man, but she would do it if it was the only way to entreat him to help her.

But the colonel was shaking his head and flicking crumbs from his waistcoat as if he could also brush her aside.

'At least can he serve his sentence in this country?' she pleaded. 'Please don't send him away to the other side of the world. It's too far!' She didn't need to add that if he was sent away it was unlikely he would ever come back and she would never see him again.

'I must ask you to leave now, Mrs Holden,' said Colonel Fletcher. 'The men of the jury made their decision after hearing the sworn evidence presented to them and Justice Mister Alexander Thomson left us in no doubt as to what the prescribed punishment is. The sentence the judge has passed must stand.' He called the maid to show her out and returned to his dinner. The aroma of mutton chops drifted into the hallway as he opened the door to his dining room and Molly was ushered out and the front door closed behind her. She sobbed as she walked away. People said that Colonel Fletcher was a fair man who would always listen to the working people, but they were wrong. He cared nothing for her plight and she had no idea where to turn next.

Chapter Six

Thomas was sitting on the thin straw mattress that had been assigned to him whilst he was held at Lancaster awaiting transportation. It was crawling with bugs and he'd been badly bitten. He scratched at his leg and wondered how long it would be before he was let out into the yard for a breath of fresh air and a glimpse of daylight.

The other Bolton men had been taken to a different cell and he didn't know anyone he was locked in with, although some of them seemed to be acquainted with one another and were talking quietly. He strained to hear what they were saying.

'Think thyself lucky tha's only got transportation,' one was saying to his companion. 'That woman who was involved with the food riot at Manchester is condemned to hang.'

'What? Hannah Smith?' he asked.

'Aye. All she did were tell some chap to sell his butter at a sensible price. She climbed up on his cart and handed it out. She paid 'im for it an' all – just not the exorbitant price he were asking. It's not like it were stealin'. It were only to feed folk for a fair price. But they found her guilty of highway robbery.'

'And she's to hang?' The man sounded incredulous.

'Aye. And all them as fired the mill at Westhoughton along with her.'

'Lord preserve 'em.'

'Aye. They're in His hands now. There's nowt anyone on earth can do to save 'em.'

Thomas heard a rustling in the straw and didn't have to see the creature to know it was a rat – a sizeable one by the sound of it. It squeaked as someone landed it a blow. He wondered how much longer he would be here until they were taken to a ship. Would there be time for his father to beg Colonel Fletcher to show him some leniency? And what about Molly and the baby? He'd paid money to the Friendly Society whenever he could, but he didn't know if they would give her any relief. He hated to think that she might be reduced to begging money from the parish to feed herself and Annie. And he was worried about what Isaac Crompton might do whilst he was away. The man was angry with Molly too and Thomas hoped that the family would protect her from him.

'Is there no letter for me?' he asked the turnkey when the man fetched him for his time in the yard.

'Not today.'

'Is tha sure? I'm expecting letters from my wife and my parents. I can pay the postage,' he said. He'd received a letter from Molly and four shillings by return of post the last time he'd written to her. He'd sent a reply, but he'd heard nothing. He was beginning to worry that he'd been abandoned.

'When will I go?' he asked the man. 'I need to let my family know.'

'It could be any day,' the man told him. 'But tha'll be going to the hulks first.'

'The hulks?'

'Aye, prison ships near Portsmouth. Tha'll be held there until tha gets thy transport ship,' he told him.

Thomas was pushed through the door out into the yard. The daylight was bright and hurt his eyes after the gloom of the cell. It was a while before they adjusted and he could see anything properly. His legs were itching badly and when he rolled up the rough, prison-issue trousers he saw he was covered in raised red weals where he had been bitten. He covered the bites and began to pace the yard in an effort to take his mind from his discomfort.

There were a few others in the yard and he recognised some Bolton men and Jack Fisher. They weren't allowed to speak but Jack managed to whisper in passing that they were due to leave for the hulks later that week. He must write to Molly again, thought Thomas. He must let her know that he could be taken from here any day, and he must find out whether his father had been to see Colonel Fletcher to ask if he would petition for his sentence to be reduced.

When he was taken back inside, he asked if he could send a letter. After a long wait, the turnkey brought a sheet of paper and some ink and when Thomas had paid him a shilling he dipped the nib into the inkpot and scribed the words that Thomas dictated.

Lancaster Castle. June 14th 1812.

Dear Wife,

Nothing in this life gives me such uneasiness as not hearing from you. Surely you have not forgot me so soon. I earnestly request that you will let me know if Colonel Fletcher gives you any favourable answer or if there is any hope of my time being shortened. I do not know how soon I may leave here for the Hulks. I will expect to see you. If not it will break my heart that I may have taken my

last farewell of you, for I never shall think of seeing
any of you after I leave this place. I will expect to
hear from you by return of post. From your true,
loving husband till death. Thos Holden.

–

Molly was thankful when Uncle Richard handed her a letter. She'd walked down to the Golden Lion every day, hoping for a reply from Thomas and when two weeks had passed without any word from him, she'd grown increasingly alarmed and imagined him either ill, or sent away from Lancaster without the chance to tell her where he was being taken.

She sat down to read it, but Thomas's words filled her with dismay. It was clear that not all the letters she'd sent had been delivered – and there had been money in some of them.

'He's still hoping Fletcher might intervene,' said Molly when she got back to Hag End and showed the letter to her parents-in-law.

'He'll do nowt for him,' said John, who had also been to plead with the Colonel but met with the same negative response.

Molly felt completely helpless now. At first it had seemed unreal. She'd found it hard to reconcile herself to the thought of Thomas being transported and, despite Colonel Fletcher refusing to intervene, she'd still hoped that he would eventually realise that there had been a mistake and Thomas would come home. But as the days had turned to weeks, she'd been forced to acknowledge that it was not the case. The half-finished quilt that hung from Thomas's loom taunted her with his absence. It needed to be completed. She needed the money that it would bring. But when that was gone, she wasn't sure what she would do. She couldn't rely on her parents-in-law to feed her, or her sister, Nancy. They were hard enough pressed as it was and there wasn't enough to go round. She would have to go to the parish and beg for relief if she wasn't to starve.

Chapter Seven

Thomas watched as the turnkey handed letters to the other prisoners in the cell. He hoped that Molly had written to reassure him that she and the baby were well. He was worried sick about them, and felt so guilty for leaving them alone. But when he'd gone to that meeting, he could never have foreseen that it would end like this. And he couldn't understand why Colonel Fletcher had believed the words of someone like Isaac Crompton; he must know that he wasn't to be trusted.

His mood lifted when the turnkey approached him with a parcel as well as a letter. He hoped that Molly had sent him some money too. He was running short and although he had no choice but to buy the overpriced watery gruel and inferior oatcakes, it was better than going hungry.

'Open it,' the turnkey told him. 'I need to see what's inside.'

Thomas put the letter on his pallet and tore back the brown paper wrapping of the parcel. Inside he saw his two linen shirts, freshly laundered and ironed. He raised them to his face to inhale the smell of his home.

'Tha can't keep them,' the turnkey told him. 'Uniform only.'

'No!' Thomas protested as the man took the shirts from him. The clothing he'd been given to wear was riddled with lice and when he went out into the yard he could see that it wasn't clean. He shuddered every time he contemplated who might have worn it before him and what their fate had been. The sight of his own clean clothes had been such a comfort and now they were being taken from him. He ached to snatch them back, but he knew it would do no good.

'Uniform only,' repeated the turnkey. 'Tell 'em not to send no more.'

All the joy drained from Thomas as the man went out with his shirts. How he would have loved to put one on, to feel it against his skin knowing that the last hand that had touched it had been Molly's. Now he wasn't sure what would happen to them. Would they even be returned to him? He hated to think of the waste of money if they weren't.

He turned to the letter, relieved to see that it contained five shillings. At least he wouldn't starve just yet. Molly reassured him that she and the baby were both well, and that she'd been to plead with Colonel Fletcher for leniency, but he had refused. Thomas almost wept with disappointment. He'd been holding on to the hope that his wife would be able to make Colonel Fletcher see reason and that she would be able to persuade him to get his time shortened. Even if he was forced to spend some time in gaol it would be better than being sent so far away as New South Wales. And he was worried that he would be moved any day now. Seven of his cell mates had been told that they would be going tomorrow and he was anxious that his time would come without him having the chance to bid a farewell to his family, who he might never see again in this life.

He used some of the money he'd been sent to get a letter written.

Lancaster Castle. June 15th 1812.

Dear Wife,

I take this opportunity of writing a few lines to let you know that I expect to go from here every day as there are seven going tomorrow. I beg of you not to send me no clothes as we are not allowed to wear our own clothes, but if you would be kind enough to send me more money it would be a blessing, but you must send it immediately. So no more at present, from your ever loving and affectionate husband, Thomas Holden.

Then he asked for the paper to be turned over and began a letter to his parents.

Dear Father and Mother, I write a few lines to you, hoping they will find you in good health as it leaves me at present. But my spirits is low with thinking how I am sent from my Native Country, and I am innocent, dear Mother. I do not think of seeing you in this world any more, except if you can get my time shortened and if you can get me off I beg you will do it immediately. I have kissed this letter a thousand times and I hope you will do the same and may the Lord bless you all, and so no more at present from your ever loving and affectionate son, Thomas Holden. I love you all.

To be left at the Golden Lion, Churchgate, Bolton le Moors for Molly Holden.

Thomas kissed the letters again before they went into the bag for the mail coach. He prayed that they would arrive safely.

There was a sombre mood in his cell as the other prisoners contemplated their journey. The next morning they would go south to the hulks. Some of them had said their farewells to their families. Others lay on their beds and tried not to let their companions see them weep. Thomas knew that it would soon be his turn. His hopes of a reprieve were fading. It seemed that Fletcher would not listen and would not believe that he was innocent. Thomas cursed Isaac Crompton for what he had done. This was not justice. It was wickedness.

—

Molly wept without reserve as she sat at a table in the Golden Lion and read her husband's words. She kissed the letters that he had kissed, wishing that she could hold him in her arms and comfort him and tell him that she would stand by him, no matter what happened.

Ellen wept too when she heard what Thomas had written. 'I'll never see him again. My precious lad,' she said as she raised her apron to dry her eyes. 'I curse Fletcher and that Isaac Crompton for what they've done. I hope summat bad happens to both of 'em!'

'Don't take on so,' John told her, patting her shoulder, but Molly could see that he was struggling to contain his own grief.

'Is there no one else who can help us?' Molly asked them. 'What about Major Watkins? He's a magistrate as well. Would he put in a good word for Thomas?'

'I could go to see him, I suppose,' said John. 'But he's a friend of Fletcher so I doubt he'll say owt different.'

'I'll go,' said Molly. 'He might listen if I plead with him.'

–

Next morning, Molly pulled on the chain that rang a bell somewhere deep within Mayfield House. After an age, in which she contemplated leaving and going home without completing her task, she heard footsteps and a moment later the door was opened by a man she thought was the major.

'I'm Molly Holden,' she said. 'Please may I speak to you about my husband, Thomas?'

'I think it's Major Watkins you want,' sneered the man, looking at her with contempt. 'I suppose you'd better step inside. Wipe your feet,' he added, pointing to the coir matting that was placed behind the door.

Molly did as she was bid and didn't dare to move from the mat as the door was closed behind her and the man walked across the hall to find the major. It was an even more splendid house than the Hollins, thought Molly, as she stared at the carved bannister and the elaborate crystal chandelier that lit the stairwell. These men had made plenty of money from their coal mines and cotton mills but little of it trickled down to the workers.

A man who was younger and more slender than Colonel Fletcher came out of a doorway and eyed her suspiciously. His hair was dark and he sported fine whiskers above his flawless, starched collar.

'Major Watkins?' she asked, reluctant to make a fool of herself a second time.

'How can I help you?' he asked.

'My name's Molly Holden. My husband Thomas was found guilty at the Lancaster Assizes and sentenced to seven years transportation. I've come to ask if owt can be done for him. I've got the baby,' she added. 'I don't know how I'll manage.'

The major glanced at Annie, who had begun to cry.

'I'm sorry,' Molly apologised. 'She's frettin'. She misses her father.'

'She's not old enough to know her father.'

The words angered Molly. Annie did know her father, and Thomas was the one who was better at getting her quiet and off to sleep. He would walk around their little parlour with her held against his shoulder and sing until her eyes gradually began to close and she fell fast asleep. Major Watkins probably left his own children in the care of a nursery maid and had no idea what it took to be a proper father, thought Molly.

'And was your husband guilty?' the major asked her.

'He went to a meeting,' Molly admitted, 'but it were only from curiosity. He didn't mean to cause harm. He's a good worker. He's not a troublemaker. I don't know how I'll manage if Thomas is sent away,' she told him again, hoping that he might be moved to pity her.

'There's always the workhouse,' he replied.

'I'll not go there! Why should I be a burden on the parish when I've a husband who could work to provide for us?'

Major Watkins seemed thoughtful. Her words appeared to have made him reconsider and for a moment she was hopeful that he might agree to petition for some leniency.

'We could do without more burdens on the parish funds,' he agreed. 'Have you no family?'

'Only a sister, and Thomas's parents. But they can't afford to keep us. They're strugglin' to feed themselves.'

'You could petition to go with him.'

'With him?' Molly didn't understand what the major was saying.

'With your husband,' he told her. 'They may agree to give you free passage on the ship with him if there's room.'

'Would that be possible?' Hope filled her at the prospect of being with Thomas. She was terrified at the thought of leaving her home to travel so far, but if they could be together then maybe things wouldn't be so bad after all.

'You must send a letter to the Prince Regent describing your circumstances and he may consider the case,' he told her, as he ushered her towards the door.

–

'Might it be possible?' she asked when she got back to John and Ellen's house and told them what Major Watkins had said. 'Dost think they'd really let me go with him?'

'I don't know,' said John. He seemed doubtful.

'But it must be worth asking?' persisted Molly, even though she could see that her parents-in-law weren't keen on the idea.

John frowned. 'I suppose it's worth a try,' he said at last. He got up and opened the top drawer of the chest and rummaged about inside for a sheet of clean paper. Molly exchanged a glance with Ellen who was nursing Annie on her lap.

'It would mean losing thee and the baby too,' she said sadly, raining kisses on Annie's head at the thought of it.

'I don't really want to go away,' Molly told her, 'but I can't bear the thought of being parted from Thomas for seven years. And if it's to be his fate, then I'll gladly share it.'

John spread the paper on the table and got the pen and ink. 'What do we have to say?' he asked.

'I don't know,' said Molly.

'We could do with someone who writes a fair hand and knows how to phrase these things.' John stared at the blank sheet in front of him.

'What about yon parson?' asked Ellen.

'At t' church?'

'Aye,' Ellen nodded. 'He would know how to write it.'

Molly wasn't sure whether it was a good idea. They weren't churchgoing folk and she didn't know if the vicar would agree to help. He'd married her and Thomas but they'd hardly set foot in the church since, apart from going to get Annie baptised.

'I think tha should go and ask him,' said John to Molly. 'If tha's to stand any chance it needs to be done right, and it would look better coming from someone like him.'

Molly agreed. 'I'll go tomorrow, in the morning,' she said.

–

Molly walked past the Golden Lion and on down the cobbled street to the church as the clock struck ten. She walked up the path, through the graveyard, and turned the handle on the wooden door. She hoped that the Reverend Brocklehurst would be there at this time of the day.

She pushed open the heavy door and stepped inside. The church smelt of polish and fading flowers. At first she thought there was no one there as she walked down the central aisle towards the altar, then she heard a cough and the vicar came out from his vestry, holding his spectacles in his hand.

'Can I help you?' he asked.

'I hope so,' Molly told him. 'I'm Mrs Holden. My husband Thomas has been sentenced to seven years transportation and I've been told if I write a letter I may be allowed to go with him.' She hesitated. 'But I need some help, to get it right,' she explained.

'Come in,' said the vicar and Molly followed him into his vestry. 'I heard what happened,' he continued, 'and I'm very sorry for it. Your husband always seemed a decent, hard-working young man.'

'He is!' protested Molly. 'He's innocent,' she added, hoping that the vicar believed her. 'What was said at the Assizes wasn't true. What Isaac Crompton said was a lie – and under oath as well! I went to see Colonel Fletcher, to beg for some leniency. But he'd have none of it and it seems that Thomas will be sent away any day now.'

'Sit down,' said the vicar, pulling out a bentwood chair and ushering her towards it. 'It's not for me to question the decision of the jury,' he told her, 'but I have heard that Colonel Fletcher has used methods that are not entirely to be approved of.' The vicar frowned. 'Colonel Fletcher's heart is hardened against anyone he believes may be a revolutionary,' he said. 'I don't think there is anything you could have said that would have made him change his mind, and I'm sorry for it. Your husband doesn't deserve this – and neither do you. You have a baby too?'

'Aye. A little lass. Annie. Tha baptised her.'

'I did. I remember.' The vicar took a seat opposite her and began to polish his spectacles on a handkerchief. 'Are you sure you want to go to New South Wales?' he asked. 'It's a long and hazardous voyage. Not one I would recommend for a woman with a young child.

The accommodation will not be much – just a simple hammock below decks at best.'

'I'm sure,' Molly told him without hesitation. 'I can't let Thomas go alone if there's a chance I can be with him. It'll break my heart to be parted from him and in his letters he sounds in very low spirits. He says as he'll never see his family again in this world if nowt can be done.'

The Reverend Brocklehurst nodded and turned to find a sheet of writing paper. 'You're not the first wife I've written a letter for,' he told her, 'and I doubt that you will be the last. It saddens me. It really does. And I must warn you that such petitions are not always successful.'

'But it's worth a try?' said Molly. She felt desperate. She didn't know what else she could do if this failed.

'Yes. It's always worth a try,' said the vicar as he dipped his pen into the inkwell. 'Perhaps your prayers will be answered.'

Chapter Eight

'Tha's goin' tomorrow,' the turnkey told Thomas when he brought in his tea of stale oatcakes and boiled water. It was all Thomas had been able to afford with the last few pennies in his pocket.

'I need to let my family know. I need to write to my wife.'

'Aye. I'll make sure tha gets a pen and paper,' promised the man.

Thomas thanked him. He'd been kind – as kind as a turnkey could be, although the amount of kindness a prisoner received was unequivocally linked to the amount of cash they put in their guard's pocket and the man had taken all the money that Thomas had. He'd been praying that a letter would come for him with some more, but there'd been nothing and now it seemed that if anything had been sent it would arrive after his departure and be wasted. The thought worried him. They had little enough as it was.

The cell was quiet since the others had been moved on and he sat at the rough table and began to write in his own uncertain hand to Molly by the light of a flickering tallow candle. It stank, but he supposed it was better than the utter blackness that would descend once it was done. He had no money for another.

Lancaster Castle. June 18th 1812

Six o'clock at night.

Dear Wife, I am very sorry to inform you that I am going off tomorrow morning, but I hope to meet again before long when innocence is rewarded. I am surprised that you have not sent me any money. I am now going off without any at all. I expected to have received some by now.

Dear Father and Mother, I bid you farewell and all friends likewise. I cannot say that I go in good spirits on account of leaving my native country on this false charge that has been said against me. Dear Father, if you cannot get me off before I leave this country I think I shall never see you or my mother again. Till death shall part us. T. Holden.

p.s. Arthur Taylor owes me 5s – 6d. I request that you will get it and send it to me as I am in much need of it at present.

To be left at the Golden Lion, Churchgate, Bolton for Molly Holden.

Thomas folded the letter and banged on the door for the turnkey. 'Can tha make sure it catches the night post? Please?' he asked.

'Give it here, then,' said the man, jangling his keys and unlocking the door for Thomas to hand him the letter.

'Thank you,' said Thomas. 'If a letter comes for me after I'm gone and there's money, take it as thy own,' he said.

'Aye.' The man nodded. Thomas knew that he would have taken the money anyway, but he hoped that it was enough to sweeten him so that he would see the letter onto the mail coach.

The door banged and as Thomas heard the turnkey's footsteps walk away, the candle fluttered and failed. The acrid smell overcame the stench of the cell for a moment and Thomas groped his way towards his straw mattress to lie down. He had no idea what tomorrow would bring, but he knew he must cling to the hope that his father might convince Fletcher to see reason and at least get his sentence reduced. How could it be justice to treat an innocent man like this?

Early the next morning, they came for him. He was still groggy with sleep, having lain awake for much of the night but then drifted off into troubled dreams as dawn approached. It wasn't the turnkey he was familiar with and the two strangers were rough with him. They hauled him to his feet and fastened the heavy irons around his legs, then a neck collar and an armlet with chains that manacled his wrists in front of him. They hurried him along although he could only take short steps and had to make a strange sideways running gait to keep up with them. There was no mention of breakfast and he was pushed onto the cart that was waiting inside the castle gates as if he were a parcel or a piece of luggage. He tried to make himself comfortable as two other men were put up beside him. One was only a boy and trying to hide his tears. None of them spoke or made eye contact, except to glance up and then look quickly away again. They were all dirty and unkempt in their prison uniforms, beards unshaved, hair uncut and scratching at the bites of the lice and fleas that infested them.

Thomas glanced up at the rising sun. The morning was already warm and he was glad to be out of the fetid cell, but the cart was hard and he was jolted relentlessly as they rolled out over the cobbles. It would grow hot before long and he wondered how far they were to travel and how long it would take them, but he knew better than to ask questions. His stomach growled with hunger and he already felt thirsty. He had no money to buy food and hoped that he would at least be allowed a drink of water along the way.

They headed south and Thomas thought of Molly and his child waiting at home for him. It seemed that he would not have the opportunity to bid them a last farewell after all and he felt as if his heart would break. Unless his family could succeed in an appeal for clemency, it seemed his fate was to be sent away from them, for ever. He glanced up at the rolling hills and the fading greens of the hot summer. The countryside was beautiful and he would miss it. He had no idea what the land was like in New South Wales but he thought that nothing could compare with his home.

'Where are we goin'?' whispered the boy after they had been jolted and bruised for hours.

'The hulks,' replied the other man. 'But we're headed for the New Bailey today.'

Thomas felt a surge of hope. If he could get word to his family that he was in Salford, perhaps there was a chance that he might be able to see them for one last time.

–

'I must go,' said Molly when they were sent word that Thomas was to be held at the New Bailey for a few days. 'It might be the last chance I ever have to see him.'

Ellen agreed. 'I wish I could come with thee to visit him,' she said, 'but I don't think I could walk that far

53

at the moment.' She looked ashen, thought Molly. The loss of her son was almost more than she could bear, and Molly feared for her health. Once bright and optimistic, despite her pain and all their hardships, Ellen had now taken to sitting beside the cold hearth with her shawl wrapped tightly around her and staring, unseeingly, into the distance, hardly speaking a word. Molly knew that she was mourning for Thomas as if he was already dead. And although she expressed hope that Molly would soon hear she was to be allowed to go with him, Molly knew that she also mourned the prospect of losing her little grandchild.

'I must take him some more money,' said Molly. She'd been horrified at the news that he had none and had gone hungry. 'And I'll make some fresh oatcakes and happen try to get a bit o' cheese to take to go with them.' The thought that she could see Thomas and do something practical to help him made her feel better. 'I'll take Annie too,' she said. 'I know he'll want to see her.'

'She's gettin' heavy to carry. It'd be easier to leave her here with me, especially if tha's a basket to carry an' all,' suggested Ellen.

Molly shook her head. 'Thomas'll want to see her,' she said. Ellen nodded. They both knew it might be last time he was able to set eyes on his daughter.

Before she left, Molly called at the Taylors' house to ask for the money that Arthur owed to Thomas. Mrs Taylor answered the door and her face saddened when she saw Molly. 'Come in,' she said. 'Sit thee down.'

'I'm not stoppin',' said Molly. From the cellar below she could hear the familiar beat of the loom as Arthur worked. It was such a familiar sound that she found herself crying at the thought she might never hear her own husband at his work again.

'There, there. I'll make thee a cup o' tea,' said Mrs Taylor.

'I can't stop,' Molly told her again. 'I've come because Thomas is at the New Bailey and I'm going to see him, but he needs money. He said as Arthur owes him five and six.' She felt embarrassed at having to ask for it and hoped that even if the Taylors could pay that she wouldn't leave them short.

'Aye, that's right,' said Arthur as he appeared at the top of the cellar steps. He opened a drawer. 'Here,' he said. 'Give him that and tell him thanks. Tell him as I'm right sorry about what's happened and that I sends my best wishes.'

'I will.' Molly put the coins into her purse and thanked Mrs Taylor for the offer of tea but said that she must get on.

She hurried down the fold towards home to collect Annie and the food she was taking for Thomas, but as she turned the corner she was taken by surprise as she walked right into someone. 'Sorry,' she said before realising that it was Isaac Crompton.

'Tha needs to look where tha's goin',' he told her. 'Where's tha rushin' off to, anyroad?'

'I'm on my way home.'

'Oh, aye. How much longer will it be thy home, though?' he asked. 'Tha can't afford to keep a house on without a man to support thee.'

He looked so pleased with himself that Molly wanted to slap him. Her fingers tightened around the purse with the coins in it. She could deal him a nasty blow with that, she thought.

'How will tha manage?' he persisted.

'I wouldn't need to manage if tha hadn't told lies about Thomas,' she said.

'I've never said owt as wasn't true. He were at yon meetin'. I saw him wi' my own eyes.'

'Aye. Eyes that were busy spyin' on decent workin' folk for the likes of Colonel Fletcher!'

'I tek it he didn't respond well to thy pleadin' then?'

Molly itched to knock the self-satisfied look from Isaac's face, but she realised that it was what he wanted. He was taunting her. He used to do it before. He would go on and on until she lost her temper and then he would tell her that she had no self-control and that she needed to grow up.

She tried to pass him by, but he grasped her arm and she almost dropped the purse. Whatever happened she mustn't let him see the money, she thought.

'What does tha want?' she asked.

'I can help thee out,' he said.

'Oh, aye. If tha thinks tha can pick up wi' me where we left off, tha can think again,' she told him. 'I want nowt more to do with thee – especially after this.'

'Tha'll change tha mind when tha's famished,' he said. 'I always said as I'd tek care of thee, and I will. Not that babby, mind. It can stay with its grandparents. I'll mek sure tha gets another one to replace it if that's what tha'd like.'

She shook free of his arm and saw him smile.

'Tha'll not be so high and mighty in a while when tha's going wi'out,' he warned her as she walked away from him.

She hurried down the street and broke into a run once she was out of his sight. She hated him. But she was scared of him too, and now that Thomas wasn't here to protect her, she was afraid of what he might do.

Molly set off towards Salford with the basket of food over one arm and Annie balanced on her other hip. Hopefully she would be there by early afternoon. She followed the bank of the river Irwell until she saw the prison in the distance, a sombre building, flanked by towers, with iron spikes jutting from its high walls. She was weary from the long walk in the oppressive heat of the June day. Her arms were leaden with the weight of the baby and the basket of food, but with the end of her journey in sight, she increased her pace, eager to see Thomas.

She approached the cage-like gates and gave her name. A man with a set of jangling keys opened them a fraction to allow her to squeeze through and then locked them behind her. Molly was taken to an inner courtyard from where a turnkey led her up a winding stone staircase. She was relieved to see that it looked clean and the floors had been freshly sanded. At the top there was a long arched gallery and the turnkey led her past a line of strong, nailed doors until he paused outside one and unlocked it. He motioned her to step through. Then he swung the door closed behind her with a bang that echoed down the corridor.

'Molly!' Thomas leapt up from the bed and put his arms around her and the child. 'Oh Molly. I'm that glad to see thee,' he said. 'Hast walked all this way? Sit thee down.'

Annie had woken with a jump as the door slammed and had begun to cry. Thomas took her in his arms and began to shush her, but was unable to pace with her as he would have done at home. The cell was tiny. It held the bed and nothing more. Opposite the door was a half circle window, unglazed but with iron bars to prevent anyone trying to get through it, and wooden shutters to keep out the wind – although today they were open and any breath of a breeze was welcome in the heat. Beneath the window was a stone ledge that might serve as a seat and Thomas sat down here with his child in his arms. He looked filthy and was unshaven and she could see the bites on his arms where his sleeves were rolled up. She hoped nothing would bite Annie, but she couldn't bring herself to take the child back from him.

'Did tha bring money?' he asked her.

'Aye. I got what tha were owed from Arthur Taylor.' She got out her purse and gave it to him. 'I brought some food an' all,' she said, uncovering the basket and offering him the oatcakes and cheese which he began to eat with one hand, whilst still holding onto Annie with the other.

'Hast tha been to see Fletcher?' he asked, with his mouth full.

'Aye, I've been twice. Tha father's been too, but he'll not listen,' Molly told him. 'He believes every word that Isaac Crompton said.'

'What Crompton said were untrue and he knows it. He were at that meeting himself, but he's never been accused of nowt.'

'He's a spy,' said Molly. 'Fletcher's paying him to go to yon meetings and inform on folk. And he's borne thee a grudge ever since that trouble,' she added, deciding not to worry her husband with the news that Isaac was pestering her again. 'Colonel Fletcher told me not to go back. It's useless to ask him again,' she went on. 'He's determined to send away anyone he thinks may be a revolutionary. He's afraid for himself and the other gentry, especially since Mr Perceval, the prime minster, got shot.'

Thomas nodded. The joy that had lit his face when he'd seen her come through the door had faded and only disappointment and despair were left in its place. 'So it doesn't look like tha can get me off?'

She shook her head. 'I'm sorry,' she said. 'I've tried. I really have.' She began to cry at the thought of her failure, even though she'd vowed to stay cheerful so as not to upset him.

'Oh Molly.' He came to sit beside her on the bed and put an arm around her and kissed her tears. 'How has it come to this?' he asked. 'It'll break my heart to be parted from thee.'

'We might not have to be parted,' she told him, remembering that he didn't know about her petition. 'I went to see Major Watkins. He didn't agree to plead for thee, but he told me there's a chance I can go with thee.'

'What? To New South Wales?' Thomas stared at her, his face transformed by the hope that they might be allowed to be together.

Molly nodded. 'I've petitioned to go with thee,' she told him. 'Reverend Brocklehurst penned a letter for me to send to the Prince Regent. I haven't heard owt back yet, but if he says aye then at least we'll be together.'

'Let's hope he does,' said Thomas, seeming more optimistic. 'I don't want to leave this country, but if we can go together then I can bear it. And happen we can come back when my time's done.'

'Not many come back. It's a long way,' said Molly. She didn't repeat what the vicar had told her about the conditions on board the ships. She didn't want to worry him. 'I just hope the answer comes in time,' she told him.

'If it doesn't, tha might be able to follow on another ship,' he said. 'Don't give up hope, Molly. Besides, I may not be leavin' straight away,' he told her.

'Will tha stay here?' she asked, thinking that if he did she might be able to visit him again.

'No, I'm to leave here any day. Maybe even be tomorrow,' he said. 'But I'm to go the hulks, the prison ships, to wait until I'm transported. They say as there's so many being sent to New South Wales that tha has to wait thy turn.'

Molly took his hand in hers and held it tightly. 'I don't know what I'll do without thee,' she said, fighting back more tears. 'I promise I'll come to thee if I can.' Another door banged on the corridor and she leaned against him. He seemed thinner. He'd lost weight and his face looked pale.

'Happen we'll not be parted,' he said. 'Happen we'll get to go together, and it'll be like an adventure.'

She knew that he was trying to be cheerful, but the prospect terrified her. She wasn't sure which she feared the most – losing him or making the sea voyage.

The key turned in the cell door. 'Time's up!' shouted the turnkey.

'Already?' She knew she hadn't been there long.

They stood up and Thomas put Annie on the bed so he could embrace Molly properly. She clung to him, running her hands over his shoulders and down his back, breathing in the scent of him and trying to commit it to her memory in case she never saw him again.

'Give my love to my parents,' he instructed her. 'Tell them I'm sorry they couldn't come.'

'It was too far for thy mother. She's still in a lot of pain.'

'Aye. Tell them I'll remember them in my prayers every night. Thee an' all, and t' child.' He eased himself from her grasp and picked up his daughter and kissed her, then held Annie against him for a moment, his eyes closed and tears seeping from beneath his lashes, before he handed her to Molly. Then he kissed them both again as the turnkey jangled his keys to hurry them. 'Write to me,' he said. 'When I get to th' hulks I'll send a letter so tha knows where to address it.'

'I will,' she promised. 'And if I get word that I can go with thee, I'll come straight away.'

He nodded. 'I pray that I'll see thee again – in this world.' He broke down and began to weep along with her. She didn't want to leave. She grasped Thomas's hand and held onto it until the last moment, until their fingers parted, as the turnkey ushered her out into the corridor and the door was slammed shut. She sobbed as the turnkey locked the door and escorted her back down the steps, across the courtyard and out of the main gate, which clanged shut behind her. She stood beyond its bars and stared back at the prison, wondering how long it would be before she saw her husband again. But she must not give in to despair, she told herself as she hitched Annie further up into her arms and began to retrace her steps towards home, glad the basket was lighter and hoping that there would soon be an answer to her petition.

Chapter Nine

Thomas lay awake most of the night after Molly had gone. It had been so good to see her, but the thought that it might have been for the very last time haunted him. After talking to her, his hope of a reprieve had faded. He knew that Isaac Crompton hated him, but he'd expected him to stand with his fellow weavers against the gentry. Molly's revelation that Crompton was a spy disturbed him. And he was worried about his intentions. Had he purposely given evidence against him so he had the chance of taking up with Molly again? It was another reason that he prayed she would get permission to go with him. He couldn't bear the thought of her being with Isaac Crompton, but with him gone for seven years, or even more, he knew that it would be hard for her to manage alone and that she might be tempted.

It was a relief from his tormenting thoughts when he heard the jangling of keys outside his cell door just as dawn broke through the high window. The turnkey took him down to the yard, where he was glad to see Jack Fisher amongst the men who were to travel with him. They exchanged a welcome glance although there was no chance of a conversation as the irons were fastened around their legs. But Thomas was relieved to see a familiar face and hoped that they were both headed for the same hulk.

A coach was waiting for them at the main gate and the warder handed them into the custody of two king's messengers who were to escort them on their journey. At least it wouldn't be as uncomfortable as the cart that had brought them here, thought Thomas as they were pushed up onto the outside seats, encumbered by their heavy chains.

The prison gates clanged shut and the coach moved off through the streets that were almost empty at that time of the morning, except for a couple of weary night-watchmen making their way home and a maid on her hands and knees scrubbing a doorstep. They headed south as the sun rose higher. At least the weather was still fine, thought Thomas, although there would be no shade from the fierce sun as the day grew hotter.

When they reached Stockport and stopped for the horses to be changed, a crowd of curious onlookers came to stare at them. Some expressed their sympathy, whilst others were of the opinion that it served the prisoners right and that they'd received their just desserts. They went on to Disley, where they were allowed to get down to relieve themselves and given portions of bread and cheese for breakfast and a cup of ale each. Thomas ate hungrily and was able to have a few words with Jack Fisher.

'I were only found guilty on the word of Isaac Crompton,' Thomas told his friend. 'Molly told me that he's a spy for Fletcher.'

'Aye. So I heard. What sort of man does that?' asked Jack. 'I've known him and his family all my life. I thought he were one of us.'

'It's surprising what folk'll do for a few pounds,' replied Thomas, although he didn't say what he thought the real reason was for Crompton's betrayal. 'I hope we're kept together,' he went on. 'It'll make it a bit easier.'

'Aye, we can look out for one another,' said Jack as the men came to load them back onto the coach.

They reached Leicester by the end of the day and Thomas was glad to see the sun go down in a dazzling display of gold and orange. It had been hot and the sun had burned his skin, leaving his cheeks and the back of his neck sore. And although there had been a mustering of dark clouds on the western horizon as they'd travelled, the threat of a thunderstorm, with an accompanying down-pour, had not materialised.

They stopped at the Head Inn, where they were herded into a tap room; the landlord ejected a number of stable workers and others to make room for them. Ale was put in front of them and they drank thirstily. Thomas was parched, and aching from being jolted all day. He was hungry too and welcomed the hot stew when it arrived on a pewter plate. It tasted good and he ate as much as he was able, glad to rest on a more comfortable seat. But once the food was finished they were taken back out to the coach. It seemed that there would be no respite and they would travel on through the night.

The sky was starlit and bright as a full moon rose and illuminated the small white cottages scattered around the farmsteads. Thomas heard the sound of hymn-singing as they passed a roadside chapel and he thought about the people he glimpsed as they passed, going about their lives just as he had done not long since. How things had changed for him, he thought, and all on the word of one man.

The other prisoners he was chained to shifted this way and that as they tried to get comfortable, propping one another up as they dozed before being jolted from sleep again by another rut in the road. Their movement pulled on the chains and one of Thomas's ankles was sore and swollen where the irons were cutting into his skin.

Just before dawn a thunderstorm broke. The heavens opened and they were drenched to the skin as the coach continued on its way – the only respite being that the roads were better here as they made the final approach towards the city of London and there was less jolting. Thomas was exhausted and chilled to the bones with the heavy rain, which had brought such a drop in temperature that he found himself craving a return of the burning sun. He slept a little, waking to find himself leaning on the shoulder of the man beside him who was snoring loudly. He shifted as his wet shirt clung to his back and his trousers to his legs. He would have loved to get into dry clothes, but there was no opportunity even when they did stop to eat some breakfast. Thomas feared that this was what his life would be like from now on. There were moments when he wondered if those who had been hanged had received a better bargain, but then he told himself that he mustn't think like that. He must survive this, for the sake of Molly and the child as well as himself.

It was approaching dinner time when they reached the Coldbath Fields Prison. The turnkey led them through winding passages until they came out into a small yard with a cell at the far end. The door was open and they were herded inside and their irons unlocked and taken away. Thomas sat down on one of the wooden chairs that were arranged around a rough table and examined his leg. The skin was broken and had bled a little, but apart from the swelling there seemed to be no infection and the turnkey promised him that a doctor would examine it before nightfall.

The others had flopped down onto the beds that were arranged against the walls – three on each side of the long, narrow cell. Everyone was weary and wet and although there was a fireplace with wood piled up beside it, it hadn't been lit.

Thomas longed to change into something dry and he expected his small bag of belongings to be brought soon, but although the other prisoners received theirs, the turnkey shrugged when Thomas enquired about it and told him that it must have been lost. He sat disconsolately on the edge of his allotted bed. His clothes were drier now, but felt stiff and awkward. He would have peeled them off, but the cell grew cold and it was late before any food was brought and the fire lit to allow them to put a kettle to boil to make themselves tea.

They stayed at the prison for four nights and food appeared at every mealtime – something that Thomas was grateful for because he found that not only his bag but his money had gone missing. He knew that his friend Jack Fisher would never have taken it, so he found himself watching the other men with suspicion and hoping that one might betray himself. But they all seemed as poor as he was himself, and in the end he decided that his pocket must have picked during one of their stops at the inns on the way. The loss grieved him because he knew how hard it was for Molly to spare the cash. He hoped that she had enough to feed herself and that his parents would care for her and Annie until she could join him. He longed to be with her again. This ordeal was like a nightmare from which he couldn't wake no matter how hard he tried to rouse himself. His only consolation was the hope that he and his wife could remain together.

On the Thursday afternoon, the turnkey came and told them to gather their belongings together. Then the irons were locked around their legs once more and they were taken back through the maze of passageways to a waiting cart. The rain was pouring down from a dismal sky and by the time they were seated on the benches and the flap on the back of the cart was bolted, Thomas was soaked through to the skin once more. He knew that there were prison hulks moored in the river Thames and he was expecting that they would be taken there, but it seemed that their journey was to be a longer one, as the cart was driven out of the crowded streets of the city and on to the open road. They travelled through the night again, dozing as they leaned against one another. Thomas allowed himself to sleep, no longer worried about his belongings now that he had nothing left to steal and so wet that the relentless rain couldn't make him any wetter.

As dawn broke, he caught a glimpse of silver on the horizon and smelt the salt in the air. By mid morning he could see the masts and sails of ships on the horizon and around midday they rolled down to the harbour where they were unloaded from the cart and stood soaked, tired and bewildered on the quayside.

They were loaded onto a boat and rowed out to the hulk of a huge ship moored in the harbour. Thomas had seen pictures of war ships in full sail in the papers that his father sometimes brought home from town, but the *Portland*, stripped of its masts and sails, looked bleak and unimpressive as they approached. Thomas had no idea how they would get on board until he saw the rope ladder that snaked down the wooden hull from a platform on the middle deck. In turn they were urged up the ladder as the rowing boat rose and fell on the sway of the waves. Thomas wasn't sure that he would manage it, but he was left in no doubt as to what was expected of him and he grasped hold of the ladder and hauled himself up, encumbered as he was by his leg irons. The ladder was wet and his fingers struggled to grasp each rung as he climbed them one at a time. As he reached the platform, he felt someone grasp him by the shirt and haul him on board, shouting at him to line up with the others.

When all the prisoners were on board, they were taken down steep wooden steps. Thomas counted three decks in total as they descended. In the bowels of the ship, he could hear the water slapping against the wooden hull and saw several places where the sea was coming through and streaming across the floor. They were led down a central corridor with cells on either side – empty at this time of the day – and allocated one which seemed sufficient for only three or four men at most. They were unchained from one another but the irons were left around their legs. The door slammed shut and they found themselves in semi-darkness with only one high grille to let in light and salt-laden spray as the ship moved and creaked on the rising tide.

They stood and stared at one another, unsure what to do.

'At least we're still together,' said Jack Fisher, attempting to sound optimistic, but Thomas saw that his friend, like him, was close to tears of despair as they wondered what new horrors would face them.

After a while they were moved to a galley and seated at a long table where they were allowed a chunk of stale bread and a cup of watered ale. After that a scribe came in and they were allowed to write one letter to their families to tell them where they were. Thomas hated having to voice his thoughts to a stranger, especially in the hearing of the other prisoners. Although his own writing was laborious, he would have preferred to try to form the words himself and keep his feelings between his heart and the page. There was so much more he wanted to say to his wife and his parents, but he found it hard to speak the words out loud.

When the letters had been taken for the post, they were lined up again and marched to a room under the forecastle where there were troughs of water against the wall. They were told to strip off their clothing and wash themselves. Some of the others grumbled, but Thomas was glad to get out of the filthy things he'd been wearing for over two weeks. He scrubbed at the grime on his body with the rough cloth and harsh soap that he was handed, then dressed in the prison-issue uniform – a shirt, trousers with the name *Portland* on them, striped socks and a brown jacket. They weren't new, but seemed fairly clean, certainly cleaner than the clothes he had taken off.

After that, they were allowed to go on the upper deck until it was time for the other prisoners to return from their work.

'It could be worse, I suppose,' said Jack as they watched some of the other convicts loading heavy sacks onto a ship moored further down the quayside.

'Could it?' Thomas was struggling to see anything good about their situation. He gazed at the expanse of water between him and the harbourside. Some men knew how to swim, but it wasn't something he'd ever learned. He had always been afraid of the water since he'd fallen into a pond as a small child. He recalled the muffling of everything that was familiar to him as the water closed over his head and the panic that he would never breathe the air again. It had seemed an eternity, but was probably only moments before he felt himself grabbed and lifted from the murky prison that had replaced the bright sun of a summer's day. He'd coughed and coughed and been taken home for his sodden clothing to be changed. Some people had laughed at him, he recalled, as if it had been funny, but when he had nightmares, they were always dreams of being under the water and not being able to break the surface.

Now he wondered if he could manage to reach the shore if he threw himself into the harbour. Probably not, he thought, and the iron chains around his legs would weigh him down like an anchor and surely drown him. He wouldn't risk that, not whilst there was still a chance that Molly and his daughter might join him.

Chapter Ten

Molly stared at the letter from Carlton House. She'd already read it once but she went through it again, tracing each word with her finger, to see if she could discern some different meaning.

'Bad news?' asked Uncle Richard, coming to sit beside her.

'I think it means my petition's been turned down,' she said as all the hope she'd been clutching on to during the past weeks was torn away from her in a few, lofty words.

'Let's have a look.' He picked up the letter and she watched as he read it, a frown forming on his face.

'Aye,' he said, flinging it down onto the table with a gesture of disgust. 'It says as seven years ain't long enough for thee to be allowed a free passage to go with him. Says tha can go if tha pays. Thirty-five pounds!'

It was an enormous sum of money. Thomas would be lucky if he earned anywhere near it in a year and Molly had no idea how she could possibly raise so much.

'But I have to try,' she told Ellen and John when she got back to Hag End Fold. 'Thomas is expecting me to go. I can sell t' loom,' she suggested though she knew the price wouldn't amount to thirty-five pounds, nowhere near. There was the furniture and the bedding and her cookpots. She wouldn't need those. And maybe she could sell some of her clothes because she didn't think she'd be able to take much with her. But she was at a loss to know where the rest might come from. Maybe folk would lend her some if she promised that she'd pay them back as soon as she could, but it was a lot to ask when times were hard.

'Tha can't sell yon loom until t' quilt's finished,' said John. 'It'd be a waste to take it off not complete. I'll finish it myself, but I've some orders of my own to do first so it might be a week or two.'

Molly felt frustrated. The loom was probably the most valuable thing she had to sell and without the money from that there was no chance that she could raise enough for her passage, and she was terrified that Thomas's ship might sail before she could join him.

She crossed the fold to her own cottage feeling disconsolate. She'd been so sure that she would be granted the passage and now she felt as hopeless as she had when Thomas had first been sentenced to transportation.

She gazed around her parlour. The little house was her pride and joy and she loved to keep everything spick and span, but what use was any of it to her without her husband? She ran a hand over the burnished surfaces of her table and chairs. She kept them well polished and they were good quality. She hoped they would fetch a decent price, and there was no reason she couldn't eat her solitary meals on her lap beside the fire.

Molly went down the stone steps into the cellar where Thomas had his loom. Light flooded in from the long windows that were built into the wall above ground level at the back, where the land sloped away down the hill. They were south facing and caught most of the daylight – and at this time of the year Thomas would work long hours, from dawn until dusk, weaving the quilts. The one he'd been working on before his arrest stretched across the broadloom; both the shuttles had full bobbins – one wound with the binding thread and the other with the thicker, folded thread that was picked up by hand with the reed hook to create the knops that made the pattern.

The edge of the quilt almost reached the floor and she could see that there was a border of garlanded leaves and the centre was a rose. It was a design he'd used many times before and the tattered paper pattern was pinned up on the side of the loom's frame to guide him. Sometimes, if he was trying to get a quilt finished in time for an order, she'd help him with the knopping. It wasn't that difficult, but it had to be done by hand. None of the fancy power looms that they were bringing into the factories could produce work like it – and she knew that Mr Ainsworth at the warehouse had plenty of orders in his book for caddow quilts.

Molly sighed. Thomas had been so stupid to go to that meeting. His work wasn't threatened by the new machines, and although the price of bread and potatoes had almost doubled in the last few years, they'd been managing.

–

Molly didn't sleep well that night. She'd heard nothing from Thomas since she'd seen him at the New Bailey and more than a week had gone by. She had no idea where he was, whether he was still on his journey or whether he'd arrived at the prison hulks. She would be so relieved when she got a letter saying that he was safe – even though he was so far away, if she could hold a letter that he'd sent she would feel closer to him.

Next morning, she left Annie with Ellen and made her daily walk to the Golden Lion, hoping that today a letter from Thomas might have come.

'Sorry, Molly. Nowt today,' Uncle Richard told her when she went in. He poured a half pint of ale and insisted that she sit down to rest and drink it before she walked back. He refused her offer of payment.

'I wish there were more I could do,' he said.

When she'd drained the cup she came back out into the hot sun and began to retrace her steps towards home, paying little attention to where she was going. The way was so familiar she could have walked it in her sleep.

'Hello, Molly.'

She was jolted from her thoughts by the familiar voice – the person she least desired to see. Isaac Crompton. He was blocking the way ahead of her and seemed to have appeared from nowhere. She wondered if he'd been lingering and waiting for her. Everywhere she went she seemed to catch glimpses of him and she was beginning to think that he was following her.

Molly wished that he would get out of the way. She walked on without a word, hoping that he would let her past, but he fell in alongside her as the path rose towards Hag End Brow.

'How's tha managin'?' he asked her. 'If tha needs owt, tha only has to ask.'

'What makes thee think I'm that desperate?' she said, conscious of the bulk of his body walking beside her. She knew that he could overpower her in a moment if he chose to. There was nobody else about and she felt vulnerable in his company.

'I heard tha'd been askin' about for money,' he said. 'I'll not see thee go short of owt. Tha only needs to ask me and I'll help thee.'

'I don't need owt from thee,' she told him, knowing that he would never give her any money if he knew why she needed it.

'But I don't want to see thee shamed by havin' to beg or ask t' parish for relief.'

'It's nowt to do with thee,' she retorted.

'But I worries about thee, Molly.'

'Tha weren't worryin' about me when tha told them lies about Thomas.'

'I only said what were true,' he repeated. 'He were at that meetin', and I saw him with my own eyes with his hand on a book, swearing an oath.'

'And what were thee doin' there?' she demanded. 'Except spyin' for Colonel Fletcher. Tha should be ashamed of thyself – informing on folk who're thy friends and neighbours.'

'There's a law against oath-takin',' he said. 'I were only upholdin' t' law.'

'Tha were doin' it for money,' she replied. 'No wonder tha can afford to say tha can help me out. I'd rather starve than take thy tainted money!'

'Tha'll think different when tha's an empty belly and nowt in thy purse to buy food.'

'I'll not go hungry. There's better folk than thee that'll help me.'

'Tha can't survive on generosity for ever,' he warned her. 'He'll not come home, tha knows, so there's no point hopin' for it. Transportation's a one-way ticket. Nobody comes back.'

'It doesn't matter,' she snapped. 'Because I'm going with him.'

Isaac hesitated in his stride, but she kept walking and he increased his pace to draw level with her again.

'What's tha mean, goin' with 'im?' He sounded perturbed and Molly felt a moment of triumph that she had wrong-footed him.

'Didst tha not know? Wives are allowed to go an' all,' she told him, although she didn't reveal that she'd been refused the free passage and needed to raise thirty-five pounds. 'Reverend Brocklehurst sent a petition on my behalf.'

'Tha's tellin' me a lie,' he accused her. 'I don't believe it.'

'Believe what tha wants,' she replied, exhilarated to have got the better of him. She turned into the fold and he stayed behind. At the door to John and Ellen's she glanced back, and he was still standing there, watching her.

'Any word?' asked Ellen when she went in.

Molly shook her head, sad to have to disappoint her again. 'Nothing today. Has Annie been all right?' she asked, going to check on the baby.

'Aye, not a whimper.'

'She'll be awake soon enough and bawlin' for milk,' said Molly as she hung up her shawl and went to fill the kettle. She wanted to tell Ellen about her encounter with Isaac Crompton, but something stopped her. She didn't want her mother-in-law to think that she was encouraging him in any way. It was a problem she would have to deal with alone, because it was becoming increasingly obvious that with Thomas out of the way, Isaac fancied his chances of taking up with her again, and if she didn't manage to raise the money for her passage she worried that he might never leave her alone.

Chapter Eleven

It was another ten days before the letter came from Thomas. Molly fell on it with relief when Uncle Richard handed it to her and sat down to open it with trembling fingers.

Langstone Harbour. June 28ᵗʰ 1812

Dear Wife, I have taken this first opportunity of writing to you to inform you that I am arrived at the place of destination. Hoping this will find you and my dear child in good health as this leaves me at present. Thanks be to God for it. Dear Wife, we arrived in London on Sunday last and remained there until Thursday night when we set out for this place where we arrived this day about twelve o' clock. Dear Wife, I have to inform you that I have had a bad misfortune for I have lost my money. I hope you will send me some more as quick as possible. But I beg you will not think of coming to see me at this place as the distance is so great, being nearly three hundred miles, and it will attend with a great expense as well and give me a great deal of uneasiness. Dear Wife, Father and Mother, I beg you will let me know as soon as possible if there is any thing done for me or not. Our journey has

been very wet and uncomfortable and I have been
eight days and nights without having the clothes off
my back, so I will leave you to judge what state I
am in at present, but I hope to be better in a few
days. Your loving husband, Thos. Holden.

    Direct for me on board HMS The Portland,

    Laying in Langstone Harbour, near Ports-
mouth, Hants.

At least he was safe, thought Molly, although she wept at the thought of him wet and uncomfortable with no change of clothes and his money all lost. How had that happened? Even though he was often generous to those in need, he was always careful with his money and it was unlike him to lose even a penny. It must have been stolen from him, she thought, wondering what kind of thieves and ne'er-do-wells he had travelled with, who would take money from another man who was as badly off as they were. She cursed them. Thomas must be really struggling with nothing and although he hadn't said that he was hungry, she worried that he might have gone without food. It wouldn't do for him to be hungry, she thought. He must keep up his strength to stay well.

His need for more money was a setback. As she walked home she thought of the three pounds and ten shillings that the table and chairs had fetched from the pawnbroker. Well, three pounds, nine and six really, because she'd had to give sixpence to the carter. She'd stashed it away as her first step towards raising the thirty-five pounds she needed to join Thomas on the ship, but now it seemed that she would have to send some of it to him. But hopefully there would be money for the quilt once it was finished and the price that she could get for the loom. There was the bed too, but she needed that to sleep in for the present and although she could pawn the blankets, she would need to redeem them if she hadn't saved enough money before the winter came. She had a few things that had been her mother's – her wedding ring, a mirror and a teapot. They would fetch something but nowhere near as much as she needed.

It seemed an impossible task, but she was determined not to give up. She'd even considered finding work, wondering if she could get a place as a maid, and leave Annie with her grandparents. She hated the thought of being parted from the child, but it would only be until she'd earned enough money to join Thomas.

'I have a pound that I'll send him straight away,' said John when she went to show her parents-in-law the letter. 'I'd been saving it to give thee for t' passage, but Thomas needs it now.'

Molly was grateful.

'I hate to think of him in that state,' said Ellen. 'Let's get it in the post straight away.'

'I'll take it,' said Molly. 'It should go today if I'm quick.'

John sat down to write a letter. When it was done, Molly hurried to the post office where she exchanged the pound for a money order and spent ten pennies of her own money to send it post paid, knowing that Thomas would not receive it otherwise.

When she came back out onto Wood Street, she saw Isaac Crompton lingering near the corner and her spirits plummeted even further. She was sure now that he was following her. She wondered if she could hurry away without being seen, but it was too late. He was already striding towards her.

'Molly!' he called and she knew that it was useless to pretend that she hadn't heard him. 'Sendin' a letter to thy Thomas?' He grinned.

'Aye.' She kept walking.

'Not gone to join 'im yet, then?' he asked. His tone was mocking and it was clear that he didn't believe that she would go. 'They don't let wives have free passage if it's only a short sentence,' he told her. 'It's only for lifers.'

He must have asked Fletcher or someone else about it, thought Molly.

'If tha's been told otherwise then tha's holdin' on to false hope. Best forget him,' he advised. 'I've told thee as I'll tek care of thee. Tha should have wed me in t' first place, anyroad. I don't know what tha ever saw in Thomas Holden.'

'He's kind, and considerate. And he loves me!'

'But I loves thee, Molly.' He grasped her arm to stop her walking and spun her to face him. 'I loved thee t' first.'

'It doesn't work like that,' she told him. 'I'm not some possession to argue the ownership of!'

He frowned. She suspected he did see her as a possession and that was why he was so angry with Thomas for taking her away from him.

'What choice dost tha have?' he challenged her.

'I've plenty of choices,' she replied. 'I can get work and save up enough money to go to him. And I will!' she told him. 'There's no need for thee to concern thyself.'

'And how much will it cost?' he asked. 'Tha'll never save that much. And what work can tha get wi' a baby? There's no call for hand spinnin' no more. Tha'll not even earn enough to keep a roof over thy head, never mind save owt.'

'I can move in with John and Ellen if I can't afford t' cottage, or with my sister Nancy and her husband. They'll all take care of me, neighbours too. Everyone knows that Thomas is innocent and they've pledged to do all they can to help.'

'Folk'll be reluctant to be seen helpin' yon Luddites,' he warned her. 'There's none of 'em'll want to risk the same fate.' His voice held the hint of a threat and Molly slowed her steps.

'Nobody's frightened of thee,' she said, although she knew that it was probably not true. Folk were becoming afraid and there were mutterings about babblers and men who could no longer be trusted. Isaac Crompton's name came up time and again and although there were plenty who agreed that he was in the pay of Colonel Fletcher, there were those who wouldn't hear a word against him. It was wrong to rise up in revolution like the French, they said. Look what it had led to. First all the damage to their livelihood and then the terrible murder of the prime minister. Fletcher was right to try to discover the troublemakers and get them sent away where they could cause no more harm. And even though most folk were supportive of Molly, she knew that some were avoiding her because they thought that Thomas was guilty. Folk who had been neighbours all their lives and whose families had known one another for generations were growing suspicious of one another and it was beginning to tear their small community apart.

Isaac laughed. 'Tha'll change thy mind in a bit,' he told her. 'And I'll be waitin' for thee.'

He turned and walked away. Molly watched him go. He no longer wore the rough clothes of a weaver, she saw. His jacket was new and his trousers were without patches.

He was beginning to take on the look of the gentry and he never seemed to be at work at his loom. Isaac clearly thought he could rise on this wave of trouble. He'd always been like that. His first thought was always for himself and he'd do whatever he could to raise his position in life even if it meant stamping all over his friends and neighbours. He was always so sure of himself, and he believed that she would go back to him. It struck fear in Molly's heart. She knew he wasn't a man to be thwarted when he set his mind to something. She knew that she would struggle to keep him at bay and it was all the more reason to try to get together enough money to go with Thomas.

Chapter Twelve

On the Friday morning, John came across to Molly's cottage to say that he would finish off Thomas's quilt.

'There's plenty of daylight and if I work on it through Sunday, it'll be done for thee to take it down to Mr Ainsworth at the warehouse on Monday mornin',' he said.

'I can help,' Molly told him. John looked doubtful. 'I sometimes helped Thomas,' she went on. 'Not with the weavin', but raisin' the knops. It's easy enough when there's a pattern to follow.'

'I think I'd best do it myself,' said her father-in-law. 'Wilt tha fetch me a cup o' tea?'

'Aye.' Molly went back up the steps to put the kettle on. John hadn't needed to say that he was afraid she would spoil the quilt if she worked on it. His meaning had been clear enough.

As she spooned tea into the pot she heard the familiar rhythm of the loom start up below her. Just for a moment she indulged herself and imagined that it was Thomas down there, and that everything was all right.

Molly let the tea brew and then took a cup down.

'Put it over there,' said John, nodding towards the table that stood at the side of the cellar. 'I don't want owt spilled on it.'

Molly did as she was bid and then stood a while to watch as he raised the knops with the hook. He was a skilled worker and completed the row much faster than she could have done. She wondered whether Thomas had ever really needed her help or if he'd just liked to have her sitting beside him on the bench.

She would have liked to linger, as she'd often lingered watching her husband. The whole process fascinated her and she loved to watch as the shuttle flew back and forth and the treadles raised and lowered the frame to gradually turn the spun bobbins of thread into a thing of beauty. But she heard Annie upstairs, waking from her nap, and so left John to his task. The sooner it was done, the sooner she would have the money for it, and for the loom too when it was sold. The thought excited her. It would give a huge boost to the savings she already had.

–

John finished the quilt by dusk on Sunday and took it down from the loom. Molly folded it ready to take it the warehouse the next morning.

'Don't take a penny under twelve shillings,' John warned her, 'and make sure tha gets some bobbins for me an' all. It'll save me t' trek down to Tonge.'

When Molly reached the warehouse the next morning it looked busy. There was a cart outside delivering bales of cotton ready to be spun and she waited until the men had finished hefting the huge sacks onto their shoulders and carrying them inside before she approached. The cotton had left a haze of fine dust hanging in the air and she sneezed again and again as she waited for Mr Ainsworth to notice her.

'Mrs Holden,' he said, his eyes straying to the package that she was carrying. 'What can I do for thee?' he asked.

'I've fetched this quilt that Thomas were workin' on,' she told him.

'Is it finished?'

'Aye. His father finished it off,' she explained as Mr Ainsworth spread it out on a table to examine it.

'It's good work,' he agreed, 'as I'd expect. I can pay thee eleven and six.'

Molly remembered John's words, but the price offered was only a sixpence short and she was reluctant to haggle.

'I'll include more bobbins,' he offered, seeing her reluctance.

'Aye, all right then,' said Molly, nodding her agreement. John had given her money to buy bobbins so she knew that she had a good deal.

With the money in her pocket and bobbins in her basket she hurried back to Hag End. After she'd taken the bobbins to John and given him back his money and he'd insisted on returning sixpence to her, she took Annie home and sat down on the upturned box, which was the only furniture left in her parlour apart from Annie's crib. She emptied the money from her purse into her lap, added the eleven shillings and began to count it, even though she knew how much was there – ten pounds, fifteen shillings and tuppence ha'penny. It was still a long way off the amount she needed and she hated having to dip into it for rent and to buy food. Perhaps it was time to go and see the Reverend Brocklehurst again, she thought, and ask if she could get some relief from the parish now that she no longer had a husband to provide for her.

First, she called at the Golden Lion to check if there was a letter from Thomas.

'Nothing,' said Uncle Richard.

'Perhaps that's good news,' said Molly, trying to comfort herself. 'Perhaps it means he's not been told that there's a ship yet.'

'Aye, that'll be it,' said Uncle Richard, although Molly knew that he was probably thinking the same as she was – that Thomas might have gone without having the chance to send another letter.

'Dost tha want a drink?' he offered. 'It looks like a hot 'un out there again.'

Molly shook her head. 'I'm on my way to see the vicar,' she said. 'Best not go smellin' of ale if I'm to ask for parish relief.'

'Call on t' way back then,' he said. 'Tha knows it's always on th' house.'

Molly walked down to the church and pushed open the door. It was a relief to step out of the sun and she stood there for a moment, enjoying the coolness of the stone building, until she heard slow footsteps and saw the vicar approaching down the side aisle.

'Oh, it's you, Mrs Holden. I thought I heard the door.'

'Can you spare me a moment?' she asked, embarrassed at the thought of having to ask for charity, but reminding herself that it was the only way she would be able to save enough to get her passage with Thomas.

'Of course. Come up to the vestry.' He walked ahead of her and pulled out the same bentwood chair as last time for her to sit down. 'I'm sorry that the petition wasn't successful,' he said. 'You must be disappointed.'

'I am,' agreed Molly. 'But they say I can go if I pay thirty-five pounds.'

The vicar sadly shook his head. 'So what will you do?' he asked, dismissing as impossible any idea that she might successfully find so large an amount.

'I'll sell Thomas's loom,' she told him, eager to explain how determined she was. 'I've already sold most of my furniture and got eleven shillings and sixpence for a quilt, and once t' loom's gone I'll be able to stop rentin' t' cottage. That'll save me a bit.'

'Where will you live? Do you have family who will take you in?' asked the vicar.

'There's Thomas's parents, and I've a sister,' she said. Her conscience was pricked by the thought of Nancy who was heavily pregnant and found it difficult to walk from Springfield. She really ought to go and see her and check that she was all right and had everything she needed for the coming child. 'Thing is,' Molly went on, 'I wondered if there was any chance of me gettin' some help from the parish in the meantime – for rent and food.'

The vicar stared at her for a moment. He seemed surprised by her request. 'Parish relief is only for those who have nothing,' he told her.

'But I've nowt now that Thomas has been sent away.'

'You just told me you were paid eleven shillings and sixpence for a quilt, and that you're to sell the loom.'

'Aye, but that's to go towards paying for my passage.'

The vicar frowned. 'I don't think you understand,' he said gently. 'If you have money then you're not eligible for relief.'

'But I need to save up so I can go with Thomas. It's not my fault I've been turned down for a free passage.'

'I understand that, and you have my sympathy,' said the vicar. 'But you can't get relief when you already have money. When it's all been spent you can come again and I'll speak to the guardians then.'

'But it isn't fair,' protested Molly.

'It would hardly be fair for you to be given money from the parish fund when there are others who need it more,' the vicar told her. 'There are women asking for help whose husbands have died and who are left with six or seven children or more and nothing at all to feed them with. How can the parish guardians deny them whilst giving the money to you?'

Molly could see the logic in it, but the words hurt. She was desperate to go with Thomas and couldn't bear the thought of her savings dwindling away.

'How am I going to get the thirty-five pounds then?' she asked, wiping her nose on a rag from her pocket.

The vicar shook his head. 'I don't think it's possible.' He reached out and laid a hand over hers. 'Please don't think I'm uncaring,' he said. 'I know how much you want to be with your husband and that is commendable, but I think you need to be realistic. You're going to struggle to keep yourself and the child. And thirty-five pounds is an enormous sum of money.'

'So tha thinks I should just give up?' she asked him.

He looked uncomfortable and withdrew his hand. 'I admire your spirit,' he told her. 'Is there anyone else who could petition again on your behalf? Someone whose word might carry more weight than that of a mere parish priest?'

'I don't know no fancy folk,' said Molly, thinking that if a vicar wasn't good enough, she had little chance of doing better. 'There's the schoolmaster,' she suggested.

'I was thinking more of someone like Colonel Fletcher. Would he put in a good word for you? He's well regarded in London.'

Molly shook her head. 'I've been twice to plead for Thomas. He told me not to go again.'

'Then Major Watkins? Or Mr Gooden?'

'It were Major Watkins as suggested the petition in the first place. Dost think it's worth me seeing him again?'

'Maybe,' said the vicar. 'Perhaps if you expressed some regret for what your husband did, it might soften him. I'll write a letter for you to take, explaining your situation,' he said. 'Don't mention the savings,' he warned her, 'and I will suggest that his recommendation of a free passage might lift the burden from the meagre parish fund.'

'Thank you!' Molly found that the seed of hope she was keeping alive had begun to flourish a little. If she could get free passage after all then the savings would get her and Annie to Portsmouth quickly, and hopefully before Thomas's ship sailed.

–

That afternoon she took the letter from the vicar and went once more to Major Watkins's house. She was trembling as she approached the flight of stone steps that led up to the front door. She wasn't sure if it was fear or indignation. The vicar had counselled her that if her petition was to have any chance, she must admit Thomas's guilt and show her remorse for what he had done.

She pulled on the chain and heard the bell chime inside. Moments later, the door was opened by the same man as last time. He regarded her with distaste.

'I'm here to see Major Watkins. I have a letter from the Reverend Brocklehurst.' She waved it under his nose like a charm.

'What name?'

'Molly Holden.'

'Step inside.' He opened the door fractionally wider, but Molly still had to squeeze past him and she got the impression that he was enjoying it. 'Wipe your feet,' he instructed. 'Wait there.'

Molly stood on the coir mat once again and stared at the splendour. She guessed that just one of the ornaments on display or one of the many pictures on the walls would fetch far more than the thirty-five pounds she needed. How was it that some men had so much? Thomas and John worked all day, every day, except for the Sabbath, but even if they were to work that and all night too, they could never hope to have a fraction of the wealth on display here.

A door opened and Major Watkins came out. 'Mrs Holden?'

'I'm sorry to bother you again,' she said. 'But the vicar, Mr Brocklehurst, said you might be able to help. He's explained it all in here.' Molly handed him the letter and watched as he eased it open and skimmed the contents.

'Yes, I remember you coming last time. I'm sorry your petition was unsuccessful.' He glanced at her. 'The Reverend Brocklehurst thinks that your case might do better if it came from me.'

'He told me you are a very influential gentleman, sir.' Molly hated having to demean herself like this, but she knew that it had to be done if she was to have any chance of success.

'Your husband was involved in the burning of the mill at Westhoughton, wasn't he?'

'No!' she protested. 'He didn't do owt like that! He went to a meeting on t' moor, that's all. There were a man there, who they say's a spy for Colonel Fletcher, who gave evidence against him.'

Major Watkins frowned, but didn't dispute her allegation that Isaac Crompton was a spy. 'Those meetings are illegal,' he said. 'And I seem to recall now that your husband was found guilty of swearing a Luddite oath.'

'I don't know if it's true,' said Molly. 'I wasn't there. So I can't say.'

'But this man, this witness, swore in court that it was what he'd seen?'

She nodded. She wanted to argue some more that Thomas was innocent, but the vicar had counselled her to be contrite.

'I have no means of supporting myself,' she told Major Watkins. 'I'll just be a burden on the parish if I stay here – or so the vicar tells me. He said that there's a need for women in New South Wales, that I'd do well there.'

'The trouble is, Mrs Holden, that free passage is only being given to those whose husbands are given life sentences. Your husband was given seven years, I think. That's not long enough.'

Molly made no comment. She could see that he was mostly thinking out loud and she hoped that he might come up with a solution. He only needed to hand her the vase that was on the side table beside his elbow and she could sell it for more than she would ever need. She glanced about, wondering if there was something smaller and whether she might help herself to it. The man would probably never miss it. He had more than he could ever need. But she quickly dismissed the thought from her mind. No matter what difficulty she was in, she was honest and she knew that she would never dare to do such a thing anyway.

'I will write another petition on your behalf,' said Major Watkins, 'if I can say that you are sorry for what your husband did.'

'I am sorry,' she told him. 'I am that. I wish he'd never gone to that meeting.'

'And you, yourself, have no dealings with these Luddites?'

'No. I know nothing about them.' She wanted to add that Thomas had known nothing about them either and had only gone out of curiosity, but she realised that the time had passed to plead his innocence yet again. These men would not listen. They just wanted Thomas out of the country so that they could continue to enjoy their wealth without protest.

Chapter Thirteen

Thomas barely slept in the overcrowded cabin. He found it impossible to get comfortable in the flimsy hammock that was strung up between two hooks attached to the ceiling. Every time he nodded off he was afraid that he might try to turn over his sleep and fall out, and the fear woke him with a jolt.

Soon after dawn – Thomas guessed it was around five o' clock – they were roused and told to roll up and store away their hammocks. They washed and dressed and were told to sit down on either side of the long trestle table. No speaking was allowed. A tin filled with cocoa was brought to the table and Jack Fisher given the task of pouring some into each man's cup. They were all given a hunk of dry bread and that was breakfast. Thomas chewed the bread, glad of the hot cocoa to help it down and grateful for any food at all, meagre though the ration was.

When they'd washed their plates and stored them away, they were taken to an upper deck and set to work with mops and buckets. The sun was rising steadily and it looked like it would be another fine day. As he worked, Thomas stole a glance at the horizon beyond the ship. The water seemed to go on for ever and out there somewhere was New South Wales. He could see sailing ships, big and small, moored in the port and he wondered what cargoes they carried and where they were bound. It was all new to him and he would have found it fascinating under different circumstances, but then he heard himself being bawled at by an overseer for shirking his task and felt the stinging blow of a whip across his back. He cried out with the pain and quickly began to mop even harder, reminding himself that he needed to be diligent and stay out of trouble if he was to survive this ordeal.

Around half past seven they were mustered into a work group and taken to one of the boats that ferried prisoners between ship and shore. Thomas climbed awkwardly aboard with the irons around his legs and his back still stinging from the whip. They were rowed to the dockyard where they were assigned to a man who told them that their task was to remove the wood and other ballast from the hold of a ship that was moored there. As he carried the planks of dark-coloured wood ashore and piled it up as instructed, Thomas wondered where it had come from. It wasn't English wood, like oak or elm. It must have been loaded on some other shore, but he had no idea where, and as no unnecessary conversation was allowed, he resigned himself to never knowing.

They worked all day, with a short break for dinner – more dry bread – and at around five in the afternoon they were mustered once more, searched and taken back to the hulk where they were allowed to wash before sitting down again at the long table in their mess. Thomas was tired, hungry and thirsty. Although he considered himself to be fit, he was unused to the hard toil of manual work and his arms ached from lifting and carrying the wood. His mouth watered at the smell of the potatoes, although there were barely enough to go round and he knew that he would go to bed wanting more.

Some of the other men also grumbled about the lack of rations.

'You can always have more,' they were told, 'if you can pay for it.'

Thomas hoped that Molly would send him money soon. It looked like he would starve without the means to buy extra food.

After they'd finished eating and cleared the table, Thomas was hoping to rest, but they were lined up once more and taken to a higher deck where they passed into a room as splendid as the parish church back home in Bolton. This was the chapel and they were crowded onto benches to bow their heads in prayer, to ask for God's forgiveness and to give thanks for the opportunity they had been given to redeem their souls.

–

Molly was in the back kitchen when she heard the knock on her cottage door. Wondering who it could be, she hurried to open it whilst wiping her hands on the rough sackcloth apron that she had tied around her waist.

'Molly.'

'Isaac.' She stared at him in dismay as he stood, filling her doorway. He'd never been to her home before and she was unsure what to do. She glanced behind her, at Annie, sleeping in her crib – and then across the fold, wondering if John was about and if he would come if she cried out for help.

'Tha's no need to look so worrit,' Isaac told her. 'I've come about t' loom. The one tha's sellin',' he added as she continued to stare at him.

'Oh, t' loom,' she said.

'Well, is tha goin' to ask me in? To look at yon loom.'

'Aye. Come in.' Molly stepped back and allowed him to cross her threshold. She didn't want this man in her house, but he must have heard that the loom was for sale and it would have been pointless to deny it. Besides, he might give her a good price for it. He wasn't short of money.

'It's down in the cellar,' she told Isaac, showing him the way down the steps.

The loom looked strangely bare, stripped of its warp and weft. Isaac went across and gave it a cursory glance. 'I'll give thee two pounds and take it away for thee,' he said.

'Two pounds?' Molly knew the price was an insult, but she was afraid of antagonising him. She shouldn't have come down here with him, she thought. She should have stayed upstairs and waited whilst he took a look; she should have run across the fold to fetch John to help her drive a fair bargain.

'There's not much use for handlooms now,' he said.

'There is. Factory looms can't produce them prinilled bedspreads,' she told him. 'It's too skilled.'

He shrugged his shoulders. 'They will be doing soon enough. Like I say, I'm willing to pay thee summat and take the loom away. Tha'll not get a better offer.'

Molly hesitated to contradict him. The truth was, she'd had no other offers, but she knew that the loom was worth much more than two pounds – and two pounds was nowhere near enough the amount she needed.

She shook her head. 'If I can't get a better price I think I might keep it,' she said.

'What use is it to thee?' Isaac demanded. 'Tha doesn't think Thomas'll be comin' back to tek up his weavin' again, does tha?' He made it sound as if she was stupid or a child who couldn't see the truth of something.

'He might.'

'Oh, Molly.' Isaac sighed. 'I'm impressed by thy loyalty. I am. It's quite touching. But he'll not come back. Tha must see that now. He's done summat stupid and he's let thee down. What's t' point of hopin' someone like that'll come back? Best move on,' he advised her. 'Two pounds.' He took the money from his pocket and held it out to her. 'It'll help thee until tha makes up thy mind what tha's goin' to do.'

Molly knew that he meant her deciding whether to go back to him, not whether or not she should sell him the loom. But she was determined not to give in to him. Besides, now that Major Watkins had sent another petition she might not need the full thirty-five pounds to go to Thomas.

'What does tha say?' asked Isaac. He'd moved away from the loom and was standing much too close to her.

'I don't know,' she said, taking a step back towards the stairs. 'It doesn't seem enough.'

'It's a fair price. Tek it or leave it.'

'I think I might leave it.' She flinched at the sight of the scowl on his face.

'Now tha's just bein' stubborn,' he said, moving so that his bulk blocked out most of the light from the window. 'Two pound in thy purse is better than nowt – and better than havin' to beg for parish relief.'

She didn't say that she'd already asked and been turned down.

'Where's tha goin'?' he asked as she put a foot on the bottom step.

'I thought I heard t' baby cry.'

'I heard nowt.' He closed his fingers around her wrist. His grip was tight. She would have a bruise, she thought as she tried to pull her hand away. 'I'm tryin' to help thee, Molly,' he told her. 'Tha's no one else now.'

'That's not true. There's John and Ellen, and Nancy.'

'There's none as has money to keep thee. I could look after thee,' he said. 'Tha'd go short of nowt. All tha needs to do is admit tha made a mistake and tha'll find that I'm a forgivin' man. We'll pretend it never happened – never speak of it again. Tha can be my wife as if tha'd never even heard of Thomas Holden.' He almost spat at the name of his enemy on his tongue.

'What about Annie? I'm not giving up my child,' she warned him.

'She can go to her grandparents. It's not as if I'm sayin' she'd be put in t' workhouse.'

'No.' Molly pulled her hand free of his grip and rubbed her wrist. 'No,' she repeated. 'I'm Thomas's wife and I'll stand by him. Major Watkins has written another petition and if I get a free passage then I'll go to New South Wales too.' For the first time, the thought of putting an ocean between herself and this place seemed an appealing idea.

'And what if tha gets turned down a second time?' he mocked. 'How will tha manage then?'

'I'll find work,' she told him.

He laughed out loud and Molly fled up the steep steps as Annie really did begin to cry. Isaac followed and watched as she lifted the child. Annie was hungry and Molly was aware that her blouse was damp where the milk had begun to flow. She stared at Isaac. She wouldn't unbutton her clothing until he'd gone. After a few minutes he averted his gaze and sighed. He was unused to being denied anything and Molly knew it made him angry.

'Come and see me when tha comes to thy senses,' he told her as he put the money away. 'Tha knows where I lives. It's a good solid cottage and tha'd be happy there. Tha can't be stubborn for ever,' he added as he went to the door.

Molly sat down on the box once she'd heard his footsteps fade. She put Annie to her breast and kissed the child's head as she suckled. 'I'll not give thee away like a stray kitten,' she promised her. 'If we can't go with thy father then we'll manage until he can come home to us. I'll never go back to Isaac Crompton.'

–

That afternoon, Molly took Annie up to Springfield to visit her sister, Nancy. She needed to talk to someone about Isaac – someone who understood what he was like.

The house she'd grown up in looked unchanged, set at the far end of a fold with three steps leading up to the green painted front door. She knocked briefly; it felt strange to knock on her own front door. Then she opened it and called out to her sister.

'Nancy? It's only me.' Nancy was sitting by the range. A small fire was burning and she was sewing – baby clothes, thought Molly, as she glanced at the swell of her sister's belly. She bent to kiss Nancy's cheek and her sister put the sewing aside and reached out her arms to take Annie onto her lap. The child laughed up at her auntie as Nancy took off her bonnet and smoothed her hair.

'She's grown!'

'It's not *that* long since tha's seen her.' Molly knew she was taking offence where none was intended, but she felt guilty that it was over three weeks since she'd been to visit her sister.

'Hast tha heard from Thomas?' asked Nancy as Molly put the kettle on to make them tea.

'Aye. He's on a hulk at Portsmouth.'

'Will tha be goin' to join him?' Molly could see that Nancy was worried.

She shook her head. 'It seems impossible to get the money together for a passage,' she admitted. 'And they've turned me down for relief because I have savings so I'll have to pay out for t' rent. Major Watkins has sent another petition for me but I don't know if it will be any more successful than the last one.'

'Then tha might still be here when my baby comes.' Nancy sounded relieved and Molly knew that her sister wanted her to be there for the birth. Molly wanted to be there too. Without their mother she knew that her sister needed her. Nancy had helped her after Annie was born and she longed to do the same, but she was worried that the likelihood of Thomas sailing without her was growing as each day passed. 'But tha must go if tha gets the chance,' added Nancy.

Molly set the tea to brew. 'If they turn me down again I don't know what I'll do,' she said.

'Tha'll manage,' replied Nancy. 'We'll all look after thee. Nobody'll let thee and little Annie go hungry.'

'Isaac Crompton's been round,' she told her sister.

'No!'

'Aye, it's true. And I keep seeing him. I think he's following me.'

'I wouldn't put it past him,' said Nancy. 'Dost tha think he gave evidence against Thomas because...' She didn't finish. She didn't need to. They both understood the implications. 'He said he'd get his own back,' added

Nancy, 'but this is low, even for him. Did he come to Hag End?'

Molly nodded. 'Right to the door. He pretended it were about buying Thomas's loom, but it weren't. He wants me to take up with him again.'

'But tha's married to Thomas.'

'That's what I said, but he says nobody comes back from New South Wales. He says I might as well call myself a widow and be wed to him,' said Molly remembering Isaac's parting words as he'd left her cottage. She fumbled in her pocket for a rag to blow her nose as tears threatened to surface. 'What will I do, Nancy?' she asked. 'Tha knows what he's like. He'll not take no for an answer and I don't know how to keep him away.'

'I thought tha were well rid of him when tha married Thomas.'

'Aye. It were a relief then, but now I'm on my own he'll not stop away. Comin' round about yon loom is just the start of it. He'll not rest until he wears me down. I'm frightened, Nancy,' she admitted. 'I don't know what to do.'

'Perhaps tha'll get the free passage.' Her sister's optimism rang hollow.

'But it'll break my heart to leave thee.' Molly wiped away fresh tears. She so wanted to be with Thomas, but she could hardly bear the thought of being without her sister. 'Why does life have to be so unfair?' she asked. 'We've done nowt wrong. Why are we being punished?'

'Life isn't always fair,' agreed Nancy. 'Yon preacher tells me that God has His plan and that we should accept it, but it's hard.' She shook her head. 'What do Thomas's parents say about Isaac Crompton?'

'Well, they hate him for what he said in the courtroom.'

'But what do they say about him calling on thee?'

'I've not told them. I don't think they saw him – I hope not anyway. I don't want them thinkin' that I've encouraged him. I couldn't bear it if they turned against me – and they would if I took up with him again. And who could blame them?'

Chapter Fourteen

Almost two weeks passed before Major Watkins sent word that he would like to speak to Molly.

'It must be about the petition for passage!' she told Ellen excitedly. She'd gone across the fold to ask if Ellen would mind Annie for an hour so that she could run all the way to Mayfield House. But when she saw that Ellen was having a bad day and was in pain, she realised that her mother-in-law was going to struggle with the baby and that she would have to take Annie with her.

'Do I look all right?' she asked Ellen. She'd changed into her best calico frock and was wearing her summer bonnet. The weather was still warm so she didn't need a shawl and she hoped that she looked like a lady.

'Tha looks a treat,' Ellen assured her. 'I hope it's the news tha's waitin' for.'

Molly bent to kiss her. She looked so sad, but Molly's spirits had been lifted at the prospect of good news.

She hitched Annie onto her hip and set off towards Major Watkins's house. *Please let it be my free passage*, she repeated in her head with every step of the way. She'd had no letter yet from Thomas to say when he would sail. As far as she knew, he was still on board the *Portland* and it might be possible for her to sail with him. She wanted to see him so much. He'd sounded so sad and hopeless in his last letter. All she wanted to do was hug him and tell him that she would stand by him, whatever happened.

She was breathless by the time she rang the bell. It seemed an age before she heard footsteps and the door was opened for her. 'Major Watkins wants to see me!' she burst out.

'Step inside.' The man glanced at the mat and Molly wiped her feet vigorously even though the day was dry and there wasn't a trace of mud on her shoes. 'Wait here,' he instructed.

Molly waited, hardly able to contain herself. It must be good news. It must be. Major Watkins wouldn't have sent for her otherwise.

A door opened and the major came out into the hall. As soon as she saw his face, Molly knew that she'd been foolish to hope. He barely managed to smile at her.

'Come into my study,' he told her. 'Sit down.'

Molly perched on the edge of the chair that faced his polished oak desk and watched as Major Watkins sat down behind it. There was an official-looking letter in front of him and he glanced at it with a frown.

'I'm so sorry, Mrs Holden. The petition has been turned down.'

As if she understood his words, Annie began to cry – a heartfelt wailing that Molly couldn't prevent. 'I'm sorry,' she apologised as she tried to shush the child.

'Does she need something? Is she hungry?'

'I think it's just being in a strange place. She'll be quiet in a minute,' said Molly over the gathering cries of her daughter.

'I wanted to tell you myself,' continued Major Watkins. 'I really hoped that it would be better news, but they say the same as last time. Only the wives of lifers are being given free passage.' Out of the corner of her eye, Molly could see the little feather on her bonnet trembling. 'What will you do now?' asked the major.

'I'll have to get work,' she said. 'I'll try to save up enough to pay for a passage.'

'What about the baby?'

'I'm not sure. My mother-in-law's not well. My sister might mind her, but she's about to have a child of her own and it'll be hard for her.'

'What sort of work can you do?' he asked.

'Anything. I can spin. I can work as a maid.'

'I think Colonel Fletcher has need of a kitchen maid,' he said. 'Would you like me to speak to him?'

Molly nodded. She didn't say that the last person she wanted to work for was Fletcher, but she supposed that any job was better than none. 'It may be a live-in job,' he warned her.

'I can't leave the baby with my sister full-time,' she said. 'I'd need to go home at night.'

'Well, go to speak to the colonel tomorrow morning,' said Major Watkins. 'Perhaps something could be arranged. I'll send a note, telling him to expect you.'

'Thank you.' Realising that she was being dismissed, Molly stood up. 'I am grateful,' she told Major Watkins. She knew she couldn't blame him for the decision. He'd done his best to help her.

'I wish I could have done more,' he said.

Molly nodded again, but as she crossed the hallway she saw the vases and the paintings and she knew that the price of her passage would be nothing to him.

She walked slowly back to Hag End Fold. Her legs were heavy and her mood even heavier. Her last hope had been torn away and she wept, knowing that she would never see Thomas again.

'Why did he go to that meeting?' she asked Annie as she sobbed. 'Why didn't he stay at home with us?'

–

As soon as he saw her coming, John came hurrying towards her with a flimsy sheet of paper in his hand. 'A letter came,' he said as he handed it to her and took Annie into his arms. 'Did Major Watkins have good news?'

She shook her head. 'Let's go inside, out of the sun,' she said, opening the door to her cottage. She was anxious to read what Thomas had written to her. She hoped it wasn't news that he was about to sail, but she needed a moment to stay the trembling of her hand so that she could focus on the words.

> *On board the* Portland. *July 14th 1812*
>
> *Dear Wife,*
>
> *My sorrow is greatly increased by parting with you. For what comfort can I enjoy when we are separate? If nothing can be done for us there is nothing surer than I will have to go to Botany Bay, and I will not know it until the morning that we have to go. But dear Wife, if it is in your power to make exertions on my behalf to get some friends of respectability to represent my case, my restoration would be the happiest sight to both you and me that we ever saw. If government was made sensible of my innocence it would not detain me one more hour. Dear and loving Wife, when I come to reflect on being banished from you and my native*

country it breaks my heart, and all for not doing the smallest injury to government or subjects. Please to let me know how the dear child is getting on when you write to me again – and remember my love to your sister Nancy. Your ever loving husband, Thomas Holden.

Molly wiped away her tears. She couldn't bear to think of Thomas being so sad and disconsolate. 'Have you read it?' she asked John.

He shook his head. 'Only the letter to me and his mother. You can read that.' Molly turned the paper over.

Dear Father and Mother,

I received your kind letter on the 13ᵗʰ and was happy to hear of your welfare as I am in good health at present. I also received one pound safe for which I return you the most heartfelt thanks for I assure you it will be of the greatest service to me. We have not the smallest way of making one penny here and the ship's allowance is too scanty to suffice. We are not debarred from having any necessary food if we have a little money to provide it, but everything is extremely dear. We pay ten pence for a quart of flour and that weighs only about one pound and eleven pounds – and everything is proportionate to that. Dear Father, you have sent me word to keep my spirits up but if you could see how my situation is placed you would think it was fit to make anyone low. All I can say is that as far as I have experienced, all the officers over us seem to be very humane men and we think that even good conduct here will be of use to us, for every three months a return is made of all the men's characters on board and the captain was pleased to speak favourably of us even for the little time we have been here. The characters are laid before the Secretary of State in London. I beg that you will leave nothing undone that lieth in your power to do for me. My heart is almost broken by my unfortunate circumstances. Your loving son until death, Thomas Holden.

'We must send more money,' said Molly. It would be an extra burden on top of trying to save, but they would have to find it from somewhere. She couldn't bear the thought of Thomas going hungry. 'I'm going to get work,' she told him. 'Major Watkins said that Colonel Fletcher has need of a kitchen maid and he's writing a letter to recommend me. I have to go to the Hollins tomorrow to enquire. Dost tha think Ellen is well enough to look after Annie?'

John frowned. 'She has a lot of pain,' he admitted. 'She never grumbles, but I can see it on her face. And she's beside herself about our Thomas. She's makin' herself proper poorly.'

Molly knew that he was right. It was unfair to expect her mother-in-law to mind the baby when she was unwell.

John sat down on the box and the parlour filled with an atmosphere of gloom. 'Thomas sounds very low. I wish I could go in his place,' he said.

'Don't say that. Ellen needs thee. Annie and I need thee an' all.' Molly rested a hand on his shoulder and wished that things could be different.

'I worry that I'll never see him again,' he admitted. Molly didn't reply. The same thought haunted her by day and spoiled her sleep at night. She'd never thought when Thomas had taken his cap from the peg behind the door that evening, and told her that he'd see her later, that he would never come home.

'We have to hope,' she said. She kept on saying it, like a charm, but the truth was that her hope faded with every day that passed.

–

'I don't think I can manage to mind her all the time,' said Ellen when Molly and John went across the fold to tell her the bad news.

'I know tha can't. I'm not expectin' it,' Molly told her. 'I'm goin' to ask Nancy if she'll take her.'

'But will she manage?' asked John. 'With her own child on the way? Maids usually live in, and they work long hours.'

'I'll not take a live-in job,' she replied. 'I can't be parted from Annie as well as Thomas.'

'Tha could move in here,' suggested John.

'But I'd still need to work,' Molly told him. 'I can't sit about doin' nowt and expect other folk to feed and clothe me – not if it's for seven years.'

Ellen began to cry at the thought of Thomas being away for so long. 'I'll not live to see him again.'

'Don't fret, Mother. He'll come back,' said John, although his voice didn't hold much conviction and Molly knew that Thomas would have to raise thirty-five pounds himself to pay his passage back if he was to return at the end of his sentence, and she doubted that it would be possible.

Molly got up early the next morning and took Annie to Nancy before she went to see Colonel Fletcher. Her stomach was fluttering with anxiety as she approached his door. She hoped he'd got the note from Major Watkins, otherwise she was sure that she would never be allowed over the doorstep.

She knocked so tentatively the first time that no one heard her and after waiting for a long time she dared to ring the bell, hearing it clang sonorously inside the house and hoping that she wouldn't be shouted at for making so much clamour. She should probably have gone to the back door, she realised.

The maid opened the door and asked what she wanted. Molly explained that she'd come to see Colonel Fletcher and that he was expecting her.

'Step inside,' she said, doubtfully. 'Wait there.'

Molly could hear her heart pounding as she waited in the cool hallway. She was dreading seeing Colonel Fletcher again after the last time.

He came into the hall with a frown. 'Mrs Holden. You're here again.'

'I'm sorry. Major Watkins told me to come. He said he'd send a note...'

'Aye. I got it,' said the colonel. 'But there's no work here for you.'

Molly felt her cheeks flame with indignation. Yet she wasn't surprised by his response.

'I'm sorry,' she mumbled. 'I shouldn't have troubled you.'

'There's work at the pit,' he told her as she turned away, wondering if she should open the door herself or if she would be forced to stand there, squirming with embarrassment, until the maid came back.

'The pit?' She turned to face him.

'Aye. The coal pit,' he said, as if she was stupid. 'If you go down to see the manager, he'll find work for you – Major Watkins says you need work.'

'I do. I'll not be a burden on the parish,' she told him, looking him in the eye. 'If I'm not to be allowed to join my husband then I'll work hard and pay my own way.'

Fletcher nodded. 'Best get along then,' he said.

—

'Down t' coal pit?' asked Nancy when she went back to tell her what Colonel Fletcher had said. 'Tha can't do that!'

'I've no choice,' said Molly. 'I need to work and it seems that pit work is all I'm going to be offered.'

'But it's dirty work, back-breakin',' protested Nancy.

'I'm young and strong. I can do it,' said Molly. 'And at least I can come home in the evenings. I was wondering,' she said. 'Dost think tha could mind Annie for me? I'd ask Ellen but she's in that much pain that she'll not manage. I could bring her on my way to t' pit and collect her on t' way back.'

'Will tha keep thy cottage on?' asked Nancy.

Molly shook her head. 'I don't think I can afford it. If all my wages go on rent I'll never save owt. John suggested I move in with them.'

'I've a better idea,' said her sister. 'I'll ask William if tha can come back here. It were thy home as well and it's nearer to t' pit than Hag End.'

'I don't want to impose,' Molly said.

'I'm sure he won't mind. Tha can have the back room.'

Molly thought of the smaller of the two bedrooms upstairs. It had been hers and Nancy's when they were children. And although the thought of giving up her own home grieved her, she was tempted by the thought of the little room with its lime-washed walls and flower-patterned curtains. The same bed was still there, covered by the quilt that Thomas had woven for Nancy and William as a wedding gift. He'd intended it to be used on their marriage bed, but Nancy had said it was too nice for everyday and put it on the bed in the back room for any guests that came. And she would be safe here from Isaac Crompton, she thought. William would protect her.

'I'd pay thee for my keep,' she said. 'I'll not be a burden. And it would only be until I've saved up enough money to go to Thomas.'

'Tha's never still hopin' to raise thirty-five pounds?'

'I have to try,' she told her sister. 'I have to hope.'

–

Molly left Annie with Nancy after they'd had some dinner and set off to walk to the pit at Ladyshore. It was about three miles away and she was hot and tired well before she reached the pit head with its smoking chimney and the gin that raised and lowered the buckets that brought coal up from below. Apart from a group of men loading coal onto a cart, the place seemed almost deserted. Most of the workers were in the pit. The banksman looked at her enquiringly as she approached him. He wore fustian trousers and a neckerchief that he used to wipe his face. His hands were grimy beyond the wrists from tinkering with the engine that pounded relentlessly beside him.

'I'm looking for work,' she told him. 'Colonel Fletcher sent me.'

'Aye.' He looked her up and down doubtfully, taking in the gown she'd dressed in that morning to impress Colonel Fletcher. She hadn't had time to go back home to change it.

'Dost know what it's like down there?' he asked.

Molly shook her head. 'I'm a spinner – or at least I was until the mills took my work.'

'It's dirty. Tha needs to wear old clothes. Tha can't go down like that.'

'I've got workaday things,' she said.

'All right,' he conceded. 'Tha'd best go and speak to t' manager.'

Molly approached the small hut with trepidation and knocked on the door. A voice shouted for her to come in and she saw a man in his shirt sleeves sitting at a desk spread with plans and drawings that she guessed were of the workings of the mine. She shivered as she thought about what it would be like down there, under the ground, but this was the only work she'd been offered and if it made the difference between going with Thomas and being left behind, then she would do it no matter how unpleasant it was.

The manager also looked at her clothes, but he said nothing. He must have received some instruction from Colonel Fletcher about setting her on, no matter how unsuitable she seemed and Molly couldn't help but wonder if the man had done it to punish her.

'Come tomorrow. Early,' the manager told her. 'The women are mostly down by six to begin their shift.'

'How much does it pay?' she asked.

'Five bob a week for a drawer,' he said. 'Sundays off and tha can carry a bucket of coal home with thee.'

Molly nodded. 'I'll be here,' she told him, even though she felt unsure about it. And only five shillings, she thought as she walked home. If she gave three to Nancy for their keep, it would take her a year to save just short of five pounds. It would take her years to save her passage to New South Wales. Thomas's sentence would be nearly over, but she still might be able to join him if he decided to stay, or at least send the money to him to pay his fare home. They would be together again. She was determined. It would be hard work, but she would never give up trying.

She went home and fetched her oldest clothes to go to work in. She glanced around the cottage. It wouldn't take her long to pack up what was left so that the house could be put up for rent again. Maybe someone would take the loom on as well, she thought when she went down the cellar steps to take a look at it before she left.

She closed her eyes and tried to imagine Thomas sitting there with the sun streaming in through the window as he painstakingly raised the knops on a quilt. He used to whistle whilst he worked and she loved to hear it as she went about her own tasks, though he never whistled when she went down to help him. They would sit side by side, with their thighs warm against one another, exchanging a word now and again as the pattern formed as if by magic on the quilt.

Molly opened her eyes and gazed at the empty and silent loom. 'Oh Thomas,' she whispered. 'I miss thee so much.'

Chapter Fifteen

Molly was up with the sunrise to feed Annie before she set off to her work. She felt anxious as she approached the pit head, unsure what she would have to do down below. A crowd of other women began to surround her as they walked. They were mostly silent. They looked tired to death before the day had even begun and their faces were partly pale and partly black where the coal dust had sunk into their skin. One or two gave her a nod of greeting, but most kept their heads down as they approached the shaft, where they climbed into a bucket and were lowered by the winch two or three at a time.

Molly waited at the back of the line. She was trembling with fear. Part of her wanted to turn and run away rather than be lowered into the bowels of the earth, but she knew that if she didn't take this job she would be forced to spend every penny of her savings before she was even considered for parish relief – and even then there would be nothing for her if there was work to be had. She had no choice. She had to do this to have any chance of joining Thomas.

The bucket came swinging up for the last time and she was told to get in quickly. She had to pull her skirts up to clamber over the edge. She saw that many of the other women wore trousers, like men, and that they were barefoot. Each held a candle and the light flickered on the dark, wet walls as there was a jerk and the bucket began to descend on its thick rope, squeaking and squealing as it did.

'First time?' asked one of the other women.

'Aye,' whispered Molly as they went lower and lower until she feared the rope would run out and they would be plunged into the depths of hell – for this must be what hell was like she thought as they went down, down under the earth. The bucket stopped suddenly and Molly lurched forward, having to grab the sides to prevent herself falling. The other women laughed at her.

'Tha'll get accustomed to it,' the one who'd spoken earlier told her.

Molly climbed out of the bucket, still encumbered by her skirts and found that she couldn't stand upright in the low tunnel. Her feet had landed in water, which was now seeping through the soles of her boots and she realised why the other women chose to work barefoot. Someone nudged her and handed her a stout leather belt with a thick chain attached. 'Here, fix that on. Put the chain between tha legs and the other end hooks on the cart, like this.'

Molly peered into the gloom to try to see who was speaking and where the cart was. 'There!' instructed the impatient voice. 'Get it hooked on. Tha's workin' on yon mine today. Tek the cart down and fetch t' coal back. It isn't that difficult to master! Even t' childer do it.'

'Down there?' she asked. The low tunnel was barely big enough to take the cart. She would have to bend almost double to pull it along.

'Aye, get a move on. Tha's twenty loads to bring out afore tha's finished.'

Molly struggled to attach the chain to the cart in the darkness and when she was sure it was secure she found that she was still hindered by her skirts and had to pull them up and tuck the material under the belt.

Once she was ready she began to make her way nervously down the tunnel. 'Tha'll have to be faster than that!' the man called after her. 'Or the next shift'll be startin' afore this one's done!'

The other women had gone off down different tunnels. She could hear their carts rumbling along and she wished that she could have worked with someone else until she learned what to do. The mine seemed to get lower and lower and narrower as she went along, almost on hands and knees, wading through ankle-deep water and pulling the cart behind her. As complete darkness closed in she felt her heart racing with thoughts of being trapped if the tunnel caved in behind her. She'd heard stories of accidents in the pit, but now that it was real she was badly frightened. Yet it was impossible to go back. She couldn't turn around in the confined space and all she could do was move on towards the faint flickering light of the next candle fixed to a makeshift sconce on the tunnel wall.

Eventually she heard a thudding sound ahead of her and realised that she was approaching the place where the miners were hewing the coal. There was a stronger light and she headed towards it, hoping that there was enough air to breathe in this underground warren.

The thudding paused and the men turned as she came up to them.

'Well, who have we here?' asked one. 'Tha's a sight for sore eyes,' he said to her. 'What's thy name?'

'I'm Molly.'

'Well, Molly, fetch that cart right up and we'll load it for thee.'

'Hast been down afore?' another asked her.

'No.' She tried to avert her eyes from him, realising that he was naked as the day he was born, the sweat running down his chest, creating a striped effect where it was washing away the coal dust.

'Tha's done the easy bit,' he told her. 'Tha'll find it harder goin' on t' return, but we'll expect thee back again without delay.'

He shovelled coal into the cart and threw in his tally stick. 'Be sharp,' he said as he showed her how to reattach the chain for the return journey. 'Time's money, and the more loads we get out, the more we get paid.'

'Trust us to get stuck wi' a lass who looks like she couldn't pull a plug never mind a cart,' she heard one of them grumble as she set off back down the tunnel. 'I'll be right miffed if I lose a load's pay 'cause she's not quick enough…'

Molly cried as she hauled the heavy load. At times, she felt as if she couldn't move it at all, never mind drag it all the way back to the entrance. The muscles in her legs burned with pain as she struggled along, determined not to make the men angry by letting them down.

By the fifth load she was crying without restraint and wondered if she might die of exhaustion. She'd thought that she was fit and healthy, but this work was like nothing she'd ever had to endure before. But she was determined not to give in. Other women did it – and she'd seen children as young as seven or eight doing the work too. She would get used to it, she told herself. She needed to earn the money.

Molly lost count of how many loads she'd drawn after she'd counted to fifteen, or it might only have been fourteen. She wasn't sure any more. Her clothes were clinging to her body as she sweated in heat that was worse than the sun of the summer's day above ground. She saw that some of the other women coming out of other seams with their cart loads of coal had stripped off all their clothing except for their trousers. Their breasts hung pendulous and filthy as they heaved their loads towards the waiting bucket that took the coal to the surface. Molly felt ashamed for them in the presence of men and children, but no one seemed to think it was unusual.

There must be hundreds of people down here, she thought, toiling away like ants. Men, women and children working like animals to provide the fuel that kept the fires burning and the engines turning in the new mills. It was filthy work and exhausting – and she had no idea how she was going to continue to do it day after day. But when she looked at the other women, some of them obviously with child, she reminded herself not to be so soft. She had to do this for Thomas. He was waiting for her, hoping that she would come, and somehow she had to raise enough money to join him.

'That's it. Twenty loads,' the man at the bottom of the shaft told her when she eventually managed to haul out her last cart. 'Tha's done well, for thy first day,' he said and the faint praise rang her in ears brighter than a dozen compliments. She unhooked the chain and struggled to unfasten the thick leather belt from around her waist. Her fingers were shaking and she felt as if her legs would buckle beneath her and she would never stand upright again. The pain in her back was almost as bad as the agony of giving birth to Annie – with not as much to show for it. There would be no pay until the end of the week.

When she was told to get into the bucket, she couldn't even lift her leg and the man laughed, grasped her around the waist and lifted her, dropping her in beside another woman.

'Up tha goes!' he said, pulling on the rope and a moment later it tightened, groaned, and little by little, they went up and up through the dark walls until there was a glow of light above them. It was still light on the surface, Molly realised. For some reason she'd expected it to be as dark above as it was below, but the light intensified as they reached the pit head and her eyes streamed with the glare of it.

'It's gets easier,' the other woman told her as she wiped her eyes. 'First time's always worst. Get home and have a rest and tha'll be ready for owt come tomorrow.'

Molly thought that she'd never be ready for anything again. She more or less fell out of the bucket as the banksmen tipped it over and she sat on the ground, dazed and confused until she dragged herself to her feet and tried to straighten herself out. She was as filthy as all the others. Her clothing was streaked with coal dust, her hands grimed and her boots squelched from being submerged in water all day long. She doubted that they would ever be the same again.

'No home to go to?' asked the banksman.

'Aye,' she replied, as she wiped her eyes again and looked around for the path she needed to take. She was hungry and thirsty, she realised. The bread and butter that she'd fetched for her dinner had been eaten long ago. She saw that some of the men were heading into the Wheat Sheaf for a pint of ale, but most of the women were turning for home where other duties were waiting for them. Annie would be hungry, thought Molly as she set off towards Springfield. Her daughter had begun to take some solid food and Nancy had promised to try her with a little milk from the dairy, but she would need a feed of her mother's milk by now – and at least it would give her the chance to sit down for a while.

'Good lord!' exclaimed Nancy when she saw her. 'Hast seen thyself? Tha's filthy!'

'Aye. Anyone would think I'd been down a pit,' she replied, surprised that she still had the strength to make the jest.

'I'll get a basin of water,' said Nancy. 'Tha'd best get washed in t' back kitchen.'

As she limped through the parlour, Molly glanced at her daughter asleep in her crib. 'Has she been all right?'

'Good as gold. She ate some pobbies at dinner time and she's slept most of the afternoon. She'll be wakening up hungry in a minute, though. Tha'd best get cleaned up.'

'Give me summat to drink first. I've had nowt all day and my mouth's filled wi' coal dust.'

'Tea?'

'Nay, get us a big cup o' water,' said Molly sitting down on a wooden three-legged stool and gulping down the warm offering that her sister drew from a bucket beneath her slopstone.

Nancy watched her as she unfastened the filthy gown and let it fall to the floor. Her legs were covered in grime and when she peeled off the petticoat she saw that her arms and breasts were equally mucky. Although she barely had the strength to lift the cloth to her armpits and rub, Molly knew that she had to get herself clean before she could feed her daughter.

'What were it like?' asked Nancy, her face filled with horror at the sight of her sister.

'Dark, hot, dirty. There were childer down there too,' she said. 'I don't know how they do it. I don't know how I'm going to do it again come tomorrow.'

'Tha doesn't have to go,' said Nancy. 'I never thought tha'd come home in a state like this. Don't go again.'

'But I have to,' said Molly. 'How else can I raise t' money?'

'Tha doesn't have to go with him,' said Nancy, meaning Thomas. 'He were a fool to be anywhere near that meetin', so William says. He's got his punishment, but tha doesn't have to be punished as well.'

'But I need to work.'

'There's other work,' insisted Nancy. 'Tha can't do this, our Molly. It'll kill thee!'

Annie woke at the sound of their voices and began to cry. Molly rubbed herself dry on a towel and put on clean clothes. This job was going to create a lot of laundry, she thought. Her legs were still shaking with fatigue as she went through to the parlour and picked up her child. Annie eagerly sought her breast and began to suck, and Molly was glad to sit there without having to feel guilty for not helping Nancy to get the tea ready.

William came in from the paper mill and greeted her. He hung up his cap and went to the back kitchen to wash his hands. 'What's all this?' she heard him ask.

'They're what our Molly wore down yon pit,' Nancy told him. 'I'll take them out into t' yard and put them to soak in a minute.'

'Can't she do it for herself?'

'She's tired out,' said Nancy. 'Let her have a rest – for her first day, at least.'

Annie finished feeding and Molly propped the child against her shoulder and rubbed her back. As soon as her daughter was asleep she would go to bed herself and hope that she would feel all right come the morning. Even though the thought of being lowered down into the pit again in that swinging bucket filled her with dread, she was determined to go and earn her wages.

She lay down in bed with a sigh. The curtain were closed but it was still daylight outside and she could hear people calling to one another. Beside her, Annie fidgeted in the crib. She was sure to wake in the night and want feeding again, thought Molly. The child was fretful. It was the first time she'd been left and although Nancy wasn't a stranger, Molly knew that her daughter had missed her. After a while she fell into a light sleep, but she dreamed that she was down the mine again and the walls were closing in around her. She woke with a jump, her heart pounding. It was barely twilight and she thought that she hadn't slept long, although the house was quiet and her sister and William must have gone to bed. She leaned over the crib to check on Annie. The child was deep asleep, breathing steadily and she was thankful for that. She turned over, pushing away the covers to allow herself to cool. Every bone in her body seemed to ache.

She woke again to the sound of birdsong and eased herself from the mattress, feeling stiff and dull all over. She went out to the privy. It was early yet and a low mist was coating the fields. When she went back in she woke Annie and fed her before putting her back in the crib and dressing herself. She wanted to walk up to Hag End to find some old clothes of Thomas's that she could wear. Her skirts had been such an encumbrance yesterday that they had made her work much harder and although she felt troubled at the thought of wearing men's trousers, she hoped that it would make her task easier.

Molly enjoyed the slight chill as she made her way back home, her joints easing as she walked. Hag End Fold was quiet as she unlocked the front door and stepped inside. She climbed the stairs to the bedroom, oddly reassured by the familiar squeak at the fifth step, and opened the chest. It smelled of the camphor she'd put in to keep the moths away, but the only clothes in it now were the old ones that Thomas wore for gardening and other outside work. Molly pulled out the patched trousers and held them against her, before stepping into them. They were too long, but she could roll them up and though the waist was a tight fit, it would do for now. Running her hands over the coarse cotton, she wondered what Thomas would say if he could see her. She wished she still had the old mirror to look at herself. She must be a sight, she thought as she pushed her hair under her cotton cap.

Not wanting any of her neighbours to see her – especially not Ellen and John, who would be horrified – Molly knew that she needed to leave quickly. She folded her own clothes and left them on the bed to collect later. She mustn't be late for her work.

Molly went back down the stairs and hesitated at the top of the cellar steps. Then she went down to look at the loom. She ran a hand over the seat, where dust had gathered, then sat down for a moment. She tried to imagine Thomas sitting beside her, but couldn't. He'd only been gone for a little over three months and it worried her that the memory of him was already fading. She tried to recall the exact colour of his eyes, the fall of his hair, the gap between his front teeth, but all the details were becoming as hazy as the morning mist.

With a last caress of the loom she stood up and went back to the empty parlour and out through the front door.

People were beginning to stir and she hurried away in the direction of the pit. She hated the thought of spending the day underground now that the sun was rising higher and the birds were singing, but doubted she would have been better off working as a maid in Fletcher's kitchens. She wouldn't have had much leisure there to enjoy the day either.

The night workers were coming away from the pit as Molly approached. She hurried, slightly breathless, so that she wouldn't lose money by being late. One or two of the other women gave her a nod of approval when they saw her clothing.

'Tha'll find it easier to draw yon carts like that,' said one.

They queued for their turn to be taken down. Molly climbed into the bucket for the descent with sore limbs and a heavy heart. It was for Thomas, she reminded herself as she fought back her tears. It was so that they could be together again.

Chapter Sixteen

Molly joined the queue for her wages at the end of the week. She counted the shillings into her purse with gratitude, feeling thankful that the next day was Sunday and she wouldn't have to go down the pit. Although Colonel Fletcher had his workers toiling day and night, even he would not allow them to defile the Lord's Day.

She trudged back to Nancy's house where her sister had plenty of water on to boil and had fetched in the tub from the back yard so that she could have a bath.

'I've sent William out,' she said as she added boiling water to the cold that was already in the tub. 'I told him tha needed a bit o' peace to get properly clean.'

Gratefully, Molly stripped off the shirt and trousers that she'd borrowed from Thomas. Nancy scooped them up from her clean floor and took them into the back. 'I'll put them to soak,' she said. 'If t' weather stays fine they'll be clean and dry for thee by Monday.'

'Folk'll talk if tha pegs out washin' on a Sunday,' Molly warned her as she tested the water with her hand and then a toe. It was a bit too hot but she enjoyed the sensation as she gingerly lowered herself into it and reached for the soap and the cloth.

'Let them talk,' called Nancy from the other room. 'Folk like that find fault in everything anyway.'

Molly began to soap herself up, watching the scum float to the top of the water. She lathered her long hair and Nancy came in with a pitcher of clean water to rinse it off.

'I'm that tired I could sleep here,' admitted Molly, enjoying the soothing heat of the water on her tired muscles. 'Hast tha fed Annie?'

'Aye, she's eaten and I've put her to bed. We'll not wake her for a feed if she sleeps through,' said Nancy. 'It'll do thee good to get a full night's sleep. Have a lie in, an' all. I'll bring thee a sup o' tea in bed in t' mornin'. Tha deserves it.'

'Tha's a good sister,' said Molly as she watched Nancy go to refill the pitcher. 'But I'm worried that tha's tirin' thyself out.'

'I'm all right,' she said. 'It's not like I'm workin' down yon pit.'

'There are women down there who're expectin',' Molly told her. 'One were tellin' us she give birth down there last year and carried t' baby out wrapped in her skirt.'

'No!' Nancy came back and Molly leant her head forward and held her nose whilst the water was poured over her. Then she got up, dripping wet, and began to towel herself dry in front of the fire.

'Leave that,' she said, nodding towards the full tub. 'It's too heavy. I'll help William carry it out when he gets back.'

'No, tha needs to get to bed. Tha's worn out,' said Nancy. 'Sit there by the fire until thy hair dries. Then when tha's had summat t' eat tha needs to go up.'

'Thanks, our Nancy,' said Molly, reaching out to grasp her sister's hand. 'I couldn't have done this without thee.'

Molly was so tired that she barely had the strength to bend and kiss her sleeping daughter before she got into bed. When she woke the house was quiet so she guessed it must still be early. She sighed, happy that she didn't have to get up and go to the pit, but Annie was waking and she pushed back the covers to pick her up and feed her before she woke Nancy and William with her crying.

She'd rest this morning, thought Molly. And after dinner she'd go to up to John and Ellen's. She knew that they would be anxious to see Annie.

She relished the fresh air as she walked over to Hag End Fold. Turning her face up towards the heat of the sun, she let it shine on her and pushed the thought of the pit to the back of her mind. Time enough to worry about that tomorrow, she thought. Today was hers to enjoy and she'd been able to add some money to her savings.

She'd walked some distance before becoming aware that someone was following her. Glancing back with dread, she saw Isaac Crompton, steadily gaining on her.

'Molly!' he called out. 'Hold on a bit. I need to talk to thee.'

Reluctantly, she waited for him to catch up with her. In his Sunday best, he looked quite the gentleman. *A fine figure of a man*, some would say.

'What dost tha want?' she asked him. 'Hast tha come to make a sensible offer for t' loom?'

'What's this I've heard about thee goin' down yon pit?' he demanded. 'Is it true?'

'What business is it of thine?' she asked as she began to walk on.

'Molly!' He grasped her arm to turn her back to him.

'Be careful! Don't make me drop the child!'

'Molly,' he repeated. 'Please tell me it's not true.' He searched her face and she could see the concern in his blue eyes.

'It's true enough,' she told him, pulling away from his grasp.

'But why?'

'Why dost tha think?' she demanded. 'I've to earn a livin' now that I'm on my own.'

'But tha could have gone to the parish.'

'They refused me,' she told him.

'Refused thee?' She could hear the rising anger in his voice. 'Why would they refuse thee?'

'Because I've summat put by. I told thee I were savin' to go with Thomas.'

'So tha took work drawing coal carts?' She could see the disbelief on his face.

'I might not have had to if tha'd made a better offer for t' loom,' she replied.

He stared at her for a moment. 'Don't throw this back on me,' he warned.

'Why not? It's thy fault, isn't it?' She put a hand protectively around Annie's face and began to move away.

'Tha can't keep blamin' me for tellin' the truth!' he told her, following her as she walked on. 'Thomas were at that meetin' and they were swearin' oaths.'

'Tha could have kept quiet about it. Tha didn't have to give evidence against him.'

'I had to tell t' truth when I were called,' he protested.

'Tha should be ashamed of thyself,' Molly told him. 'Tha's a workin' man thyself and tha should stand by thy neighbours not be spyin' on them for Fletcher.'

'Don't call me a spy!'

'Why not. It's true enough, isn't it?' She turned to glare at him. 'I want nowt more to do with a man who'll betray his own,' she told him.

She increased her pace, hoping that he wouldn't continue to follow her, but he wasn't so easily shaken off.

'I can't bear t' thought o' thee bein' down that pit, workin' like that under t' ground,' he persisted as he drew level with her again where the path widened.

'Others do it. Childer an' all. Why not me?'

'Because tha deserves better than that, Molly. Tha's no need to be gettin' mucky and tirin' thyself out down there. I've told thee once and I'll say it again. I can help thee.'

'I want no help from thee, Isaac Crompton. Stay away from me.'

'Tha needs to put aside thy pride,' he told her. 'I knows it's only pride that's keepin' thee from agreein'. Tha knows it were a mistake to leave me to get mixed up with Thomas Holden. Look where it's got thee, Molly.' His voice reverted to the wheedling tone that she'd heard so often before. 'Molly, tha knows that I'll take care of thee. Leave that child wi' its grandparents and come home wi' me. There's no need for thee to go back down that pit.'

For just a moment, Molly was tempted by the thought of not having to return to the mine the next morning. She was dreading having to climb into the bucket and swing down past the rock face where the water constantly seeped through the cracks and ran down into the pit below. She dreaded the thought of working for hour after hour, hauling the wagons laden with coal through the tunnels that were ankle-deep in water and never seeing daylight except during her long walk to and from her work. She'd never been so tired in her life as she'd been this last week

– and although Isaac could be overbearing sometimes and occasionally lose his temper, she wondered if it would be worth it to be released from her toil. But it would mean admitting that she would never see Thomas again. It would mean giving up hope of joining him in New South Wales, and it would mean being parted from Annie. It was the last that she could never bear. She would never give up her daughter.

'I'd rather go and live down yon pit than live with thee!' she told Isaac as she saw that they were approaching Hag End. 'And I'll never give up my child for thee.'

She hurried towards John and Ellen's house, but he still pursued her. She wished that he would go on his way. She didn't want her parents-in-law to see her with him.

'What about yon cottage?' he asked her. 'I heard tha's givin' it up.'

'Who told thee that?'

'I don't need tellin'. I'm workin' for Colonel Fletcher. He's got me collectin' rents.'

No wonder he looked so well dressed, she thought. He'd done all right for himself by cosying up to Fletcher. And it was a job that suited him, she thought. The first requirement for a rent collector was to be a bully and to give folk no leeway if they hadn't enough money to pay up.

'I'm back livin' with my sister, Nancy. For t' time bein' at least,' she added. 'I'll be gone soon, when I've got my money together for a passage.'

'Tha'll never get enough,' he told her. 'Tha'll come back to me sooner or later. I know tha will. I only need to be patient.'

He raised his hat to her and strode off as they reached the fold. Molly watched him go. He would never give up pestering her, she thought. The sooner she could get away from him the better.

She went into John and Ellen's cottage and called out a greeting.

'Molly!' They welcomed her with pleasure and Ellen held out her arms for the baby.

'I've missed this little one,' she said as she settled Annie on her knee and kissed her head. 'Hast tha missed thy grandma?' she asked her in a singsong voice and Annie laughed and reached out to grasp the little brooch that Ellen wore pinned to her Sunday frock.

'Hast tha been to ask if there's a letter come?' Molly asked John. Every day as she'd walked to the pit she'd wished that she could go to the Golden Lion instead to ask if Thomas had written to them, even though she dreaded receiving the news that he was to sail away from her.

John shook his head. 'Nothing,' he said. 'I went yesterday.'

'I hope he's all right,' said Molly. 'What if they've sailed and he had no chance to send word?'

'He would have sent a letter.' John tried to reassure her, even though he looked concerned himself. 'I'm sure they would have allowed them to tell their families.'

Molly wasn't so certain. The government and the gentry didn't care. She'd learned that the hard way.

'What was it like down t' pit?' asked Ellen.

'It were easy enough,' Molly replied, not wanting to worry them by describing how bad it was down there. But as the afternoon wore on and she knew it was only hours before she had to go underground again, a feeling of dread began to creep over her. She wished that she could raise the money some other way.

'Did anyone come to enquire about t' loom?' she asked John. If she could sell that it would help.

'Not a one. I can't understand it,' he told her. 'It's a good sturdy frame.'

'Young uns are more interested in gettin' work in one o' t' new mills than learnin' t' traditional ways,' said Ellen.

'Aye, some are,' conceded John, 'but weavin' caddow quilts is a skill that can't be replicated by yon machinery. There'll always be a need for quilt weavers.'

'Yet no one's shown any interest.'

'It's odd. I thought it'd sell easily.'

'It needs to go so's I can give up rentin' the cottage,' said Molly. 'It's daft to keep payin' out when I'm tryin' so hard to save up.'

Even so, the thought of giving up the home she'd shared with Thomas made Molly sad and she worried whether it was the right thing to do. What if he got his reprieve and came back and she'd let the house go? Where would they live then? They'd waited months for it to become available so that they could live in the fold and not every cottage caught the daylight so well for working on the loom.

'Happen if we take t' loom down we can find room to store it here,' said John. 'It could lean against t' wall downstairs.'

'Would it not be in thy way?' asked Molly. John already had two looms in his cellar and she doubted that another one would fit even if it was dismantled.

'It'd be better than smashing it up and using it for firewood,' he said.

'No!' Molly was horrified. 'We can't do that,' she said, thinking how upset Thomas would be if he learned that his loom had been burned.

'Well, if it's not gone by the end of the month summat'll have to be done.'

'Dost tha think anyone might take it on with t' cottage?' asked Ellen.

'I doubt that would be a solution,' Molly told her. 'Did tha know that Isaac Crompton's been made rent collector? He'll do nowt to help me.'

'Is that so?' asked John. 'So that's his reward for givin' his evidence against our Thomas.' He looked worried. 'He'll do nowt to help this family,' he agreed.

Oh, but he would, thought Molly. She only had to give in to his demands and he would make sure that she wanted for nothing. And it wouldn't surprise her if Isaac Crompton was the reason that no one would buy the loom. She knew that she wasn't the only person who was afraid of him, and now that he had the power to turn folk out of their homes on a whim nobody would defy him if he was warning them not to buy it. He would make sure that the house wasn't rented with the loom in the cellar too. He was sure to insist that it was taken away. Being made rent collector had given him even more power than he'd had before and she knew that he would use all the influence he had to try to force her to go back to him rather than sail with Thomas.

Chapter Seventeen

Thomas was woken by the customary banging on the ward door. He swung his feet over the edge of the hammock with his eyes closed. He was still almost asleep, but he'd learned it was better to get up straight away. Lingering just made it harder and any tardiness was likely to be rewarded by a blow across the shoulders.

He lined up behind Jack Fisher. They'd become used to the routine now — wash, breakfast, a deck to be swabbed, then on shore for their day's work. Sometimes they were assigned to the same work party, sometimes not. But they came together at the end of the day when they were allowed a little leisure before the wards were locked for the night.

A couple of nights before, they'd been on the lower deck, admiring the sunset and watching a boat come in — a middle-sized ship by the name of the *Fortune*. She had three masts and two decks and appeared square at the stern. Thomas stared at her. She seemed sturdy enough for the harbour but he could barely imagine what it would be like to sail in her out on the sea, where, he'd been told, you could sail for weeks on end and never see a glimpse of land. Thomas could hardly conceive of such a thing. He'd never even seen the sea until he'd been brought to this place and he struggled to picture how vast the oceans were and how far they would have to travel to reach New South Wales.

'Dost tha think she might be the one?' he'd asked Jack.

'She's not as big as some we've seen.'

'Aye. Happen she's not for us,' Thomas had said, hoping that he might be given more time before he was taken away. He'd wanted to ask someone if they knew anything about the *Fortune* and where she was bound next. The non-convict workers that they laboured alongside knew plenty, but the prisoners were not allowed to speak to them for fear that they were hatching some plan to escape.

He washed his face and neck in the cold water in the trough. He could feel the roughness of the stubble on his chin. It was a Friday and the next day they would be allowed to shave, under close supervision, ready to attend the fine chapel for Sunday service, where they were told that they must mend their ways. Thomas wasn't sure how he could do that, having done nothing wrong.

He sat down at the table and was given his ration of bread and cocoa. Thomas ate without relish. It was pretty tasteless. He ate only to give himself energy for the day ahead.

'Gather any belongings you have and muster on the deck!' they were told when they'd cleared the plates and cups away. Thomas exchanged a glance with Jack Fisher. His heart had begun to race. Was this it? Were they to be transferred to the ship they would sail on?

They went back to the ward and Thomas gathered his things and put them in a cloth bag. He glanced around the place that become his home for the past few weeks. It had grown familiar and a part of him was reluctant to leave it to be faced with heaven only knew what.

'Get a move on!' called one of the guards and Thomas followed Jack Fisher up to the deck, hoping that they would be kept together.

They were searched and chained together before being taken ashore and marched down the docks under armed escort. Thomas hardly dared to look around him, at the ships on the sparkling sea and the green mound of the Isle of Wight in the distance, although he knew that this might well be his last glimpse of England – the busy port was filled with large vessels, the sunlight glittering on their chequered sides and their colours flying in the wind.

Thomas recognised the *Fortune* as they approached. There was a man in a blue and gold naval uniform, his buttons shining in the sunlight, who watched as they came aboard. Thomas thought that he must be the ship's captain.

They were lined up on quarterdeck as the man looked them over. Then they were required to give their name and the offence they had been found guilty of.

'Thomas Holden. Swearing an illegal oath.' The captain met his eyes for a moment and Thomas wanted to add that he was innocent, but the next man was already speaking. The moment had passed, and he knew that it would do no good anyway.

They were taken down to the lower deck. Thomas looked around for Jack Fisher and was glad to see him at the end of the line. It seemed that the men who had been arrested at Bolton were to be kept together, but none of the others were his friends. He had hardly spoken to any of them whilst they'd been on board the *Portland*. He didn't want to be associated with them. For the most part they ignored him too, although one or two who knew Jack Fisher sometimes exchanged a few words with him.

A hatch was raised and revealed a steep wooden staircase that led below the deck, to the lowest part of the ship. They were pushed down, some almost stumbling and falling until they were all below in the gloom, bending almost double under the low ceiling. In the darkness Thomas could make out what looked like cages. The prisoners were lined up and as each man reached the narrow doorway of the cell, his manacles were taken off, though the irons were left around their legs and Thomas wondered if they were to be shackled all the way to New South Wales.

The warder closed the gate on them and locked it and the men stood around, huddled too close together for comfort, each uneasy about what their future held.

Thomas felt the ship move as it rose on the incoming tide.

'I don't feel so good,' he told Jack Fisher as his stomach heaved. 'I feel sick and we haven't even set sail yet.'

'Tha'll be all right,' said Jack, peering at him in the gloom. 'It's probably nowt.'

Thomas hoped that he was right. Sickness was rife on the hulks and he hoped he hadn't caught some disease from the rats that he'd seen and heard running through the ship and climbing up and down the ropes.

He sat down on the floor, it being the only place to rest, and put his head on his knees. Perhaps it was just the worry that was making him feel so rotten. Perhaps this was what heartbreak felt like.

He remained there as the other men began to sit down one by one. The ship was rocking gently. It might have been soothing if it hadn't been so frightening, thought Thomas. He'd grown used to the sound of the waves slapping against the hull of the *Portland*, but he dreaded going to sea. He was still hoping that a reprieve might come before they set sail, but he knew that time was growing short and once they were underway there was nothing that would help him.

After a while the warder returned and they were issued with bedding – a hammock and two blankets and a pillow for each man, which were to be stowed away for now on the shelves that ran the length of the ship. It was too dark to see if they were clean, but they didn't smell too bad, thought Thomas, wearily wishing that it was time for them to go to bed. He wanted to lie down, but the floor was wet.

They were issued with a plate, a beaker and a spoon. The warder said he wanted one man to act as mess officer and he pointed at Jack Fisher. Jack was taken out of the cell and the door locked again. Thomas watched as he climbed the ladder to the hatch to fetch down their rations.

Jack returned with bread which he doled out and a barrel of weak ale was rolled in and ladled into their beakers. Thomas broke off small pieces of the dry bread and dipped them in the ale to soften them before trying to eat.

'What's to do?' Jack asked him.

'I can't eat it,' said Thomas. 'I feel that sickly.'

'Tha needs to keep thy strength up,' Jack warned him. 'We've a long journey ahead of us.'

'Aye.' Thomas contemplated the sea voyage and wondered if he would survive it.

'Think of thy Molly and the little lass,' urged Jack. 'If she gets leave to join thee she won't want to find thee poorly.'

Thomas knew that his friend was right. He ate a little more of the bread, although he had no appetite for it and hoped that if Molly did come, she would be provided with better accommodation than this.

After the meal was over, Jack was told to gather the cups and utensils and take them up on deck to wash them. Thomas envied him the breath of fresh air that it allowed him. The bucket that served as their latrine was already beginning to stink.

Chapter Eighteen

'There's a letter come,' John told Molly as soon as she reached the cottage on the fold a few weeks later. 'I picked it up yesterday. I'll get it for thee.'

Molly sat down at the table and took off her bonnet to read it. She was tired out. The work in the pit didn't seem to get any easier and she worried about how long she could keep doing it. If it hadn't been for the thought of Thomas anxiously waiting to hear if she could go with him, she would have given it up long since.

> *On board the* Fortune. *November 22ⁿᵈ 1812*
>
> *Dear and loving Wife, I take this opportunity of writing a few lines to you hoping to find you and my dear child in a good state of health. I have been very poorly ever since I came on board this ship, but thank God, I am getting a deal better now. You desire me to write at all opportunities and you may depend I shall, but it is a great deal of trouble to get to write a letter here. Dear Wife, it does not trouble me as much being confined here as being parted from you and my dear child. But if I live to serve out my time, as I trust in God I shall, you may depend upon it I shall return to England and then I hope we shall spend the remainder of our*

days in this world in love and happiness together.
If you send me any more money, I beg you will
send it in a note and not a post office order and
pay the postage. Dear Wife, as soon as I reach my
journey's end I will write to you and if there is any
prospect of you coming to me and us doing well I
will send for you, so I would have you get all the
money you can gathered together.

You ever loving and affectionate husband until
death, Thomas Holden.

Molly kissed the letter and put it on the table. She must
not let him down, she thought. He was counting on her
to get enough money together to either go with him, or
to follow him, and she must not disappoint him.

After spending the afternoon with her parents-in-law
she kissed them goodbye and with Annie sleeping in her
arms, she walked home to Nancy's.

As soon as she got back and saw William's face she
knew that something was wrong.

'Where's Nancy?' she asked, alarmed at not seeing her
sister in the parlour.

'Upstairs. Ma Flitcroft's with her. T' baby's comin'.'

'Here, look after Annie,' she said as she pushed her
daughter into his bewildered arms. She hung her bonnet
on the peg and with her skirts grasped in her hands, she
hurried up the stairs to the front bedroom. Nancy was
standing by the bed, her hands grasping the flock in the
mattress as she leaned over and groaned with the pain of
a contraction.

'Is she all right?' Molly asked the midwife.

'Aye. She's doin' just fine.'

'There were no sign when I went out,' said Molly, feeling guilty about having left her sister for so long. 'We didn't think it were due for another few weeks.'

'Aye, well, they come when they're ready,' Ma Flitcroft said.

'Tha doesn't think it's too soon?'

'No. I think it's about the right time,' the midwife reassured her.

'Molly,' said her sister, reaching out a hand as the worst of the pain eased for a few minutes. 'Tha never told me it would be this bad.'

Molly looked at the midwife again, alarmed at her sister's words.

'How long will it be?'

'It won't be long. Is everything ready?' asked the midwife. 'I asked yon husband, but he seemed lost for words.'

Molly managed a slight smile at the thought of William's face. 'Aye, there's clothing and caps and bedding for a little crib,' she said. 'It's all here in t' drawer.'

'Leave it for now,' warned Ma Flitcroft, as if she thought it might bring bad luck to take out the clothes just yet. 'We'll need towels and an old sheet and hot water first. I asked yon husband to put t' kettle on to boil, but I'm not sure it got through.'

'I'll go and see,' said Molly as Nancy began another contraction. She hoped that the baby would come soon. She hated to see her sister in so much pain and although she knew that it would pass, it reminded her of her own time with Annie and she knew how much it hurt.

'Hast tha got t' kettle on?' Molly asked William when she went back down.

'Aye, there's hot in t' basin and another one on t' hob.' William was sitting by the hearth and still had Annie in his arms. 'Is she all right?' he asked. 'I keep hearing her cry out.'

'She's doin' fine,' Molly reassured him. 'It's only natural to cry out. She'll be better when it's born.'

William nodded. He still seemed uncertain but looking after Annie was giving him something to do and he looked calmer now. Molly gathered some towels and the basin of water and went back up, tripping over her skirt. She cursed it and wished for the trousers she'd worn all week. Even if dressing like a man was shameful, it made it easier to move about.

Ma Flitcroft was rubbing Nancy's back and reassuring her that it wouldn't be long now. They'd said the same to her, remembered Molly, but it had gone on for hours. She hoped that her sister's labour would be quicker.

'The head's crowned,' Ma Flitcroft told Molly as she put the basin on the top of the chest of drawers. 'Looks like a good head of hair too. Bound to be a boy. It's the lasses that come out bald.' She smiled reassuringly and Molly took her sister's hand.

'Tha's doin' well,' she said. 'It'll be here soon, don't tha fret.'

It was early morning before the child was born. At around four o' clock Nancy gave a final push and the baby came. It was a boy, as predicted by Ma Flitcroft, and the midwife cut the cord before placing him in Nancy's arms.

'All perfect. Tha's done well,' she told her as Molly gathered the soiled sheets and cloths to be put to soak.

William was asleep in the chair with Annie on his chest. Molly gently picked up her daughter and put her in her crib, hoping she wouldn't wake just yet. Then she gently shook William's arm and told him he was the father of a son.

'A boy?' He was beaming – all sleepiness forgotten.

'Aye, tha can go up and see them now,' she told him, lighting a candle.

Molly heard his eager steps hurrying up the stairs as she went out to the back and put the soiled bedding to soak. It was pitch black beyond the door. She hardly saw daylight at all now that the autumn was drawing on, except on a Sunday. It was dark when she walked to the pit, dark all day in the mine, and dark when she came out. Soon it would be time for her to set off to work, she realised, and she would have to go without sleep. And what about Annie? She couldn't leave her with Nancy today. She would have to walk to Hag End Fold first and hope that Ellen was well enough to mind her. It would mean setting out even earlier than usual.

The shirt and trousers that she wore to work were still hanging on the line. They felt a bit damp, but they would be wetter still as soon as she got down the pit. As the weeks had passed, the water level in the mine had risen and now it was almost up to her knees. By the time she'd drawn the cart through the low tunnel to the coal face she was wet through.

Molly went up to her bedroom to get changed and feed Annie before they set off. As she passed the door to the front room she glanced in and saw William with his son in his arms. Tears welled in her eyes as she remembered how Thomas had held Annie so tenderly the night she was born. She turned away and got into the work clothes. Annie was waking and she sat down on the bed to rest a while with her head propped against the bolster as she fed her. She fought against the sleep that was threatening to overwhelm her. She mustn't be late for work or they would dock her pay.

When Annie was satisfied, Molly buttoned up her shirt and got wearily from the bed. She whispered to William that she was going and would be back later to take care of her sister. Nancy was asleep and the little boy was in his crib. The midwife had gone and the room looked peaceful with the candle casting shadows over the walls.

'But tha can't go,' said William, staring at her in surprise. 'Who's to look after Nancy? I've to get to my work,' he told her.

'Can tha not stay at home, for today at least?'

'Of course not. Tha always said tha were goin' to come and look after thy sister when t' baby came. That's why I agreed to lettin' thee stay here. Tha can't go back on thy word now, Molly.'

She stared at him. He looked angry with her and she realised that he wasn't going to agree to her going to her own job. She wondered if Nancy would be all right left on her own, but her conscience troubled her. It was true that she'd promised her sister she would take care of her and she knew that Nancy was exhausted. It would be unfair to expect her to care for the baby alone so soon.

'Aye, all right. I'll stop here and look after them,' she agreed, feeling a moment of relief sweep over her that she wasn't going down the pit. 'But I'll have to get back to my work in a day or two,' she told him. 'Tha knows I need the money.'

'A week,' he bargained. 'She'll need someone to help her for a week at least. Tha promised.'

'Aye.' Molly nodded. She was too tired to argue. 'I'll tell them as I can't go this week,' she agreed, thinking that it would now be a week longer before she had enough money for her passage.

She exchanged her working clothes for a petticoat and gown then went down to the kitchen and put the kettle on to boil again and began to make some breakfast for William. He came down, washed his face and then sat at the table. There was a strained silence between them as they ate and once he was done, he took his cap and went out. Molly allowed her head to sink onto her arms. All she wanted to do was sleep. Perhaps it was for the best that she wasn't going down the pit, she thought. She didn't think she could have worked a full shift.

The new baby woke and began to cry and Molly climbed the stairs to lift him out of the crib and take him to Nancy in the bed. She showed her sister how to get him to latch on to the breast and watched as the baby fed.

'Thanks for stoppin' home,' said Nancy, looking up from the baby's dark head. 'I was worried that tha might go off to work and leave me to manage.'

'I'll go and explain to them why I can't come for a few days,' said Molly, 'but I think I might have a nap first. It were a long night.'

'Aye. But it were worth it,' said Nancy, smiling at her son.

'I'll have to go back next week though,' Molly warned her. 'I'll help thee for a week, but I can't stop at home any longer. I'll lose too much pay.'

'I'll be on my feet again by then,' said Nancy. 'And I won't expect thee to pay owt towards thy keep whilst tha's here to care for me.'

It was something at least, thought Molly. She just hoped that a week would be enough and that Nancy would be well enough to look after both children by the following Monday.

Once the new baby was settled and Nancy had had some breakfast, Molly went to her own bed and laid down. Even though she could hear the voices of folk going about their business outside she soon fell asleep and didn't wake until she heard her own child cry. She took Annie downstairs and fed her a bowl of pobbies. Then she checked on her sister and the new baby. They were both sleeping soundly so she put on her bonnet and walked down to the pit, taking Annie with her, to explain why she hadn't turned up for work that morning.

The manager watched her approach with a surly look. 'It's no good tha showin' up at this time o' day,' he complained, glancing at her clean clothes and the child in her arms. 'Hast tha come intendin' to work?'

'No. I've come to explain why I didn't come earlier. My sister's had a baby and I'm caring for her for a few days. I'll be back next Monday.'

'Nay,' he said, shaking his head. 'It don't work like that, lass. Tha can't just pick and choose whether tha comes or not. If tha comes tha has a job, and if tha doesn't come, then tha hasn't.'

It was a moment before Molly realised he was telling her that the job was gone. 'But it's only for a week,' she protested. 'I need to take care of my sister, but I can come back next Monday.'

'Nay,' he said again as a load of coal creaked its way to the surface in the bucket. 'I needs reliable folk who'll turn up every day. Tha's no good to me. I've set another lass on in thy place.'

He walked away, dismissing her, and she stood and watched as the coal was unloaded and the bucket wound back down the shaft. She wanted to argue. She wanted to plead for the job, even though she would never have imagined herself pleading to go down the pit. But if there was no job, there was no money. Tiredness and frustration overcame her and she began to cry as she walked away. She had no idea how she was going to get the money together now.

Chapter Nineteen

Thomas felt too weak to get out of his hammock. The fevers that had plagued him ever since they'd come on board seemed to have intensified and he felt as if his blood was boiling in his head. It was a long time since he'd felt so rough and he blamed it on being closely confined with the other prisoners. There was barely a breath of fresh air on the prison deck and the stench from the bucket that served as the latrine made him heave at every breath.

'I've fetched thee a bit o' bread. Try to eat summat,' encouraged Jack Fisher.

Thomas shook his head and pushed his friend's hand away. 'I can't stomach it,' he said. 'I think I might die.'

'That's nonsense,' said Jack, although Thomas could hear the worry in his voice. He wasn't the only prisoner who was ill. Yesterday they'd seen a body carried out from one of the other cells to be taken to the pauper's graveyard. At least that poor soul had a grave, thought Thomas. He'd heard that those who died on the voyage were tossed over the side into the ocean. He hoped if he was to die, he'd go before they set sail. He couldn't bear the thought of his soul being tossed on the waves for the whole of eternity, and he'd been so tormented with the thought that he'd woken drenched in sweat from another nightmare about being trapped under the water.

'When I told 'em as tha wasn't coming up on deck today they said as surgeon'll come down to see thee,' Jack told him. The hour they were allowed out during the day was the one that every man looked forward to and if anyone chose to remain below then it was known that they were in a bad way.

'Happen he'll say as I'm not fit to sail,' said Thomas hopefully, even though he doubted he'd be any better off on the hospital deck of the hulk. At least here he had Jack to look after him.

A while later a man came down and the warder unlocked the door and held up a lamp. The surgeon stared down at Thomas and said that his name was Mr Ross. 'Yellow jaundice,' he proclaimed without laying a finger on his patient. 'See the yellow in his eyes?' he said to the warder.

'What's to be done, sir?' the warder asked.

'Let him rest,' said the surgeon. 'He's young and looks strong. I daresay he'll recover in a few days. But call me if he gets worse.'

Without a direct word to Thomas he went out and hurried back up the ladder.

'I need to write to Molly,' Thomas told Jack. 'See if tha can find someone who'll pen a letter for me. She needs to know as I'm badly.'

The warder seemed to take pity on Thomas and fetched paper, pen and ink in return for a sixpence and Thomas told him what to write.

On board the Fortune. *November 29th 1812.*

Dear and loving Wife, I take the opportunity of writing a few lines to you hoping they will find you in good health. But, dear Wife, I am very sorry to inform you that I am very bad of the yellow jaundice and have been for a fortnight. I am still getting worse and if I very soon do not get some relief I am afraid I shall not recover. I think it is with being so close confined and I have taken to my bed. I have no friend here but Jack Fisher and he waits upon me and looks after me like a brother. Dear Wife, I have heard that you have petitioned to go with me and I wish to know if you have any prospect of going with me or getting me off. It would not be too late to get my sentence mitigated if we were out of the country. I would have you do all you can for me. The captain here does not open the letters as the captain at Langstone Harbour does and dear Wife, if you have any prospect of coming to me I would have you write immediately by return of post. Your ever affectionate and loving husband until death, Thomas Holden.

Thomas began to cry quietly as he thought of Molly. 'I'll never see her or t' child again. I'm done for,' he said.

Jack took his hand and bid him to be brave. 'Tha'll get better,' he urged. 'Tha mustn't give up.'

'Is there still room on the paper?' he asked the warder.

'Aye. The back of it's still blank.'

'I must write to my father and mother then, tell them how we're sufferin' here. Tell them they must get me off before it's too late.'

Dear honoured Father and Mother, we have been seven weeks without clean shirts. We asked the captain for shirts and he said they could not be dirty yet. And I wear irons on both legs as we did before at the hulks. If you cannot do nothing for me, and very soon, I am sure you will never see me alive again. I have eaten nothing for three days, not one pennyworth of meat – and so no more at present, your ever-loving and affectionate, but unfortunate and unhappy son, til death for ever, ever more. Thomas Holden.

He sighed and closed his eyes. He'd never thought that his life would end like this. And he'd done nothing wrong. How cruel were the circumstances he found himself in, to die alone and so far from his home and his family.

Chapter Twenty

Molly sobbed as she stood in John and Ellen's parlour and read the letter. It sounded as if Thomas was very ill and thought that he was going to die. All she wanted to do was go to him as he begged her to in his letter. She wanted to nurse him, to make sure that he did eat something to keep up his strength and fight the disease. She'd heard talk of the yellow jaundice; it was usually whispered about in the tones of awe and horror that folk used when they knew something wouldn't end well. They said that it turned a person yellow all over before they finally succumbed. Molly sobbed again at the thought of Thomas suffering like that – and it sounded as if no one but Jack Fisher cared. At least he had one friend, she tried to console herself. At least he wasn't completely alone. She suddenly felt guilty because Jack Fisher had a wife and children too. They must be suffering and struggling, just as she was. She determined that she would try to go to see them and ask if they had had any more news about the *Fortune* and when she was due to sail. Though surely they wouldn't take Thomas away when he was so ill? Perhaps he would be left behind. He would get better. She might have enough money to go to Portsmouth to nurse him and then bring him home. But her hopes sank as quickly as she tried to raise them. His letter was like a farewell. He sounded so unhappy.

Ellen was crying too. 'My poor lad. I'll never see him again.'

'Don't take on so,' John told her. 'He might be gettin' better by now and then tha'll have upset thyself for nowt.' It sounded harsh, but Molly knew that it was meant kindly and she could tell from her father-in-law's face that he was desperately worried too. 'How much hast tha put by?' he asked Molly.

'Eleven pounds, four shillings and tuppence ha'penny,' she said. It was still a long way off the thirty-five pounds that she needed. Since she'd lost her job at the mine she was hard pressed to manage at all. She'd had to take some money from her savings to pay the rent and now she needed to buy flannel to sew some shirts to send to Thomas. She couldn't bear to think of him going without clean shirts.

Leaving Ellen crying, Molly crossed the fold to her own cottage. Although she'd continued to live at Nancy's and take care of her and the new baby for a few weeks after the birth, it had become clear that William didn't like her being there – especially when she wasn't contributing any money to the household. He'd never said anything directly, but he'd grumbled under his breath when he thought she couldn't hear him – and sometimes when he knew that she could.

'He doesn't want me here any more,' she'd said to Nancy one day when he'd gone to his work after making a pointed comment about how much she'd eaten for her breakfast and how it was up to him alone to put food on the table.

'Take no notice,' her sister had advised. 'This is thy home too. It always was.'

'Aye, but it's his name on the rent book now,' Molly had said. 'I've no claim to it.'

'But I need thee,' Nancy had told her. She was sitting by the fire feeding the little lad and watching as Molly cleared the table and took the pots into the back kitchen to wash them up.

'Tha's managin' all right,' Molly had replied. 'I'll still come up to see thee most days.' She'd meant when William wasn't in, but hadn't said so.

'Will tha go to live with John and Ellen?'

'I suppose I'll have to. It's a waste of money payin' rent. As soon as I can sell the loom then I'll let t' cottage go.'

—

Molly's home was as empty as she'd left it. Not only had all the furniture gone, but all her little ornaments too and some of her mother's treasured keepsakes that it had broken her heart to part with. She remembered how the pawnbroker had looked at them and commented that the mirror was flyblown, the teapot had a slight chip at the end of the spout and the paste brooch had a small stone missing. She'd wept all the way home, but the money in her purse had been some comfort because she'd thought that it was bringing her closer to Thomas. Now she wondered if the sacrifice had been worth it and whether she should go to get them back.

She had a small fire burning in the grate but it wasn't enough to warm the stone walls and they gave off a miasma of cold and dampness. The only place she could get warm was huddled over the meagre flames as she sat on the box and watched Annie crawl on the floor. It would only get worse, she thought. If she couldn't go and join

Thomas soon she would have to use some of her money to redeem the blankets or she and Annie would freeze to death when the winter came.

She started at the rap on her door. Picking up Annie to keep her safe from the fire, she went to see who was there. But even before she opened it, she knew that the bulky form casting a shadow across her front window was Isaac Crompton.

He was wearing a smart coat today and had his ledger in his hand. He smiled, but the expression didn't reach his eyes which looked cold and calculating.

'Thy rent's due,' he announced.

'Aye, I know. I'll fetch it,' she said. He followed her inside and stood whistling as she went into the back kitchen and retrieved her bag of savings from its hiding place under the slopstone.

'It's gone up. It's two and six now,' he told her after she'd counted out two shillings into his outstretched palm. Reluctantly, she took out another sixpence and added it to the gleaming coins. His fingers closed over them and she could see her chance of joining Thomas slipping further away.

'I heard tha lost t' job at t' pit,' he said.

'Aye. I had to take time off to help our Nancy with her new baby. They sacked me,' she told him.

'Well, I'm pleased to hear it. It were no job for thee. What will tha do now?' he asked. Molly knew that it wasn't a worthless enquiry. If she had no work it would be easier for him to press his suit.

'I'll find summat,' she replied.

'Not much work about, for a woman,' he commented. He let it sink in for a moment as he put away the money and entered the payment in his ledger. 'Tha could make things easy for thyself if tha stopped bein' so stubborn,' he told her once more. 'Tha knows I'll tek care of thee. I can afford to keep thee. Tha wouldn't need to work. Tell yon parson that tha's had word thy husband's dead and I'll marry thee.'

'But it would be a lie,' she said as her heart lurched at the thought of Thomas being so poorly. She prayed that he was still living.

'No one would ever know. It's not as if he's coming back. And don't say as tha's goin' to join him,' he added. 'It's been months now and tha's still here.'

'I'm savin' up,' she told him. 'As soon as I have enough, I'll go.'

'And how much has tha managed to save wi' no work and t' rent to pay?' he asked with a smirk. 'Tha needs to admit it's not possible, Molly. Stop makin' thyself miserable and let me tek care of thee.'

She shook her head. 'I'm Thomas's wife,' she reminded him. 'Even if I can't go with him he says he'll send for me. And if I can't go then he says he'll come back.'

'Nobody comes back,' Isaac repeated as he shut his book. 'Think on it, Molly. Tha knows where I am when tha sees sense and changes thy mind.'

He went out and she shut the door firmly behind him, fresh tears coursed down her cheeks as she rested her forehead against the damp wood. She wished that he would leave her alone, but she knew that he never would. She was sure it had been his plan from the very beginning to get rid of Thomas and the meeting on the moor had gifted him the ideal opportunity.

When she'd given Annie her dinner and settled her for a nap, Molly went down the cellar steps and stared at the empty loom. It would be a terrible thing to break it up for firewood, she thought.

She sat down on the bench and ran a hand over the burnished wood. Then she reached out her feet to the treadles and watched as the frame rose and fell. Thomas had always kept the loom well maintained and it was a pleasure to feel how easily it responded to her.

As she sat there, a shaft of sunlight broke through a gap in the clouds and Molly was struck by an idea. If she couldn't sell the loom then why not use it herself? At one time a broadloom had been the work of two people, but since the shuttles had become mechanised it could be worked by one weaver, who only needed to pull on a cord to send the shuttle across the width of the frame – and although it was usually a man's work, Molly wondered if it would be possible for her to master it. If she could weave some quilts and sell them there was a chance that she could raise enough money to join Thomas in New South Wales even if she couldn't go with him on the *Fortune*.

She felt excitement mounting inside her as the idea took hold. Why shouldn't she do it? She'd need to buy bobbins of cotton from the mill and even though she was reluctant to dip into her savings, it would be an investment. She could work whenever Annie was asleep. She could work early in the morning and late at night, and Ellen might be able to mind Annie sometimes; she wouldn't need to ask her to have the child all day. In fact, when she came to consider it, she was amazed and angry with herself that she hadn't thought of it before. It would be easier than hauling coal carts in the pit, a sight cleaner too, and would bring in more money if she worked hard.

As soon as Annie was awake she went across the fold to talk to John and Ellen about her idea. John looked dubious when she explained her plan to him.

'It's not easily learned,' he said, dashing her hopes. 'And folk won't pay for summat that's full o' mistakes. It would be a waste of t' money tha's saved if tha bought thread and then couldn't sell t' quilts because there were too many flaws in 'em.'

'But I'm sure I can learn – if tha'll teach me,' she implored him. She knew it was a lot to ask when he had his own work. 'I already know how to raise the knops,' she said. 'And I've watched Thomas weave often enough.'

John shook his head. 'It's not a woman's work. Tha'd be better off sellin' t' loom and savin' t' money.'

'But I've tried to sell it! It's been months now and no one'll buy it. I think Isaac Crompton's warned them off.'

'Crompton? Why would he do that?' asked John.

'He's been pesterin' me,' Molly admitted. 'I've not encouraged him!' she protested before they could make any accusations. 'I want nowt to do with him.'

John and Ellen exchanged a glance. They knew that Isaac had been courting her before she married Thomas, but she didn't think they understood how much she disliked him.

'I thought it might 'ave been spite as made 'im do what he did,' said John. 'But I didn't think he'd come botherin' thee again – not when tha's a married woman.'

'I hate him,' Molly told them. 'I'm sure he's doing his best to make things hard for me, but I'll not let him bully me this time. If I can weave and sell quilts it'll show him that I don't need his help. I can make some money and go to Thomas. Will tha help me?' she pleaded with John. She knew that he had to agree. She needed him to show her how to thread up the loom before she could even begin.

He didn't reply straight away and she could see that he was still unsure.

'I could just have a try at making one,' insisted Molly. 'I could begin with a simple pattern and if it was just for a workhouse bed it wouldn't matter if I went a bit wrong.'

'It'll take me from my own work,' he said. 'I'm not sure I can spare t' time to be teachin' thee.'

'Tha'd only need to show me once,' she persuaded him. 'I've a good memory for things.'

'Let t' lass have a go,' said Ellen and Molly could have kissed her for voicing her support. 'We don't want her to be goin' off with that Isaac Crompton.'

'All right,' agreed John at last. 'Go down to t' warehouse tomorrow and buy enough thread for one small quilt and I'll show thee what to do. But if tha doesn't make a decent job of it and turn a profit when it's sold then tha'll have to admit that it's not a good idea.'

'I'll make sure it is,' she replied, trying to sound more confident than she felt. It was one thing to have an idea, but it might be much harder to prove that it was a good one.

–

'Bobbins?' asked Mr Ainsworth the next morning after she'd walked down to Tonge. 'What dost tha want wi' bobbins? Are they for thy husband's father?'

For a moment she was tempted to lie, but she would need to deal with this man to buy her thread and sell the finished quilts so he needed to know the truth. She gathered her courage to speak.

'No,' she told him. 'They're for me. I'm going to do Thomas's work.'

Mr Ainsworth stared at her. 'Dost tha know how to weave?' he asked. He sounded incredulous.

'I've helped Thomas in the past,' she told him. 'I know what to do – and John's going to help me.'

'I'll not be able to accept quilts that aren't right,' he warned her. 'I might overlook a couple o' minor things, but if it's obvious that it's flawed then I'll not buy it. Why not just sell t' loom if tha needs money?' he asked.

'I've tried,' she told him. 'Nobody'll buy it.'

'Aye. It's all factory work now,' he admitted, scratching his head. 'Although yon machines can't make quilts like hand weavers. It'll be a lost skill soon.'

'Then more reason for me to learn,' said Molly. 'Sell me some bobbins,' she asked again. 'If the quilt isn't good enough then the fault'll be mine. Tha's nowt to lose.'

He still hesitated, but after a moment he turned to the box that held the bobbins of cotton to count them out. Molly heard him sigh. She knew that he thought she was wasting her money and that she wasn't capable of producing a good quilt, but she was determined to prove him wrong.

'I'll see thee when it's done,' she promised as she paid him.

'Aye,' he replied, watching her pick up the basket full of bobbins. He opened the door for her. 'I wish thee good luck,' he said. Molly nodded. She could see that he meant it.

–

Back at her cottage, Molly put the bobbins down beside the empty loom. She'd sometimes watched Thomas

163

threading it up and now she wished she'd paid more attention to how it was done. She was keen to get started, but she couldn't begin until John had time to come across the fold to help her.

Meanwhile, she remembered her intention to go to visit Jack Fisher's wife so she locked her door, collected Annie from Ellen and walked up to Hill Fold.

Hannah Fisher answered her knock on the door with a quizzical stare.

'I'm Molly Holden. Thomas Holden's wife,' she told her. 'He's on the *Fortune* with thy Jack. I was wonderin' if tha'd had any word from him.'

'Come in,' she said. She seemed weary and her cottage, like Molly's, appeared stripped of its valuable furnishings. A kettle hung from a chain over the small fire in the stone fireplace. 'Tea?' she offered.

'Aye, thanks,' said Molly, looking around for somewhere to sit down. There was only one stool.

'Thomas Holden, did tha say?' asked Hannah Fisher.

'Aye. He were arrested that night… tha knows…'

Hannah nodded. 'What were he found guilty of?'

'Swearin' an oath,' Molly told her.

'Same wi' Jack,' said Hannah. 'It's a harsh punishment for summat so trivial.'

'Hast tha heard from him?' asked Molly.

'He sent word that they were onboard t' ship as'll take them away. I've heard nowt since. Dost tha know if it's sailed?' she asked, handing Molly a cup of weak tea that was scarcely better than boiled water. 'I'm sorry I've no milk,' she apologised. She didn't even mention sugar.

Molly sipped the drink and shook her head. 'They hadn't sailed last I heard. But Thomas wrote to say he's very poorly with the yellow jaundice and thy Jack is nursing him.'

'He's kind like that,' Hannah told her, although Molly could see that the news worried her. 'Did tha petition to go with thy husband?' she asked after a moment.

Molly nodded. 'They refused me.'

'Aye, me an' all.' Hannah sighed. 'I'm hopin' I might get summat from the parish. I've these childer,' she said, nodding towards her three children who were sitting on a rag rug that barely covered the stone-flagged floor. Their eyes seemed huge in their pale faces. 'I can't keep them without a man's wages. How's tha managin'?' Her eyes searched Molly's.

Molly told her about the work in the pit and how she'd lost the job.

'No one cares about us,' said Hannah. 'We're just a burden.'

Hannah looked worn down by the worry of it all. It was clear that she was struggling and, as she said, it seemed that no one cared.

'Hast tha no family to help thee out?' asked Molly.

'None of my own. My parents are gone now. Jack has family, but they've nowt to spare.'

At least she had her parents-in-law and her sister to help her, thought Molly, but it seemed that Hannah had no one who could give her a bit of extra food.

'Will tha let me know if tha hears owt?' she asked after she'd finished the weak tea and set down the cup. 'I'll do t' same.'

'Aye, but I doubt it'll be good news.' Hannah wiped away tears with the hem of her apron. It was dirty and left a streak across her cheek. 'I miss him,' she said. 'If it weren't for t' childer I'd…' There was no need for her to finish. Molly could see that she'd reached the end of her tether.

'Don't give up,' she said, reaching out to grasp the other woman's hand. 'We mustn't give up hope. I'll come again,' she promised.

Molly was reluctant to leave Hannah. She felt desperately sorry for her and wished she could do more, but it wasn't in her power. She wondered if she would be able to help her if she made some money from the weaving. It would mean her savings growing more slowly, but how could she think of the woman and her children going without when it was Jack Fisher who was nursing Thomas on the ship?

Chapter Twenty-One

The next morning, John came to show her how to beam up the loom, by winding each warp thread onto its beam and passing it through the healds before fastening it to the cloth beam. Molly thought that although it was painstaking work and a bit fiddly at first, it didn't seem too difficult and after John had completed a few of the threads he let her have a go at doing some herself. When he was satisfied that she was making a decent job of it, he left her to it and said that he would call back after she'd dressed the warp to show her what needed to be done next.

It took her all of the rest of the day and the following morning to complete her task. She became quicker as she progressed but she had to break off to attend to Annie at times, although the child was mostly content to play with a couple of empty bobbins, rolling them across the floor and crawling after them.

Once she'd tied on the last thread she stood back and admired her work. The bending had made her back ache, but it was nothing compared to the pain of pulling carts in the pit. As she picked up Annie and climbed the steps to prepare the size to dress the threads, Molly felt optimistic. She was proud of what she'd achieved so far and determined to make a success of this work rather than allow herself to sink into a gloom as Hannah Fisher had. It was true that no one was going to help the wives the convicts had been forced to leave behind – they would have to help themselves.

Molly measured flour and water into a pot. She didn't need anyone to show her how to do this part. She'd always made the size for Thomas and it gave her a flutter of excitement to think that this time she was doing it for herself. She held the pot over the fire and mixed it vigorously until the flour had melted into the water and made a thick paste. Later, she would apply it to the warp to make the threads strong enough to withstand the weaving process. The fewer times they broke and had to be mended, the better her finished quilt would be. When that was done she would have to leave it to dry before she could begin. It would give her time to go and see Nancy, she thought, to check that she and the baby were still doing well.

–

Nancy greeted her with a hug. 'I'm right pleased to see thee,' she said and Molly wondered if she'd been worried that she hadn't been sooner. The cottage was neat and tidy and the little lad was sleeping in his crib by the fireside.

'He seems content,' said Molly, bending over to look at the baby who seemed to sense her presence and woke. He stared at her for a moment and then began to cry. Molly laughed and bent to lift him. 'I spoke too soon.'

'He's hungry,' said Nancy. 'Give him here.' She reached for her child and settled on the rocking chair to feed him. 'How's tha managin'?' she asked.

'I'm goin' to weave a quilt,' Molly told her sister.

'Weave?' replied Nancy in surprise. 'On Thomas's loom?'

'Aye. I reckoned that if no one would buy it, then I might as well have a go myself.'

Her sister looked doubtful. 'Well, I suppose it's better than t' pit,' she said at last.

'Much better than t' pit!' Molly agreed. 'I don't know why I didn't think of it sooner.'

'Well, it's not what women do, is it?' replied Nancy. She raised the little lad to her shoulder and began to walk up and down the small parlour as she rubbed his back. 'What does Isaac Crompton have to say about it?' she asked.

'He doesn't know,' Molly told her. 'And that's the way I'd like it to stay.'

'I'll not tell him. I never see him,' replied Nancy as the baby burped milk onto the towel she'd thrown over her shoulder. 'Has he bothered thee again?' she asked.

'I'm doin' my best to avoid him,' Molly told her, 'but it's never easy. I always have to check up and down the fold afore I dare step out of the cottage, just in case he's hangin' around.'

'I heard he were rent collectin',' said Nancy.

'Aye. Tha heard right.'

'Then tha'll not be able to avoid him for ever.'

'No. But at least t' loom's down in t' cellar. He'll not see as it's in use.'

–

The next day, John showed her how to put the bobbins in the shuttle and begin to weave. He did a few rows and then let her take his place on the bench to have a try herself. Nervously, she pushed down on the treadle with her feet and watched as the frame rose. Then she pulled the cord that sent the shuttle flying between the warp. She battened down the threads and looked at them carefully, relieved to see that she didn't seem to have caused any damage.

Under John's supervision she completed a few more rows, her confidence growing with each one. Then it was time to begin raising the pattern. She reached for the reed hook. She'd done this before, she told herself sternly. There was nothing to be afraid of. After studying the simple pattern they'd chosen for her to work on, she carefully tucked the end of the hook under a thread and pulled gently to create a knop. Then she made another and another, bent over the quilt, tongue between her teeth in concentration, until she had worked the row of pattern from one side of the quilt to the other. Then she set the shuttle in motion again until it was time to pause and raise more of the pattern.

'Tha's doin' all right,' said John and she smiled at his praise, and at the note of surprise in his voice. She knew he'd thought she would be hard to teach. 'I'll leave thee to it,' he said after a while. 'I needs to get on wi' my own quilt.'

Molly hardly noticed him go. She was too busy concentrating and lost track of time as she worked. It was only when she heard Annie cry that she slid off the bench and went back up the cellar steps.

-

Molly worked whenever she could, getting up early in the morning and creeping down to the chilly cellar before Annie woke. Whilst the child was napping or when she could persuade Ellen to mind her for an hour or two she kept weaving. Slowly the quilt began to grow and Molly felt more hopeful with every inch that she completed.

One afternoon, she was busy raising the knops on the latest row of weaving when she heard knocking on her door and her stomach lurched. It was rent day again and she knew that it would be Isaac Crompton. She put down her hook and went up the steps to let him in.

'Molly!' he greeted her with an insincere smile. 'I'm glad to catch thee at home. I've come for t' rent money.'

She didn't ask him in, but he stepped over the threshold anyway and stood looking around her parlour. 'Tha's not got much of a fire goin',' he observed. 'Is tha not cold? It's chilly outside today.'

He looked warm enough, thought Molly, taking in his coat and hat. A pin twinkled in his cravat and the gloves he was pulling off looked like they were made from kidskin.

'I'm warm enough. I'm workin' hard,' she told him.

'Workin'?' He looked around the room again for a clue as to what she might be doing. 'What's tha workin' at?' he asked, suspiciously.

Molly regretted her unthinking words. 'Just cleanin' up and that,' she told him as she went to fetch her purse.

When she came back out of the kitchen she saw him standing by her hearth. He was looking at the pot of size with the brush still in it that she'd used to dress her warp.

'What's this?' he asked.

'Just summat for t' child,' she lied. 'A bit o' gruel. She's takin' some solids now.'

He frowned. 'I thought it were size for a moment,' he said.

Molly tried to laugh it off, but she knew that her laughter sounded forced. 'What would I be doing with size?' she asked.

'Well, that's what I were wonderin'. Hast tha set someone on usin' that loom?' He glanced towards the cellar steps and Molly hoped that he wouldn't have the audacity to go down uninvited.

'No one wants work on a handloom,' she told him. 'Tha knows that. That's why I wasn't able to sell it. It got broken up for firewood,' she said, hoping to prevent him going down to take a look. 'It were a cryin' shame,' she added.

'So tha's no work that's payin' thee?' he asked, turning back to her. He seemed pleased about it. 'I hope tha's t' money for t' rent.'

'Aye. I can pay thee,' said Molly, counting out the two shillings and sixpence.

'And what will tha do when tha can't?' he asked. 'I'm surprised tha's not been to tell me as tha's givin' t' cottage up if tha's rid of yon loom.' Molly didn't reply. 'My offer still stands,' he reminded her.

'Well I hope tha won't be offended if I say I'll not be takin' thee up on it.'

Isaac put the money away and entered her payment into his ledger. 'There's summat not right here,' he said. He sounded suspicious. 'Tha said as tha would give up t' cottage when t' loom were gone.'

'Aye. That's why I were cleanin' up – to make it ready,' she told him.

'Tha needs to give notice,' he reminded her. 'Dost tha want me to put down when tha'll be movin' out?'

'Not just yet.'

He looked up, staring at her with his piercing eyes. 'There's summat tha's not tellin' me,' he accused.

'Don't talk daft.' She tried to shrug off his suspicions. 'I'll be givin' t' cottage up when I go to join Thomas.'

'But tha means to keep it on until then – wastin' money payin' rent? I thought tha were goin' to move in wi' John and Ellen.'

Molly saw him glance towards the cellar steps again and she tried to move to block his way.

'Tha's not taken up wi some other chap, hast tha?' he asked.

'No! Of course not.' She could see that he wasn't convinced.

'Well, tha'll not be able to stop here much longer without a wage.'

'I'll tell thee when I'm movin' out,' she said. 'Tha doesn't need to worry. I'll only stop as long as I can pay t' rent.'

She could see that he wasn't satisfied with her answers, but he closed the ledger and put his gloves back on. 'I'll find out,' he warned her. 'If tha's up to summat, I'll find out about it.'

Molly closed the door behind him and listened as his footsteps faded away. He would find out. She was sure of that. As soon as she took the finished quilt to the warehouse her secret would be out and everybody would know what she'd done. This wasn't the sort of place where you could keep secrets, no matter how much you wanted to.

Chapter Twenty-Two

Even though Molly was keen to finish the quilt and get payment for it, she knew that she needed to spend some time sewing shirts to send to Thomas, hoping he would be allowed to wear them, and if not, that they would be useful to him when he arrived in New South Wales. She couldn't bear to think of him without clean shirts and she bought some red flannel from the market place to make them. She didn't want him to catch cold and be poorly again.

Although she'd heard nothing further from him since the letter she'd received saying he was ill, she kept telling herself that someone would have sent word if the worst had come to pass and he wasn't getting any better. She consoled herself with the thought that if she hadn't heard news of his death then he must still be alive.

After putting in as much time as she could on the quilt during the day, she sat beside a meagre fire in the evenings, her head bent to the gleam of a rushlight, ignoring the stench of the burning tallow, as she made her neat little stitches along the seams of the shirts. She tried to sew love and hope into each one, pausing now and again to hold the cloth to her face and imagining that it would soon be touching his skin.

She sat up late one cold evening in December to try to finish the last of them, hoping to parcel them up and send them off the next morning, praying that it wouldn't be too late and that they would reach Thomas before he sailed.

Her intention to sail with him had faded so much that she'd finally been obliged to admit that it wouldn't be possible. He could go any day, and she was nowhere near the thirty-five pounds that she needed to pay for her passage aboard the *Fortune*. But she was determined to continue to work and to save, and as soon as she had enough money then she would take Annie and they would go. She would not allow anyone to keep them apart from Thomas for a moment longer than necessary.

At last, she folded the shirts, wrapped them in brown paper and tied them with string, adding a drop of wax to secure the knot. Tomorrow she would take the parcel down to the Golden Lion and ask Uncle Richard to write the address on it for her before it went to the post office to be put on the mail coach.

She checked that her door was locked and then went up the stairs with the remains of the rushlight, hoping it would last long enough to guide her to bed. She glanced at Annie who was asleep, breathing deeply. She'd grown too big for the crib so Molly had started to put her to sleep in the big bed. It meant that she could keep the child warm during the night and she'd only had to redeem enough blankets for the one bed from the pawnshop.

Next morning, she was up early and set off towards town with Annie on her hip and the package in her other hand. There had been a frost and the stiff spikes of grass glimmered on either side of the path as the sun rose. She could see her own breath on the cold air, mingling with Annie's breath. They were like dragons, breathing fire, she told the child as the baby watched with solemn eyes.

She turned into Churchgate and increased her pace, even though it was slippery underfoot. She didn't want the parcel to miss the post.

Uncle Richard opened the door in response to her determined knocking and she stepped gratefully into his warm parlour.

'This came yesterday,' he said, handing her a letter.

'Here, hold t' baby,' she said, pushing Annie into his arms before she put the parcel down on a freshly scrubbed table and opened the letter with shaking fingers. It wasn't written in Thomas's hand but it didn't look official and she hoped that it didn't contain any bad news.

> *Ship* Fortune. *Dec 12ᵗʰ 1812*
>
> *Dear Wife,*
>
> *I received your kind letter which gave me great comfort. You say that you are going to send me some flannel shirts, but if you have not sent them I hope you will not send them. It is a Hot Climate where we are going, therefore they will be very useless things, but anything else that you do have to send that is right would be very serviceable and I hope you will not fail in sending immediately as we don't know one day to another when we will sail.*

Molly reached for a chair and sat down.

'It's not bad news, is it?' asked Uncle Richard.

'No. Not really. He says he doesn't want the shirts. They're going to a hot climate.' She gazed at the carefully packed parcel and began to cry – all that time and effort; all that money, and all for nothing. There was no reason to send it now and she couldn't think of a thing that she hadn't sold or pawned that she could send to him instead.

'Is he any better in himself?' asked Uncle Richard, trying to read the letter that was still in her hand. Molly wiped her eyes and tried to focus on the rest of it.

> *I thank God that I am getting better now daily, but I hope you will pay no mind to what you hear from anyone who writes to Bolton saying how good they have been to me. For in my illness I have received no favour from any one of them. I don't hold any conversation with them. If you have got any trifle of money to send me it would be thankfully received and please not to delay in sending as we expect to sail daily. I hope and pray Colonel Fletcher will have the goodness to sign a petition for me and I hope you will let me know. I will be obliged to you to send me a Quire of Writing Paper and a few pens as they are very dear here. Remember my love to my Dear Loving Mother and Father and I conclude with remaining your ever loving husband till death, Thomas Holden. Next letter you sends to me please to put my Christian Name in full.*

> *For Molly Holden*
> *To be left at the sign of the Golden Lion*
> *Churchgate,*
> *Bolton-le-Moors*
> *Lancashire*
> *With all speed.*

At least he was getting better, thought Molly. She tried to cling to that thought as she wept at the prospect of him sailing away from her. The letter had been written three days ago and he might have already gone. He might be out there somewhere on that vast ocean. She couldn't even imagine what it was like. She'd never seen the sea, but she'd heard people talk about the waves and the emptiness, and the danger.

She took her daughter back into her arms and picked up the parcel. Maybe she could sell the shirts so that she wouldn't be out of pocket, she thought as she trudged back to Hag End Fold to share the letter with John and Ellen.

'I'd hoped as all them from Bolton would stick together,' said John, shaking his head. 'I'm surprised at our Thomas sayin' he has nowt to do with 'em.'

'He said in his last letter that Jack Fisher was looking after him,' said Molly, hoping that it was still true. She was reluctant to go and see his wife again if there'd been a falling-out. 'As for the rest of them... well, I suppose he doesn't want to be associated with them as have done wrong. I can't blame him for that. He's still hoping to clear his name.'

'I suppose that makes sense,' said John as he folded the letter and handed it back to her.

'I didn't send the shirts,' said Molly. 'I came back to get some money. I'm going to send it straight away and hope he gets it in time.' She paused. 'He's still askin' about a petition from Colonel Fletcher. Dost tha think it's worth another try?'

John shook his head. 'I doubt he'll be moved. Tha could go and ask if tha thinks it'll do any good.'

Molly didn't want to go. She didn't want to have to face the man again, especially after being sacked from the pit job. She knew that he would do nothing, yet the thought that she must do everything she could for Thomas made her wonder if she ought to make one last plea for clemency.

'I'll go when I've posted the money,' she said. 'Do we have paper and pens? He's askin' for them too.'

John went to a cupboard and took out a sheaf of writing paper and four new pens. Ellen fetched some brown paper to parcel them up. 'I'll be glad to get one o' these back wi' good news written on it,' she said as she straightened the writing paper and folded the wrapping around it.

'I think we all will, Mother,' said John as he watched her. 'I wish I were goin' in his place. I really do.'

'I wish neither of thee were goin',' said Ellen. 'I wish tha'd never gone to that meetin'. But nowt can change it now. It's that Isaac Crompton who's to blame, and look how he's been rewarded by bein' made up to rent collector. He has no shame.' She glanced at Molly. 'He were in thy house for quite a while t' other day,' she said. 'I hope he weren't causin' thee trouble.'

Molly felt her cheeks blush. 'He were askin' when I were goin' to give up rentin' and move out. I didn't tell him about the weavin', but he were suspicious.'

'So he didn't see t' loom?' asked John.

'No. I told him it'd gone for firewood.'

'It's none of his business so long as tha's payin' thy rent,' said Ellen.

'I know. But he still keeps botherin' me,' admitted Molly. It was best if they knew, she thought because they would see him if he kept coming round and she had a feeling that he would. 'He wants me to accept help from him.'

'Help? What sort of help?' demanded Ellen.

'I think he wants me to be with him again.'

'But tha's married to Thomas now,' said John.

'He keeps sayin' as Thomas won't come back.' Molly began to cry. 'I've tried to send him away time and again, but he's so persistent. I don't think he'll let it drop.'

'Dost tha want me to 'ave a word with 'im?' asked John.

'No.' Molly shook her head and wiped her face. 'No, I don't want there to be trouble. I'll keep tellin' him no, and it won't be long before I go to join Thomas. Once I start makin' money from the quilts I'll soon save up. But I don't want him to know what I'm doin' just yet. I'm sure he'll try to find a way to stop me.'

Molly took the parcel from Ellen and crossed the fold to get the money to send to Thomas. She emptied her purse onto the table and counted out her savings, alarmed to see how much they'd gone down. She'd had over eleven pounds, but with the cost of the cotton for the quilts, the food she'd had to buy and the rent, it had dwindled to less than eight. She wondered how much she could spare to send to Thomas. He needed money, and he needed it now. It would mean the difference between him having enough to eat and going hungry and it would be a long time before she could send him more. She knew that the voyage could take six months. Molly counted out five pounds in coins. She would take them to the post office and ask to exchange them for a note and send it with her letter, telling him that she would try again for a petition and that he mustn't give up hope because she would never forget him and she would join him as soon as she was able.

–

After she'd put the letter and parcel into the post, Molly walked to the Hollins and stood at the gate. She could see Colonel Fletcher's carriage on the driveway and knew that he was at home. She hated the thought of facing the man again. Annie was sure to cry – and she didn't think she'd be able to hold back her own tears.

Reluctantly, she walked to the door and rang the bell. The same maid answered the door and a moment later she was standing in the tiled hallway with its oak doors and curving staircase.

Colonel Fletcher came out and regarded her with disdain.

'What brings you again?' he asked.

'Please,' said Molly, her voice shaking with emotion. 'Please will you send a petition for Thomas. He might sail any day.' She hated to beg, but if it moved the man to help her then she would go down on her knees if necessary.

The Colonel looked at her. His whiskers quivered and for a moment she thought he might relent.

'For the sake of the child. Please help me,' she pleaded.

But he was shaking his head. 'There's nothing more I can do,' he told her.

'Then please let me go with him! Please will you petition again for me to have free passage?'

'It would do no good,' he told her. 'I've done everything that I can to help you. I even found you work, but you lost it.'

'I had to care for my sister. She had a baby.'

He waved a dismissive hand at her. 'I'm not interested in your excuses,' he said. 'If you're given a job then you're expected to turn up every day to do it. I need reliable workers, not those who think they can pick and choose when to come. I'm willing to help those who show themselves to be willing, but I will not help feckless people like you who think that their every whim and demand should be met. Your husband committed a crime and must take his punishment like a man.'

'And what about me? How will I survive?' she asked.

He shrugged his shoulders. 'There's always the workhouse,' he said as he turned away.

Molly cried as she walked back to Hag End Fold. She'd never thought that Colonel Fletcher would help her, but his words had wounded her. She hated him; he cared nothing for the troubles of ordinary working folk. All that interested him was the profits from his coal pit and keeping his wealth and privilege. He was frightened by the demands of the working people and he would ensure that they never rose out of their poverty and drudgery to challenge him. She might as well have been a thief and a criminal considering the way he spoke to her, she thought. She couldn't have been treated worse if she had been.

As she walked home, she remembered that it would be Christmas soon. She'd been so wrapped up in her troubles that she hadn't given it much thought. Not that it mattered. There would be little celebration for her this year without Thomas.

She remembered last Christmas. It seemed such a long time ago now and the happiness she'd felt then was something she doubted she would ever recover. She'd been near her time with Annie and Thomas had teased her that she would give birth on Christmas Day. She hadn't. Annie had been born the day after, on the Feast of St Stephen. If she'd been a boy they would have called her Stephen, but Molly knew that Thomas was secretly wishing for a daughter and when the baby had been placed in his arms she'd seen tears of joy in his eyes as he'd declared that it was the best Christmas gift he'd ever been given – even if it was a day late!

Molly was glad that Annie was still too young to understand what had happened. She'd missed her father at first, but Molly thought that she might have forgotten him by now and it made her cry again as she turned into the fold.

'Colonel Fletcher wouldn't be moved,' she told Ellen and John.

'It were worth a try,' said John.

'It were brave of thee to go again,' Ellen told her and hugged her, but she looked disappointed. They'd all been clinging to hope but their hope was diminished with every refusal to help.

'I got to thinkin' about last Christmas as I were comin' home,' said Molly. 'I don't know that I can even face it this year.'

'We need to mark t' child's birthday though,' said John. 'It's what Thomas would want.'

'I suppose so,' said Molly as she watched her daughter on her grandmother's knee, laughing as Ellen danced a little dolly in front of her.

'We'll have a bit of a tea for 'er,' said Ellen. 'Happen we can get some ham and a bit o' bread.'

'Aye, I'll get a bit of summat,' agreed Molly, mentally calculating how much more she dared take from her purse.

Molly worked on the quilt the next morning. It wasn't always easy to see by candlelight but she bent her head close to the cloth and worked carefully. She wanted to complete as many rows as she could before Annie woke.

When she heard her daughter cry, she put down the hook, blew out the precious candles and went up the two flights of stairs to lift her from the bed. There was a damp patch where her nappy had leaked and Molly left the bedcovers pulled back, hoping that they would dry. She took the soaking child downstairs and washed and changed her in front of the fire then got their breakfast. She was short on supplies and decided that she would have to walk down to the market to get more.

The morning was bitterly cold and there'd been a frost again. She'd left Annie with Ellen so that she would have two hands free to carry her purchases home, promising that she would fetch shopping for her mother-in-law as well. She had a list in her head of the things that she needed – bread, oatmeal, potatoes, candles. The candles were an expense she could have done without, but lighting them meant she could work during the hours that Annie was asleep. Now that her daughter had begun to pull herself to her feet it meant that she needed to be watched more closely and Molly was finding it almost impossible to get any weaving done whilst the child was awake.

She reached the market stalls and began to look for the best quality goods at the best prices. She didn't want potatoes that would be black in the middle, or bread that was showing green mould.

It was busy and folk were thronging the stalls, pushing and shoving one another out of the way. Molly saw a woman pick up a loaf and then glance around to see if anyone was watching. When she met Molly's gaze she looked guilty and put it down again. Molly was left with the impression that she'd intended to steal it and wondered why the woman had been tempted to do such a thing. Such a theft would have been severely punished, thought Molly as she stared at the bread. The woman involved in the food riots in Manchester had been hanged, although the courts were rarely so severe.

She picked up a loaf herself and for a fleeting moment wondered if stealing could be the answer to her own problem. If she was transported to New South Wales she might be reunited with Thomas without having to spend thirty-five pounds on a ticket. But she knew it would be stupid. What if they didn't allow Annie go with her? She couldn't leave the child behind. Besides, New South Wales was a big country and the chances of being in the same place as Thomas were small. She took the money from her purse and paid for two loaves – one for her and one for Ellen, then moved on to get the rest of her shopping. Thomas had done nothing wrong, she reminded herself, and she would not let him down by being dishonest herself.

Chapter Twenty-Three

'On deck! Now!' the warder told the prisoners on board the *Fortune*. Thomas and Jack Fisher exchanged a glance. By Thomas's reckoning it was Christmas Eve, but he doubted that they were to receive a gift or any good news.

His legs were still weak and trembled with the weight of the irons as he climbed the steep ladder into the open air. A fierce, biting wind met him and he shivered as he lined up with the other prisoners. The warder went down the line and released them from their shackles. Thomas watched with relief as his dropped to the deck with a clatter, lightening the load on his legs. He hoped that they were gone for good.

'Strip off your clothes!' ordered the warder.

With numbed fingers, Thomas struggled with the buttons on his filthy shirt. He hoped that at last they would be given something clean to wear. The shirt was stuck to his skin and he had to peel it away to get it off.

He watched as buckets of water were placed in front of them. They were all given a brush and a small slab of soap and ordered to scrub themselves all over. Thomas was glad to wash, but his teeth were chattering uncontrollably and there was ice floating in the water he was using. When the warder was satisfied that they were clean they were lined up again and Thomas stood, hugging himself against the icy onshore wind, as he waited his turn to have his head and beard shaved. Then they were issued with clean clothing. Thomas put on the flannel vest, the trousers, and the canvas shirt that felt stiff and awkward. He fumbled with the buttons as the warder shouted at him to be quick, then pulled the hat on, feeling the strangeness of his bare head and seeing a streak of blood on his hand where the barber had been careless and nicked his scalp.

When everyone was ready, the captain came on deck. 'Tomorrow we will set sail,' he announced. 'Our destination is New South Wales. The voyage will take us six months.' He waited whilst this information sank in. 'You will be treated well,' he assured them, 'so long as you are well behaved and follow directions. You will be issued with food rations that the quartermaster will read out to you in a moment. These must last you until we reach our destination. There will no more.'

'It's not much of a Christmas gift,' said Thomas as they returned to the prison deck. 'Dost tha think we'll ever see England again?' he asked Jack as they sat on the floor of their cell with their backs to the creaking hull.

'I don't know. The rations didn't seem to amount to much, did they? We'll have to be careful not to eat too much at first. We don't want to run out afore we get there.'

'Aye,' said Thomas. He'd lost weight whilst he was ill and hadn't regained his appetite. The thought of food was still unpleasant to him and he wondered if the seasickness would make it worse once they were out on the sea. 'Six months is a long time to travel,' he said, scratching at his head. 'But it seems this is it.'

All hope of a last minute reprieve seemed to be fading along with the possibility that Molly and the child might join him. It seemed that she had been unable to raise the money. He was grateful for the five pounds she'd sent him but wished it hadn't been at the expense of her ticket.

Thomas slept only fitfully that night. The ship was busy with folk coming and going; voices shouted, hatches were banged closed, chains rattled and the creaking and groaning grew in intensity.

'I think we're off,' he whispered to Jack as the ship rose and fell on the swell. He wanted to weep with fear.

–

In Bolton, Christmas Day dawned damp and cold. Mist clung to the walls of the cottages around Hag End Fold and the looms were silent. Some folk went down to the church, but most stayed at home, huddled around their fires with not much to celebrate.

Molly crossed the fold with Annie, to spend the day with John and Ellen, although she planned to go to see Nancy in the afternoon so long as the weather didn't close in. John had a good fire going and it was warm in the cottage. Ellen had a pot of tea brewing and there was a wonderful smell from the oven.

'Mutton pie,' said Ellen with a smile, 'and boiled potatoes.'

'Is there anything I can do?'

'Aye,' said Ellen. 'Set the table.'

Molly picked up the knives and forks and placed them around the scrubbed table where Ellen had arranged some holly in a pot to serve as a decoration. It was odd to be setting only three places and she had to bite back her tears as she thought of Thomas. Where was he? And what sort of a Christmas Day was he having? She felt guilty at their small celebration when she thought that he would have nothing. She missed him so much that it was a physical pain.

There wasn't much talk as they ate their dinner. They all seemed locked in their own grief and Molly knew that it was hard for them all to be without Thomas. She heard Ellen give a gasp and John squeezed her hand.

'Don't upset t' child,' he warned her.

After she'd helped to wash the pots, Molly walked over to see Nancy. When she arrived she was glad to see that the house had been decorated with greenery and smelled of good food. Nancy hugged her and Molly sat at the fireside for a while, nursing her nephew on her lap whilst Annie played with the new rag doll that Nancy had made for her. And even though the exchanges with William were a bit strained, he was welcoming and polite and Molly was glad of that.

'How's tha goin' on with the weavin'?' Nancy asked her.

'It's goin' all right,' she told her. 'It's taken a lot longer than I thought it would, but it's nearly done and I can't see any flaws... well, happen there's one or two, but tha'd have to look close to see them.'

'Well, let's hope Mr Ainsworth's eyesight isn't so strong these days,' replied Nancy.

'Hast heard owt from Thomas?' William asked.

'Not since his last letter. He said they might sail any day.'

William didn't reply and they all fell silent, lost in thought.

–

As the light began to fade, Molly kissed her sister and wrapped her shawl around herself and Annie to walk home. The paths were deserted whilst everyone was inside with their families so the footsteps that followed her echoed loudly from the moment she left Nancy's door.

She put her head down and hurried on, determined not to look back. She was in no doubt about who it was.

'Molly!'

She didn't turn when Isaac called her name. She pretended not to hear him even though she knew that he would not be discouraged by her ignoring him.

'Molly!' he called again. 'Wait!'

She sighed as he ran to catch up with her.

'I wanted to wish thee a Merry Christmas.'

'There's nowt merry about this Christmas,' she told him.

'Here. I got thee this.' He held out a package.

'I want nothing from thee.'

'Please Molly. I want thee to 'ave summat nice.' He pushed the package at her again. It was quite small and neatly wrapped in brown paper. She stared at it, wondering what it was and if it was something that she could sell to add to her savings. But to discover what was inside she would need to take it from him and she didn't want to do that.

She shook her head. 'I want nothin' from thee, Isaac Crompton. I thought I'd made that very clear.'

'Molly.' His voice took on the hurt note that she'd heard so many times before when he was determined to have his own way. 'Please take it.'

He pushed the package at her again, but she kept her hands firmly around Annie. She would not be lured into his trap.

'No,' she repeated. 'I want nothin' from thee.'

'Then tha's ruined my Christmas.' He sounded like a sulky child and she turned on him in anger.

'And does tha not think that tha's ruined mine!' she demanded, enjoying the surprise on his face as she shouted at him. 'Aye, and not just Christmas! Tha's ruined my life!'

'It doesn't 'ave to be like that.'

'Just go away!' she shouted at him as Annie began to cry in alarm at her raised voice. 'Go away and leave me alone!'

She set off up the track again, praying that he wouldn't follow her. 'It's all right. It's all right,' she soothed her daughter as she struggled on, not daring to glance back. She listened in dread for his footsteps behind her but when she reached the corner and risked a quick look, he was still standing on the path watching her. She really hoped that she'd got through to him this time.

She didn't want Ellen and John to see her crying, so she took Annie into their own cottage and coaxed the banked up fire into a blaze. It had been the most miserable Christmas she'd ever had. Poor Thomas could well be somewhere in the middle of the sea by now. She cried again at the thought of it as she got Annie ready for bed.

As soon as the fire burned low she made it safe for the night, locked her door and carried a rushlight up the stairs to bed. She crept in beside her daughter and blew out the flame. Enveloped by total darkness, there was no sound from outside except the wind moaning around the eaves of the cottages. She would get up early, she told herself, and work as much as possible on the quilt. She was becoming faster now although her work had been painstakingly slow to begin with. She must learn to be quicker and better so that she could make more quilts without flaws. It was the only way she was going to resolve her dilemma. Whatever it took, she would save the money and go to Thomas. And no matter how much Isaac Crompton tried to persuade her, she would never give in to him.

Early the next morning, she shivered her way down the steps to the cellar. She lit candles and rubbed her cold hands together, blowing them with her warm breath to try to ease their movement. If she worked hard she was sure that she could have the quilt finished by the next week.

—

On the following Thursday morning, Molly raised the last row of knops with her hook and finished with the plain rows of weaving. She pulled the reed hard against the weft to batten it, then stood up and stretched to ease her back. She needed John to come across and show her how to finish it off properly and then she would be able to take it down to Mr Ainsworth at the warehouse and ask him what price he would give her for it.

She'd worked every hour that she could spare to get it done. She'd worked from before dawn until long after it had gone dark in the afternoon, continuing by the light of precious candles in the hope that she could earn a good price. She'd worked in the mornings after walking up to Nancy's with Annie and some afternoons Ellen had been well enough to watch the child for an hour or two.

Molly was so grateful to her family. She would never have been able to weave this quilt without their help and they had given it without complaint, knowing how important it was that she raised the money she needed.

Her greatest fear had been that Isaac Crompton would discover what she was doing. But his rent-collecting round was regular and when he turned up at her door on a Friday she was always in the parlour. Every time he stepped inside, she saw him glance around for signs that she wasn't coping. She could see that he was longing for the day when she had to confess to him that she didn't have the money to pay. But every week she'd fetched her purse from the back kitchen and counted out the coins into his outstretched hand. And every time she'd seen him frown in frustration that he had no hold over her.

'Hast tha enough left for food?' he'd asked her the last time he'd come. 'I wouldn't like to see thee go hungry.'

'I can manage,' she'd told him, going to the fireplace to stir the stew that was cooking in a pot there, raising the lid to allow the aroma to reach him.

'Who's helpin' thee out?' he'd demanded. She could hear the jealousy in his voice.

'No one.'

'Then how can tha manage? Tha's not earnin' owt. Tha's no work.'

Molly had turned her face away so that he didn't see the smile she'd struggled to conceal. 'I've a bit put by,' she'd said.

'What tha were savin' for passage?' He'd sounded hopeful. 'Is tha spendin' it? What will tha do once it's gone?'

'Tha's no need to fret about me.'

'But I do, Molly. Let me help thee,' he'd insisted once again.

'I want no help from thee,' she'd repeated as she'd gone to open the door in a clear invitation for him to leave. He'd hesitated and her heart had begun to race as she'd feared he wasn't going to go. But after a moment he'd closed his ledger and moved towards her.

'I'll see thee next week,' he'd said as he went out of the door.

'Aye.' She'd sighed. She hated that she had to keep seeing him.

Molly heard Annie crying and, putting her worries about Isaac aside for now, she left the loom and went upstairs to get her. She'd started to say a word that sounded like *Ma* when she saw her and it made Molly smile every time. She lifted her daughter and kissed her head where the dark hair was growing thicker and curling around her face. Annie was such a pretty child and so like Thomas. Her heart ached. She wanted to share these precious moments with him, but they were moments that would be lost to him forever. She hoped that he would still recognise Annie when her saw her again, though she doubted that the child would recognise her father. She'd only been a baby when he was taken away from them and by the time they were reunited they might all be strangers.

After breakfast, she went across the fold to ask John if he would come and show her how to fasten off the quilt and remove it from the frame. She felt a bit guilty about keeping him from his own work, but she was sure that if she was shown what to do once, she would be able to manage it herself in the future.

'It doesn't look too bad,' John told her when it was done and he'd spread the quilt out.

'There are some mistakes,' she admitted.

'Aye, but nowt that spoils it.'

'Will Mr Ainsworth take it?' she asked anxiously.

'I can't say,' admitted John, 'but there's no reason he shouldn't.'

'Then I'll go this afternoon – if Ellen doesn't mind having Annie for an hour?'

'She's always glad to have her, when she's well enough. And she seems well today. I'll tell her that tha'll come after dinner.'

'Thanks,' said Molly. 'Tha knows how grateful I am, doesn't tha?'

'Aye, lass. Of course I do. But I don't need thy thanks.'

Molly climbed the steps behind him and watched as he walked back to his own house. She was grateful to him, because she knew that he and Ellen would have preferred it if she'd gone to live with them and simply waited for Thomas to come home.

She made some dinner, fed Annie and then folded up the quilt to take it down to Tonge. As she approached the warehouse door she almost lost her nerve, but she knew it would be foolish to have spent all those hours making the quilt and then not try to get the money for it. She went in and stood for a while as she watched the men working, fetching and carrying bundles ready for loading onto carts. At last someone noticed her and asked what she wanted.

'I've come with a quilt to sell,' she told the man and he went to fetch Mr Ainsworth.

'Mrs Holden, isn't it?' Mr Ainsworth greeted her as he came across. 'Hast tha brought thy quilt? Fetch it over here,' he said, 'and I'll take a look.'

She followed him to a table where he cleared some stacks of fabric aside.

'I hope it'll meet with approval,' she said, as she unfolded it and then took a step back, hoping that he would say it was fit for purpose.

Mr Ainsworth looked at her work. His expression gave nothing away. Then he took a pair of spectacles from his waistcoat pocket and hooked the wires around his ears before bending closer. Molly was sure that he didn't usually give work such close scrutiny and she realised that he was going to see the tiny flaws that would give him the excuse to reject it.

She clutched her hands together, her heart racing and her mouth dry. If he wouldn't buy it then the money she'd spent on the thread would all be wasted, as John had warned her it might.

After a few minutes, Mr Ainsworth straightened up, returned his spectacles to his pocket and turned to face her.

'Did tha really weave this thyself?' he asked.

'My father-in-law helped me beam it up,' she told him. 'But, aye, apart from that it's my work.'

'It's not bad,' he conceded. 'It's not perfect, mind,' he added, 'and I can't pay thee top price for it.' Molly waited, not daring to ask how much he was willing to pay. 'I'll give thee nine shillings for it,' he offered.

Molly felt so relieved she would almost have gone down on her knees to thank him, but she quickly reminded herself that Mr Ainsworth was doing her no favours. He was simply offering a fair price and he would sell the quilt on at a profit. It was her own hard work and effort that had brought the just reward.

'I'd never have thought a lass could weave a quilt,' he told her as he folded it up. 'I never thought it were women's work.'

Molly sensed that he still didn't quite believe that she'd made it, though that wasn't important. All that mattered was that he'd agreed to pay her for it.

'There's no reason a woman can't do it,' she told him.

'Aye. I suppose tha's right,' he said. 'It were all right for a beginner and wi' practice tha should get better. If tha gets as good as thy Thomas I'll pay thee top price,' he promised. 'Hast heard owt from him?' he asked.

'Nowt since a letter before Christmas. I think his ship must have sailed.'

'So tha'll not be goin' with him?'

'I'll follow later,' she said. 'Just as soon as I've earned enough.'

'Tha'll be wantin' more bobbins then?' he asked. He was smiling now and Molly returned the smile as she nodded enthusiastically.

'Aye, of course I will!'

'I never thought a lass could manage it,' he said again as he counted out the bobbins and paid her.

Molly walked back to Hag End feeling pleased with herself. She had her earnings in her purse and more cotton in her basket. She could do this, she told herself. It was possible.

'He bought it!' she told John and Ellen, unable to keep the smile from her face. 'I'm going to start another one now.'

'Shall I come across tomorrow to help thee beam up?' asked John.

'I'd appreciate it,' she said, 'but I'm goin' to make a start and see if I can do it myself. I'll not be a burden,' she added.

Chapter Twenty-Four

Thomas had grown used to the sound of the sea crashing against the hull of the ship and the creaking of the wooden planks as they heaved through the water. Goodness only knew where they were, he thought as he emerged from the top of the ladder onto the deck for his hourly dose of fresh air. Whichever way he looked all he could see was water. The day was grey and overcast and it was impossible to tell where the sky ended and the sea began. It was all one gloomy expanse with no landmark to break up the horizon.

They'd been at sea for almost two weeks now and the year was 1813. There was no chance now to send a letter so he was using the paper and pens that Molly had sent him to mark the passing of the days and to keep a note of his thoughts, hoping that, given time, he would be able to share them with her.

He walked up and down the deck. The wind was flapping in the sails above him and the ropes were smacking against the mast. He watched the sailors adjusting them and felt a slight tilt as the ship turned to make the most of the wind. It was a relief to breathe in the salty spray after being confined in the stench below and he wished that he could stay on deck for longer, dreading the moment he was ordered back down the ladder.

'You! Holden!' called a voice and he turned in alarm, wondering what he had done to draw the displeasure of the warder who was beckoning to him.

'Sir?' He pulled off his cap, feeling the breeze lift the short strands of hair that were growing back on his head.

'Come with me,' ordered the warder.

The man didn't look displeased with him, but anxiety fluttered in the pit of Thomas's stomach as he followed him to the upper deck. Prisoners were not allowed up here normally. It was the deck used by the paying passengers and housed their cabins.

He followed the warder to a door and watched as the man pulled off his own hat and knocked. Someone called out permission to enter and he turned to Thomas. 'This way,' he said.

Thomas went inside and was confronted by the captain at his desk.

'This is the man, sir,' said the warder.

'Holden?'

'Aye, sir,' replied Thomas. He felt himself trembling as he wondered what he'd done wrong. He'd heard rumours of scourgings and prisoners being locked in cells at the prow of the ship where they could neither stand up nor lie down.

The captain appraised him for a moment. 'You were sentenced for taking an illegal oath,' he said.

'Aye sir. But I never did!' he protested.

'That's not my concern. What I'm looking for is a man I can trust – someone not guilty of stealing.'

'I've never stolen anything in my life,' Thomas assured him.

'What work do you do?'

'I'm a weaver, sir.'

'I'm looking for a man to wait at my table,' the captain told him. 'Do you think you could do that?'

'Aye. I'm sure I could, sir.'

'Good. Make sure he's clean,' said the captain to the warder. 'Show him the way to the kitchens and they'll give him the food to fetch up to the table.' He turned to Thomas. 'You'll keep your mouth shut and your eyes down,' he told him. 'If you do a good job I'll put a word of recommendation in for you when we reach Sydney Cove.'

'Aye, sir. Thank you, sir.'

—

When Thomas carried the soup tureen into the captain's dining room, desperately trying to keep his balance as the ship rolled beneath his feet, he saw that it wasn't just the captain who had sat down to dine. There was another man at the table, in army uniform, and beside him a woman he took to be the man's wife and an array of children, from a surly-looking lad who was almost grown, to a small child of about four years. As they spoke, Thomas took their accents to be Scottish, but he had no idea who they were.

Thomas struggled to ladle out the soup into the dishes without spilling any. The woman's dress was made from fine material and he admired the weave of it as he placed her bowl in front of her. He kept his eyes averted from their faces as he'd been instructed, but although none of them spoke to him, he could feel the speculative gazes of the adults as they weighed him up. He knew it was a privilege to be promoted to this task and he was eager to do his best, hoping that this man might have some influence and might be able to help him gain his pardon.

Chapter Twenty-Five

It was March and spring was in the air as Molly walked down to Tonge with another finished quilt. The daffodils were nodding their yellow heads on the banks beside the path and up in the trees the magpies and rooks were selecting the best pliable twigs to build their nests.

Molly was feeling optimistic. Mr Ainsworth had paid her full price for the previous quilt – the full twelve shillings – and she was hoping he would pay the same for this one. She was sure it had no flaws at all.

She'd chosen Wednesday morning because she was knew that it was a time when Isaac Crompton was usually busy at Colonel Fletcher's office. She'd managed to keep her work secret from him all these weeks, although she hadn't been able to avoid him completely and she realised that he was growing ever more frustrated and suspicious about her refusals to accept his help.

'Good work again!' Mr Ainsworth told her. 'Perhaps tha could try summat a bit more fancy next time,' he suggested as he counted twelve shillings into her hand. 'I'll pay thee more for summat I can sell on to a private buyer.'

'I could give it a try,' said Molly as she pointed out the bobbins that she wanted. 'Thomas has several patterns I could follow.'

'Any word from him?' asked Mr Ainsworth.

Molly shook her head. There'd been no more letters since the one she received back in December and it was clear that the *Fortune* had sailed. She wouldn't hear from her husband again until he reached New South Wales and even then it would be more than half a year before the letter arrived.

She came out of the warehouse and set off for home with the basket of bobbins over her arm. When she'd settled Annie for a nap after dinner she would begin beaming up for a new quilt. She knew exactly which pattern she was going to weave – the one with the rose in the centre.

Lost in thought, she didn't notice Isaac Crompton lingering on the path ahead of her until it was too late.

'Molly.' He peered at the contents of her basket as she reluctantly approached him. 'Bobbins?' he asked.

'I've collected them for my father-in-law. Save him a journey,' she lied.

'I thought I saw 'im down at t' warehouse just yesterday.'

'He needed more.' She could see that Isaac doubted her words.

'Let me walk thee 'ome,' he said. 'I'll carry t' basket. It looks heavy.'

'There's no need,' she told him.

'It's no trouble. I'm goin' that way.' He reached out for the basket and she handed it to him, not wanting to get into an argument.

'I thought t' bobbins were for John Holden,' he said as she approached her own door.

'I'll take them over in a minute,' she said as she held out her hand for the basket. Isaac didn't relinquish it.

'I'll carry 'em in then,' he said, leaving Molly with no choice but to allow him inside. 'I could give thee a better home than this,' he persisted as he looked around for a place to put the basket down. 'I don't know how tha can keep livin' 'ere wi' no furniture. I've a decent table and rockin' chairs by t' fire, and a nice rug and…' He hesitated for a moment. 'And I've a new bed wi' fine cotton sheets and plenty o' beddin'. Tha'd want for nowt.'

Molly shook her head but he wouldn't let it drop.

'I'll wed thee,' he told her again. 'Tell 'em as tha's a widow.'

'But I'm not, am I?' she snapped at him.

'Hast heard owt from 'im?' asked Isaac.

'No, but he'll write once he's ashore.'

'If he survives.' The words sent a pang of anguish through Molly. Every night before she slept she prayed that Thomas would survive; she knew many convicts didn't. 'And even if he does, he'll not come back,' went on Isaac.

'Tha can't know that. Besides, I still mean to join him.'

'When tha's got thirty-five pounds.'

'I'm savin' it up.'

'How's tha savin'?' he demanded. 'Tha's no work and I don't know how tha keeps findin' t' rent money. I know tha's not gettin' parish relief.' He fell silent as Molly saw his thoughts take shape. 'Are them bobbins for thee?' he asked. 'Hast tha set someone on weavin' on Thomas's loom?'

'Don't talk daft,' she replied, alarmed that his guess was so close to the truth. 'I told thee as t' loom went for firewood to keep us warm in the winter time.'

'I've only seen thee burnin' coal when I've been for t' rent.'

She brushed his comment aside without a reply. 'I need to get on with makin' dinner,' she told him, and was glad when he reluctantly made his way to the door, although the scent of him lingered in her parlour. She went to collect Annie from across the fold, but didn't mention Isaac Crompton to John and Ellen, hoping that they hadn't seen him.

'Mr Ainsworth said I should try something more complex next time,' she told them. 'He said it'll fetch a better price.'

'Tha's done well!' said John. 'I didn't think tha'd manage it, but I'm right pleased tha's proved me wrong.'

Molly smiled at his praise.

'I just need to learn to be quicker,' she said. 'I can manage a quilt a week now, but tha's makin' two or three in that time.'

'Aye, but tha's got t' child to care for,' Ellen reminded her. 'Tha knows I'd have her more often but she's gettin' hard work now that she's walkin'. I've to watch her every minute.'

'I know,' said Molly. 'Tha knows I'm grateful that tha takes her when tha can. I'll ask Nancy if she can have her more often now that little Billy's a bit older.'

When she got back home she was puzzled to find the door ajar. She was certain that she'd closed it behind her. She pushed it cautiously and held Annie firmly in her arms before she stepped inside to be confronted by the thunder-filled face of Isaac Crompton.

'What's tha doin' back here?' she asked, wishing that she sounded more authoritative, more confident. The man had walked into her home uninvited yet she was the one who felt guilty.

'I lost my pen. I thought I might have dropped it 'ere.'

Molly didn't believe him.

'Yon loom's still down in thy cellar,' he said in an accusatory voice.

Molly felt herself trembling in the face of his anger, but she was determined not to allow him to bully her. 'Why's tha been down there?' she asked. 'It's nowt to do with thee.'

'I wanted to know if it were true that tha'd broken it up for firewood because I never saw thee burnin' any. Tha told me a lie!'

'It's nowt to do with thee,' she repeated as Annie began to cry. 'Get out,' she told him. 'Tha's upsettin' t' child.'

'Is someone weavin' on it?' he asked, standing his ground. 'Is that why tha's got bobbins? I've a right to know.'

'It's none of thy business,' protested Molly.

'Ah, but it is,' he said, coming so close to her that she felt the spray of spittle from his mouth as he shouted in her face. 'It is my business because it ain't allowed! Colonel Fletcher doesn't allow sub-lettin' in 'is cottages. Only them as live in 'em can work in 'em!' He paused to allow his words to sink in. 'Who's weavin' on it?' he asked her again.

'Did tha see anyone weavin'?' she asked. 'Is there any cloth on it?'

'No. But I can see it's in use. There's fluff and scissors, and a hook, and a pattern pinned up. And them bobbins I carried back for thee. Tha's not taken' 'em across to thy father-in-law, has tha?'

She saw him glance at the stairs that led up to the bedrooms and wondered if he meant to go and search up there to see if anyone was hidden.

'Colonel Fletcher has a right to put thee out if tha's breakin' thy rental terms,' he warned her.

'And that would suit thee down to the ground, wouldn't it?' she said. 'Don't think turfin' me out of here would make me turn to thee, Isaac Crompton. There's others who'll take me in. I don't need thee.'

'I'll find out,' he warned her. 'I'll find out if tha's moved someone in wi' thee.'

'Dost tha think I would replace Thomas just like that?' she asked. He looked doubtful. 'Tha can ask thy spies,' she told him. 'They'll tell thee as there's only me and our Annie livin' here and there's nobody comin' in to use yon loom.'

'So let me buy it from thee. I'll give thee three pounds,' he offered.

'I'll not sell it to thee,' said Molly. 'Tha had thy chance months ago. It's not for sale now.'

'I'll find out,' he warned her again, thwarted for the moment. She thought he was going to tell her that she'd be sorry, but he left his threat hanging in the air and this time, when he'd gone, she left the door open to be rid of the smell of him.

She tried to stay calm so as not to alarm Annie, but she was badly shaken and her tears kept bubbling to the surface where she brushed them from her cheeks with the back of her hand. She got Annie her dinner and sat on the box by the fire with the child on her lap to feed her. She was concerned by the turn of events. Molly was sure that she was doing nothing wrong by using the loom, but she suspected that when Isaac realised the truth he would stop at nothing to find a way to prevent her carrying on.

Molly got up early the next morning even though she'd worked until late the day before to beam up the threads and apply the size so that it could dry overnight. She pinned up the pattern with the leaf border and central rose, fixed her bobbin into the shuttle and began to weave in the early light as Annie still slept.

Absorbed in her work, she didn't register the sound of footsteps until they paused at the window above her. She glanced up, wondering who was there and recognised the boots belonging to Isaac Crompton.

Before he could bend down and peer in through the window, she slipped from the bench and pressed herself against the cold of the stone wall. She'd known that he was determined to discover who was working at the loom, but she hadn't considered that he would do this.

Her heart was pounding and she prayed that Annie wouldn't wake and begin to cry. If she had to move to the stairs Isaac would surely see her. The minutes ticked by. Her nose itched and she covered it with a hand, not daring to sneeze and give herself away. She heard Annie call for her and prayed that Isaac would move away so that she could go to her child.

After what seemed an age, she heard his footsteps retreating and she fled up the steps to her parlour, brushing the fluff from her apron, certain that he would come to her front door. She called up the stairs to Annie to be quiet, that she would come in a moment. She knew that her daughter was hungry and her nappy would be wet, but she didn't want the child to witness another exchange between her and Isaac.

He knocked briskly on her door.

'Who's there?' she called.

'It's Isaac. I want a word with thee.'

At least he hadn't walked straight in, she thought as she went across to open it.

'What's tha doin' here so early?' she asked him, trying to master her trembling voice and sound normal. 'Is summat wrong?'

He was peering past her into the interior of the cottage.

'I need to see to my child,' she told him as Annie's cries gathered intensity.

'Well, go and fetch 'er then,' he said. 'I'll wait a moment.'

Molly still hesitated. She was desperate to go to Annie, but she knew that if she left him alone he would take the opportunity to go down to the cellar again.

'She sounds distressed,' he said.

'I don't want to bring her down if tha's goin' to make a scene,' she told him.

'Why would I make a scene?'

'Well, what else has tha come for, at this time of the mornin'?'

'I were passin'. I wanted to see if there were owt tha needed.'

She met his eyes and they stared at one another for a moment. They both knew full well why he was here and both were equally determined not to give an inch.

'There's no one else here,' Molly told him at last. 'Tha can come upstairs and take a look.'

'I'd rather take a look in yon cellar,' he said as he pushed past her and went down the steps. Molly grasped at his coat tails as he passed her, but there was no stopping him. She knew it was hopeless.

She left Annie crying, although the child's distress was paining her, and followed him down. He was staring at the loom.

'Who did this?' he asked, glancing around as if he was sure that someone must be hiding. He turned and looked up the steps. 'Perhaps I will check upstairs,' he said.

'Tha's no right!'

'I've every right!' he told her. 'I'm 'ere as Colonel Fletcher's representative and if rules are bein' broken then I've a right to investigate, aye, and to put thee out if necessary.'

Molly hurried after him as he climbed the flights of stairs. She was terrified that he might touch Annie.

'Let me pick up the child!' she cried as he reached the top landing.

He stood aside and let her go into the bedroom where Annie's cries were echoing from the walls. Molly snatched her daughter up from the bed and held her close, trying to soothe her.

Isaac looked around. It was clear that there was nowhere for anyone to hide. The room was bare apart from the bed, but even so, he bent to search under it and Molly was glad that she'd taken her chamber pot down the stairs to empty it as soon as she'd got up.

'See, there's no one here,' she told him as she jogged Annie in her arms.

Isaac turned and crossed to the back room. Molly followed him, her anxiety rising. This room was almost bare as well. It contained nothing but the chest with the flannel shirts she'd sewn for Thomas.

'Don't touch those!' she cried as he raised the lid and began to rummage amongst them. 'I don't know what tha's hopin' to find. Them's Thomas's things!'

'I don't know why tha's kept these,' he said. 'They'd fetch a bit a money at t' pawn shop.'

'I made them for Thomas,' she told him.

'But he's not here.'

'I'll take them with me when I go to join him.'

Isaac shook his head as he slammed the lid down. 'Tha's talkin' nonsense,' he told her. 'Tha'll never go and it'd be better if tha admitted it.'

'No. Tha's wrong. Just like tha's wrong about somebody hidin' in here.'

He turned and stared her down. 'Someone's weavin' on yon loom,' he said. 'They might 'ave managed to slip away this time, but when I find out who it is there'll be trouble. I'll not hesitate to put thee out,' he warned her again.

'I thought tha were concerned about my welfare,' she said, thinking how quickly he could change from seeming to care to issuing his threats.

'I am concerned,' he said. 'That's why I'm tryin' to prevent thee gettin' in trouble. Tha's not allowed to sublet.'

'I'm doin' nowt wrong.'

'I'll find out,' he replied. 'It's only a matter o' time.' He sighed. 'Molly,' he began, trying to sound softer. 'I don't know why tha's bein' so stubborn.' He glanced at Annie who'd begun to cry again. 'Leave that child wi' its grandparents where it belongs and come to me.'

'This child belongs here with me!' she told him. 'And now I'd be grateful if tha'd go on thy way so I can attend to her needs.'

Defeated for now, he clumped down the stairs, but waited in the parlour until she'd followed him down.

'Think on what I've said,' he reminded her before pulling open the door and going out.

Molly slammed it shut behind him and leaned on it for a moment, thankful that he'd gone. But she knew that he would be back and it was only a matter of time before he found out the truth.

Chapter Twenty-Six

It was nearly three weeks before Molly finished the quilt. She hadn't rushed it, determined to work carefully so that it would be perfect.

She'd managed to climb up and hang some fine curtains at the cellar window so that even if Isaac Crompton looked in he wouldn't be able to make out who was sitting at the loom. And she'd learned to recognise the sound of his footsteps, so that if she heard him coming when she was at work, she would run upstairs and be tending to the fire or the cooking by the time he reached her door. He always came in, looking around suspiciously.

'Where's t' child?' he would ask if he couldn't see Annie.

'Across the fold,' she would tell him. Or, 'My sister's got her this afternoon,' she would say.

Every time he'd been unable to catch her out with someone else in the cottage she'd seen his frustration rise. She was aware that it was making him angry and she'd confessed her concerns to John and Ellen. They'd tried to reassure her that she was doing nothing wrong and Isaac would soon become bored with it. But Nancy had disagreed. She knew how persistent Isaac Crompton could be when he set his mind to something and she'd warned Molly to be vigilant.

As she walked towards Tonge, Molly wondered where Thomas was and whether he'd reached New South Wales yet. She thought not. Only four months had passed since his last letter so he must still be at sea. She knew that he was far away from her now. She could almost feel the distance between them tugging at her. It was impossible for her to imagine what his life might be like, but she prayed, every night, that he wasn't held in chains and that he had recovered from his illness.

The quilt weighed heavy in her arms. She'd worked so hard on it and she was pleased with the result. It was beautiful. She'd taken it upstairs to spread on her bed so that she could examine it carefully, and although she knew it wasn't quite perfect she hoped that it would be good enough for Mr Ainsworth to pay her a decent price for it.

When she reached the warehouse, she watched as he spread it out to examine it.

'It's good work,' he said after a few minutes and Molly found herself letting out the breath she was unaware she'd been holding as she waited for his verdict. 'Not perfect, mind,' he added. 'Thy Thomas would've done better, but I'm impressed how tha's taken to t' work,' he admitted. 'I didn't think tha'd be so skilful.'

Molly smiled. She knew it was high praise from the dour little man who held her fate in his hands. Although praise wouldn't pay her passage to New South Wales. She needed him to give her money.

'How much?' she ventured. 'It's taken me three weeks to do.'

'Aye. It's time-consuming work,' he agreed. 'But folk still want these handmade ones, especially if they're pretty.' He hesitated and Molly could hardly bear the suspense. 'I'll give thee two pound ten shillings,' he said.

It was a generous offer and Molly nodded enthusiast-ically. 'Thank you!' she said. 'And take off the price of more bobbins.'

'Tha's goin' to make another, then?' asked Mr Ainsworth.

'Aye. I'm goin' to keep makin' them until I've saved enough to join Thomas.'

She packed the bobbins into her basket as Mr Ainsworth counted out what he owed her. Neither of them heard Isaac Crompton come in until his shadow fell across the quilt and Molly spun round to see him staring at it.

'Whose is this?' he demanded. 'What's goin' on?'

Before Molly could prevent him, Mr Ainsworth said, 'I'm just payin' t' lass for her work. She's done right well with that one.' He gestured towards the quilt. 'I'd never have thought a lass could produce summat that good.'

'Dost tha think she's made it?' asked Isaac. Molly could hear the sneer in his voice.

'What's tha mean?' asked Mr Ainsworth. 'Who else could o' made it?'

'She might be passing it off as 'er work,' said Isaac, 'but she's sub-lettin' 'er cellar to someone. It's not right,' he added, glaring at Molly. 'Colonel Fletcher'll evict 'er if he finds out.'

Mr Ainsworth looked from one to the other of them, clearly concerned. 'It's good work. She's brought it in for sale and I'm buyin' it,' he told Isaac. 'I've done nowt wrong,' he added, clearly worried that he was about to be accused as well.

Molly hurriedly put the money she'd been given into her purse and picked up her basketful of bobbins.

'I suppose them's for another quilt,' said Isaac. 'Tha doesn't need to tell me they're for John Holden this time. I know they're not. There's mischief afoot,' he added, 'and I'm determined to get to t' bottom of it.'

Molly thanked Mr Ainsworth and walked towards the open doorway, away from Isaac. She was worried that he would follow her, but she knew that she couldn't stand in the warehouse all morning hoping that he would go away.

'I'll walk with thee,' he said and her hopes plummeted.

Molly remained tight-lipped as they took the narrow path towards Hag End.

'Whoever wove that quilt were a skilled artisan,' said Isaac.

'That's quite a compliment,' she replied.

'Well, 'appen tha can pass it on. But I'll find out who it is,' he added. 'I know tha's got somebody in t' cottage and I'll find out who.'

For a moment Molly had to struggle to stop herself laughing out loud. He was so consumed with jealousy that he would never see the truth. He was convinced that she had a man, a lover even, concealed in her cellar.

'Come in then,' she challenged him. 'Come in and search again if tha must. Tha'll find no one there.'

'I will an' all,' he said.

They walked in strained silence until they reached her cottage. He followed her in, looking about.

'Go down and have a look,' she invited him, waving a hand towards the cellar steps. He went down and she waited as he looked at the loom, bare of threads, and the curtain at the window. After a few moments he came back up. 'Dost tha want to search under t' bed again?' she asked.

'Don't be like that, Molly,' he said, changing to his more persuasive tone. 'I'm worried about thee. I only want to keep thee safe. I don't know who tha's got workin' on t' loom,' he said, 'but how dost tha know tha can trust 'em? There's plenty o' men wouldn't hesitate to take advantage of a woman alone.'

Molly snorted back her laughter. She could hardly believe what she was hearing.

'There's no one here,' she reminded him.

'Well, there wouldn't be, would there? Not until tha comes back wi' t' bobbins.'

'Tha's bein' ridiculous!' she told him beginning to lose patience.

His face darkened. 'I'll be watchin' thee,' he threatened. 'Don't think tha can make a fool out o' me.'

Molly almost told him that he was making a fool out of himself, but she held her tongue. She didn't want to get into an argument with him. She just wanted him to go.

'Tha'll 'ave to admit tha needs me sooner or later,' he said as he moved towards the door. 'Whatever tha's up to, it'll not last,' he warned.

Molly watched as he passed her window and walked down the fold. She knew that she could make a success of weaving the quilts. She also knew that Isaac would never catch her with another man in her cottage, but she still worried about what he might do to force her to accept his offer of help and protection.

Chapter Twenty-Seven

Some weeks later, as Thomas was taking his hour of allotted exercise on the lower deck of the *Fortune*, he looked up at the shout from the lookout in the crow's nest. The brightness made him raise a hand to shield his eyes as he stared towards the horizon. By Thomas's reckoning, it was the tenth of June and he thought that the hills he could just make out in the haze must be New South Wales.

The prisoners were kept below in their cramped cells as the ship anchored. The paying passengers were to disembark first and then the cargo was to be unloaded. And although they could hear the commotion around them, they could only guess at what they would see when they were taken off the ship.

Thomas wasn't sure what he felt. It was partly relief that he'd arrived in New South Wales and was still alive. One of the men from Bolton had died on the way and his body had been tossed without ceremony into the surging waves. But Thomas was afraid and anxious about what would happen next. On the long voyage he'd become accustomed to his role waiting on at the captain's table. It had been a privilege and meant that he was sure to have the opportunity to wash and be dressed in clean clothes. It had also meant he'd been able to filch a little extra food as he carried the plates back down to the kitchen – a risk worth taking even though he knew he would receive a flogging if he was caught. He'd even become used to the rolling of the ship and the creaking of the hull. It had become his home. But now he was faced with another unknown. He knew that he would be put to work, but what sort of work, he had no idea. The only thing that was certain was that he wouldn't be weaving caddow quilts.

After a week in quarantine to be sure none of them was carrying any disease, the hatch was opened.

'This is it,' said Jack Fisher when the warder came down, his keys jangling in his hand, and instructed them to be ready with their belongings to go up on deck. Jack held out his hand and Thomas shook it. 'Good luck!' he said.

'Aye, and thee,' replied Thomas, wondering if he would ever see his friend again.

'Line up!' shouted the warder and the prisoners shuffled themselves one behind the other – no one wanting to be first and no one wanting to be last.

Then they climbed out into the fresh air – the first they'd breathed for days. They'd not even been allowed their hour's exercise on deck since they arrived and the stench below had become sickening.

Thomas followed Jack up the ladders to the top deck. He clutched his small bundle tightly as they were put into rows, his eyes straining to see beyond the masts. Sydney Cove was busy with ships of all sizes. The larger ones, like the *Fortune*, were anchored in the bay and there were myriad smaller boats being rowed to and fro to take passengers and cargo to the shore. Beyond the wharf he could see low brick buildings seemingly scattered by some giant hand, and beyond, was forest. Thomas felt a shiver run through him as he contemplated what dangers it might contain.

They were ordered to climb down into waiting boats and taken ashore, where they were lined up in rows again a short distance from the harbour. Although it was June and Thomas had expected the weather to be hot, he shivered in the early morning air as they waited. The firm land beneath his feet seemed odd. He'd grown so used to the movement of the ship that he felt he was still moving up and down on the swell even though he knew that the cobbles were firm.

A well-dressed man of obvious importance came to inspect them. He was introduced as Governor Macquarie. His eye roved over the sorry-looking assembly. He spoke briefly to a few of the prisoners and seemed satisfied with their answers to his queries about their treatment. Then he ordered that the few still held in irons should be released from their shackles.

Next, the surgeon came with a sheaf of papers in his hand and gave one to each prisoner to hold up in front of him. Those who couldn't read were baffled, but Thomas could just about make out that his paper recorded details of himself – his age, his height, a brief description, the nature of his so-called crime and the length of time he had been sentenced to remain in New South Wales.

They were re-arranged into groups that contained the lifers, those who had to serve ten years and those sentenced to seven. Thomas could see the men from Bolton and managed to exchange a glance with Jack Fisher who stood further down his line, but speaking was forbidden unless you were asked a question by one of the gentleman who had come to choose workers.

Thomas recognised Mr Allan, the officer he'd waited on at the captain's table on the *Fortune*. He'd learned more about him as he'd served the meals during the voyage. The man had been appointed as deputy commissary general to take charge of the stores. Thomas had envisaged him to be some sort of shopkeeper, but by the way he was being treated now it seemed that he was a man of some importance.

Mr Allan walked up and down the rows, glancing at the faces of the prisoners and their credentials until he came to Thomas.

'Holden!' he exclaimed.

'Sir.' Thomas inclined his head.

'I'll take this one,' said Mr Allan and Thomas was beckoned to stand apart.

Thomas watched as Mr Allan selected some other men. He hoped that Jack Fisher would be one of them, but the men chosen were unknown to him and when there were four of them, Mr Allan instructed them to follow his carriage.

They walked up a wide track, potholed from the wheels of the traffic, past where a group of men were labouring to build a high wall to split the large houses of the gentry beyond it from the lower reaches around the harbour. It was to one of the large houses that they were led. It looked recently built of a pale red brick, with many windows and a pitched roof. Surrounded by a stone wall with a wrought-iron gate set at its centre, it seemed huge to Thomas – much larger than Colonel Fletcher's house in Bolton, he thought as he gazed up at the impressive frontage with a flight of steps leading up to imposing double doors.

The convicts were taken in through the gate and around the back to a courtyard with a stable block and other, less auspicious wings of the great house. Mr Allan had alighted from his carriage at the front door and it was driven into the yard, empty. A young lad came out to unharness the horses and the carriage was rolled away into a barn.

A man came out to greet them. He introduced himself as Mr Henderson, the steward, and told them that they would be answerable to him in the first instance and ultimately to their new master and mistress. Then they were told to strip off the clothes they were wearing. A tin bath was brought out and filled for them to wash and shave and then their hair was cut by a barber. It seemed Mr Allan was keen for them to look clean and presentable.

Afterwards, they were shown to a loft above the stables which contained six truckle beds, each with a trunk at the foot for them to keep their belongings. On the beds were laid out the uniforms they were to wear. Thomas felt the quality of the white, cotton shirts, the dark trousers, the jacket and stock. The clothes were a far cry from the rough convict uniform he'd become used to and he dressed in them, feeling quite the gentleman. He wasn't sure what would be required of him, but it certainly wouldn't be hard labour, he thought, not whilst wearing clothes like these.

'So you're the new footman?'

'Aye, sir,' said Thomas out of habit. He had no idea what a footman was. The steward, looked him up and down doubtfully. 'Do you know what's required?' he asked.

Thomas shook his head. 'No, sir. I'm a weaver by trade.'

'A weaver?' Mr Henderson looked puzzled. 'It makes me wonder why Mr Allan chose you. I need someone with experience of how to set a table and wait on the family and guests at mealtimes.'

'Oh, I can do that,' replied Thomas and explained his role as a servant to the captain on board the *Fortune*.

The steward nodded. 'That makes more sense,' he agreed. 'And you must have done the task well for Mr Allan to bring you to his house.'

'I did my best, sir,' replied Thomas, realising that his job here would be similar to the one he'd performed onboard the ship. It provided some reassurance. At least he knew what was required and it would be easier to serve soup on dry land. But it also meant that he would remain in close contact with Mrs Allan and he wondered if it was she who'd asked her husband to employ him. The thought vexed him. All his instincts told him that he should distance himself from her, but as the steward explained his full duties to him, it seemed that he would be at her beck and call all day long and forced to please her.

It wasn't that he disliked her. In fact the opposite was true. Although she was some years older than him, she was an attractive woman and Thomas was drawn to her – against his better judgement. She'd made it abundantly clear that she liked him too – the smiles, the lingering glances and the way her hand had tended to make contact with his when he was serving her meal.

When they'd been moored in Rio to take on supplies, and Mr Allan had gone ashore, Mrs Allan had stayed in her cabin and specifically asked for him to bring her dinner to her there. Thomas had seen that the captain disapproved even as he passed the order on, but the Allans were his paying passengers and he didn't dare refuse them their requests, no matter how unconventional they seemed.

'Keep your eyes down and only speak if you're spoken to,' the captain had instructed him.

'Aye, sir.' Thomas had been more than willing to comply, but Mrs Allan had plied him with questions about where he came from and why he'd been sentenced. He'd been obliged to give answers, however brief and her sympathy had unnerved him.

'It hardly seems fair,' she'd told him when he'd explained what he'd been sentenced for. 'What about your family? Do you have a wife?'

Thomas had told her about Molly and Annie, and how he hoped they could come to join him. He'd thought that Mrs Allan might be in a position to help him, but she'd dismissed his wishes, telling him that he should look to make a new life for himself in New South Wales.

'Have you got pen and paper to write home?' Mr Henderson asked, bringing Thomas back to his present situation. 'Can you even write?'

'Aye, I can write, but not well enough to scribe a good letter,' Thomas told him.

'Well, you'll have to do the best you can,' replied the steward. 'There's no one here to write a fancy letter for you. I'll put down the address for you to send to your family,' he conceded, 'but the rest must be your own work – and if I were you, I'd do it now. You'll not have a minute to call your own once Mrs Allan sends for you.'

Chapter Twenty-Eight

Molly walked home briskly from the warehouse at Tonge feeling optimistic, even though the summer was fading and the swallows were no longer swooping into their nests in the church porch, but had gone on their own long journey. Mr Ainsworth had told her that her latest quilt was faultless. Molly knew there was a small mistake in it, but she never mentioned it and accepted the payment with a smile. A full three pounds to add to her savings.

When she reached home, she took her basket of bobbins down to the cellar. If she began to get the loom beamed up straight away she could finish it tomorrow morning and then apply the size. It meant that she'd have a few hours in the afternoon to go and see Nancy whilst it dried.

But first she must put her money away, she thought. She climbed up the steps and went into the back kitchen where she wriggled a loose brick from the place where she kept her savings hidden in an old leather bag. She looked up as she thought she saw a shadow fall across her parlour, but there was no one there. The sun must have gone behind a cloud for a moment, she thought as she added the money, bringing the total to nineteen pounds, ten shillings and sixpence. More than half of her fare to New South Wales, and she reckoned that before another year had passed she would have enough to go to Thomas.

She longed for a letter from him. She was sure that he must have arrived by now and she was desperate to be reassured that he was well – and that he was alive. She'd been down to see Hannah Fisher again, to take her some food and ask if she'd had word from Jack, but she'd heard nothing either, and so they waited, long day after long day, for news.

'If it takes six months to reach New South Wales then it'll take another six for news to get back,' John had reasoned. 'It might be Christmas again before word comes.' Molly knew that it was true, but every day she hoped for a letter, and every time she walked to market she called at the Golden Lion to ask, only to have Uncle Richard shake his head and pour her a half pint of ale to try to console her.

Molly decided that she would leave Annie with her grandmother a while longer. Ellen had seemed well this morning so there was no rush to collect her daughter and it was much easier to work without having to watch her all the time. She'd fetch her for her dinner and afterwards she'd put her on the bed upstairs for a nap.

Molly went back down to the cellar and began to beam up the loom. She enjoyed doing it. It took all her attention and relieved her mind from her worries for a while at least.

She wondered if she would be able to continue to weave when she eventually joined Thomas. She smiled as she thought about how surprised he would be to see her sitting at a loom and doing a man's job. She hoped that he would be proud of her, and maybe, when he'd served his time, they could work together. They might buy two looms and sit side by side weaving quilts whilst Annie went to school. There might be another baby in the cradle too. A foreign-born child. It was a strange thought.

Although the truth was that Molly had no idea what New South Wales would be like; she'd known nothing but her Lancashire home and it was hard to imagine anything different.

'What's tha doin?'

Molly spun round in alarm as Isaac's exclamation roused her from her daydream. He was standing at the top of her cellar steps, staring at her and the loom.

'What's tha doin?' he repeated as he came down, looking about to see who else was in the cellar.

She hadn't heard him pass the window or open her front door. She cursed herself for allowing him to creep up on her. She ought to have turned the key in the lock, but she never did during the daytime.

'What's it look like I'm doin'?' she challenged him as she bent to retrieve the bobbin she'd dropped.

Isaac stared at the loom where the warp was half attached. 'Someone's beamin' it up,' he said, sounding confused as he glanced around again to try to find the culprit.

'Aye, that's right.'

'I knew tha were rentin' it out to a weaver,' he accused her, his eyes blazing.

Molly put the bobbin down on the frame of the loom and faced up to him. 'I'm rentin' nowt out to nobody,' she said.

'Then who's done this?'

Molly almost laughed at the puzzlement and confusion on his face. He really couldn't see what was right in front of him.

'I've done it myself,' she told him.

Isaac stared at her as if she'd claimed that night was day. 'Thee?' he said. 'But it's not a woman's work.'

'It's my work – and I'd like to get on with it,' she said, turning away from him to pick up her thread and continue.

'Where did tha learn to do that?' he asked, sounding amazed as he watched her.

'I watched Thomas. And it's not against t' rental agreement is it? For me to work here?' she challenged him.

'It's not thy name on t' rent book,' he said and she could see that he was still trying to calculate a way to catch her out.

'But tha's willin' enough to take the rent money from me,' she reminded him.

Isaac seemed unsure what to do or say next. He'd been convinced she was allowing someone in – a man – to weave on the loom and was struggling to believe what he was seeing.

'And it's thy quilts tha's sellin at t' warehouse?'

'Aye. That's right,' said Molly. 'Just as Mr Ainsworth told thee.'

'And tha's managin' t' earn enough to keep thyself?' He sounded disappointed.

'Aye. And to put a bit by.' Molly almost felt sorry for him. He looked like a little boy who'd had a promised treat snatched away from him. 'I'll go to join Thomas when I've saved enough,' she told him.

'How long will that be?'

'I'm not sure. It depends if tha lets me get on,' she said.

'A month? Six months? A year?' he persisted. 'It's a long time to struggle on alone,' he told her. 'Why not make it easy for thyself?'

'I'll do whatever it takes,' she replied. 'I love Thomas and I want to be with him.'

'How dost tha know he won't 'ave forgotten thee after all that time?' asked Isaac. 'Hast heard owt from 'im?'

'He'll send word when he can. It'll take a long time for a letter to come.'

Isaac was shaking his head. 'Tha doesn't want to be goin' all that way. Months and months out on t' sea. Owt could 'appen.'

Molly twisted the thread around her fingers. She wished that he would go away. He was feeding all the worries and qualms she had about going – the long sea voyage, what she would find when – if – she eventually arrived. But she was determined not to let him see her doubts. She didn't want to give him any hope that he could eventually wear her down with his persuasion.

'I'll leave thee to it, then,' he said at last when she didn't speak. He climbed the stairs and she heard him cross her parlour and shut the front door behind him. But Molly doubted that he would let it go. She knew that he was angry and frustrated that he didn't have the hold over her that he'd anticipated.

Chapter Twenty-Nine

Molly was relieved not to have to make a secret of her work any more. She finished beaming up the loom the next morning without having to listen out for Isaac. She desperately hoped that he would give up trying to persuade her to go back to him now that he knew the truth. She was independent. She had her work and she was earning money. It wasn't a situation that she'd ever thought she would find herself in, but she felt proud that she'd achieved it.

She worked on until Annie woke and then took the child outside into the sunshine where she watered the vegetables she'd planted in the little plot beside the cottage – some cabbages and peas. They were coming up well and would provide some extra food to supplement what she had to buy from the market.

After dinner, when she'd applied the size to the warp threads, Molly went to visit Nancy and little Billy whilst William was at work. When she arrived at her sister's house, she called out and went straight in. Billy was sitting up on his own now and Molly settled Annie down beside him on the hearthrug so that they could play together.

'Did tha sell thy latest quilt?' asked Nancy as she put the kettle on to boil for tea.

'Aye. For a good price an' all,' Molly told her sister with a smile. 'Mr Ainsworth said as it were perfect and paid me the full three pounds!'

'I'm right glad tha's doin' well at it,' said Nancy. 'I hated it when tha were workin' down that pit.'

'Aye,' said Molly. 'It weren't pleasant, though at the time I were sorry to be turned off.'

'Is Isaac Crompton still botherin' thee?' asked her sister.

Molly paused and then decided to tell Nancy what had happened. 'He caught me workin' on t' loom yesterday,' she said. 'He let himself in and I never heard him.'

Nancy put the kettle down and folded the cloth that she'd used to hold it. 'What did he say?' she asked with a frown.

'He could scarce believe it,' Molly told her. 'But I'm sorry as he found out. I worry about what he'll do next.'

'How can he stop thee?'

'I don't know,' said Molly. 'But likely as not he'll try. He's been tryin' to find out where the money for the rent and such were comin' from for a while. He were convinced I had some chap in. It were funny to see him so jealous of nowt, but tha knows what he's like when he's thwarted. He'll not let it drop. The sooner I can get away from him, the better.'

'How much has tha got?' asked Nancy.

'Goin' on for twenty pounds.'

'That's a tidy sum. Tha's done well.'

'Aye. It's not enough, though. I need to carry on weavin' until I've twice that much. It's not just the ticket. I'll have to get to the ship and there'll be food to buy…' Her voice trailed off as she contemplated the enormity of what lay before her.

'I'll miss thee,' said Nancy.

'Aye, I'll miss thee an' all. But I can't bear to think of Thomas all alone on t' other side of the world. As soon as word comes that's he's arrived safe then I'll write back to tell him as I'm coming. Hopefully it'll keep his spirits up.'

–

Walking home later that afternoon, she saw an unmistakeable figure in the distance. Her heart sank. Isaac must have been to her cottage again. There was no other reason for him to be on this path. She slowed her pace and swapped Annie to her opposite hip to be further away from him as he approached, but when she looked again she could see no sign of him. He seemed to have disappeared and she began to wonder whether he'd really been there or if she'd imagined him.

She walked on hesitantly. Maybe he'd hidden himself somewhere, ready to leap out and take her by surprise. There was a clump of undergrowth further ahead and she tightened her grasp on the child as she approached it. But as she came closer she realised that there was no one concealed in its flimsy branches. If Isaac Crompton had been there, then he'd disappeared into thin air. She hurried on, wondering if she'd been mistaken, but she was sure she'd seen him.

When she arrived home, she unlocked her door and pushed it slowly open, half expecting to find him in her parlour. But it was empty. Nothing had been disturbed – not that there was much left to move. She let Annie slide to the floor. The child was growing heavy now and she was glad to put her down.

'Let's have some tea,' she told her as she hung up her shawl and went through to the back kitchen to fetch some bread. Perhaps she had just imagined Isaac. Even so, she felt compelled to go down to check her loom. Everything was as she'd left it. The size was dry and she decided that if there was enough light left after tea, she would begin a new quilt.

–

She didn't see Isaac again until he called, as usual, for her rent money on the Friday evening. She'd got into the habit of putting Annie to bed before he came so that the child wouldn't be frightened by him, but today he was early and she was only just coming down the stairs. She heard him whistling as he approached her door and knew that it meant he was in a good mood.

He greeted her with a smile and took off his hat as he stepped inside. He looked pleased with himself and Molly was suspicious. She wondered if he'd discovered some way to prevent her using the loom.

'How's tha doin'?' he asked.

'I'm all right,' she replied. 'I'll just fetch what I owe thee,' she said, realising that she hadn't put the money into her purse and would need to go into the back kitchen to retrieve the leather bag with her savings in it.

She pulled the loose brick with her fingers, finding it moved more easily than she expected, and when she reached in for the bag it felt odd. She drew it out with shaking fingers, unfastened the string and stared in disbelief at the pebbles. With a cry she dropped them and watched as they cascaded to the floor and skittered across the flags. Where was her money? Her carefully saved nineteen pounds, ten shillings and sixpence? It was a moment before she realised she'd been robbed.

'Is summat t' matter?' asked Isaac. She looked up at him, standing in the doorway and, from the smirk on his face, she saw that he already knew. The truth hit her harder than any physical blow he could have dealt her and she struggled to gain enough breath to speak.

'It's gone! All my money.' She held out her hand with the few remaining pebbles. 'Someone's taken it all and left these.'

The shock was almost too much for her and she felt the world darken around its edges. She reached out to steady herself against the wall and felt strong hands grasp her as her legs began to fail.

'Sit thee down,' he said, helping her to the box beside her hearth. 'Put thy head down. I'll fetch thee a sup o' water.'

She sank her head into her hands, dropping the rest of the pebbles at her feet. She was sure that Isaac had done it. Who else could have got into her house? Who else could possibly have known where she had her money hidden? He was the only one. He'd been here many times when she'd had to fetch the rent for him. He must have crept across the parlour behind her and watched to see where she kept it.

'Drink this,' he said, giving her a cup. 'Tha'll feel better in a minute.'

Molly took the cup but didn't bring her to her lips. She didn't even trust him to fetch her water. And as for feeling better, she didn't think she would ever feel better again.

'How much were in there?' he asked, squatting down beside her. She wanted to strike out at him and tell him that he knew how much because he was the one who'd taken it, but she didn't dare to accuse him.

'A few pounds,' she whispered after a moment. She put the water down untouched and tried to gather herself together. She wanted him out of her house, but realised that now she didn't have enough to pay him the rent. 'Can I owe it 'til next week?' she asked.

He sighed as if he was genuinely troubled. 'If it were up to me, I'd let thee owe it,' he said. 'But Colonel Fletcher's made it very clear he'll not hold wi' any rent arrears. He said that tenants must pay, or leave and make way for them as will.'

'Then I'll have to go across to see if John and Ellen'll lend me summat.' She tried to get up, but found the room was still swaying.

'I'll tell thee what,' said Isaac as she sat back down. 'I'll lend it to thee for now. Tha can pay me back when tha's sold another o' thy quilts.'

'No! I'll not be indebted to thee!' she protested. 'I'll get it. Can tha come back in a bit? Come later and I'll have it for thee,' she promised.

'Don't fret thyself,' he told her. 'I'll put my own money in for now and tha can owe it to me.' He stood up and reached into his pocket for two and sixpence. She watched as he added it to the rent money and made an entry in the ledger. The last thing she wanted was to be beholden to him, but she didn't know what else to do. 'Don't worry about it,' he went on. 'Tha's had a shock.' He settled his hat back onto his head and went to the door. He pulled it shut behind him and Molly heard him whistling again as he walked away.

She stared at the pebbles on the floor and began to sob. All that money. Gone, and no way of getting it back. It was Isaac. She was sure of it. He'd ruined her chance of saving enough to go to Thomas, and put her in his debt. No wonder he was so pleased with himself.

Molly was unsure how long she'd been sitting there, twisting a handkerchief in her hand and wiping her face on her sleeve. When she eventually looked up she saw that it had grown dark and only the meagre fire was illuminating the room. She banked it up with more coal for the night, hoping it would stay in and she wouldn't have to relight it in the morning. Then she lit a rushlight to see her to bed.

She climbed the stairs wearily. Annie was fast asleep and Molly slipped out of her gown and petticoat and got in beside her. She blew out the rushlight and lay in the darkness. There must be something she could do, she thought. Perhaps John would know.

'Tha'll have to report it to Colonel Fletcher,' said John the next morning after she'd told him what had happened.

'He'll do nowt,' protested Molly. 'I've got no evidence and even if I had, he wouldn't hear a word against Isaac Crompton. He'll just tell me it were my own carelessness.'

'Aye, tha could be right,' conceded John. 'How much were taken?' he asked.

'Nineteen pounds, ten shillings and sixpence.'

John let out a low whistle. 'It's a lot to lose.'

'And I didn't have enough to pay the rent,' Molly told him. 'Isaac insisted on lending it to me, but I don't want to owe him anything.' She paused and saw that John understood her meaning. He went to his drawer and counted out two shillings and sixpence.

'Pay 'im back,' he said.

'Thanks.' Molly tightened her fingers around the coins and as she did so, she cursed Isaac Crompton for what he'd done. How could the man claim to care about her when he behaved as he did?

–

'Tha's not serious!' exclaimed Nancy when Molly saw her that afternoon. 'He's taken the lot? Is tha sure it were him?'

'Aye. I'm certain of it, but there's nowt I can do.'

Nancy shook her head. 'I didn't think he'd stoop as low as that,' she said. 'What does he need it for, anyroad? It's not like he's short.'

'It's not money he wants,' replied Molly. 'He'll not dare spend it, anyway. He'll want to be above suspicion. No, he just wants to stop me goin' to Thomas.'

'Aye, I can see that,' said Nancy.

'But I'll not give up!' exclaimed Molly. 'Never. I don't care if I've to start again without a penny. I'll work until I have enough! I'll not be satisfied until I'm on a ship to New South Wales, to where Isaac Crompton can't hurt me any more.'

'But it's taken thee over a year to save what tha had,' reasoned Nancy. 'And it were still only half what tha needed. It'll take years and years to get enough, and that's only if tha manages to keep it hidden. There's more than Isaac Crompton who'll be comin' round to thy cottage if they think there's a tidy sum stashed away in it.'

Molly stared at her sister in disbelief. 'I expected thee to give me some support!' she snapped at her.

'I'm only tryin' to be practical,' Nancy told her. 'I know tha wants to go to thy Thomas, and at first it seemed possible, but I think tha needs to be realistic now.'

'It's all right for thee!' said Molly. 'Tha's got William. I've no one!'

'Tha's no worse off than them as is widowed – better off than most. Tha's makin' money from t' quilts now. Why not spend some of it on furniture and a few rugs? Make a proper home for Annie to grow up in.'

'Tha'll be tellin' me next to consider myself a widow! Tha'll be persuadin' me to marry Isaac Crompton after all!'

'I'd not do that! Tha knows I wouldn't. But I think tha's makin' things too hard for thyself. I hate to see thee struggle when tha doesn't need to.'

'I'll not give up on Thomas. I won't!' Molly told her. 'As soon as he sends word, I'll write and tell him that I mean to come. I'll get the money one way or another!'

Molly snatched her startled daughter up from the rug and hurried out of the house. She ran until she had to stop for breath. She was sobbing. Annie was sobbing. It was all so unfair, she thought. She'd done nothing wrong, but she was being punished, and now even her own sister had turned against her. But it wouldn't stop her, she vowed to herself as she picked Annie up again and headed for home. She would get the money for her passage. She would not let Thomas down.

Chapter Thirty

Molly was still angry and upset when she got back from seeing her sister. She'd expected Nancy to support her in her efforts to save enough money to join Thomas and her advice, no matter how well intentioned, had not been welcome. She knew that Nancy would miss her when she was gone. She would miss her sister too, but she was Thomas's wife. Her place was with her husband, no matter what Colonel Fletcher and his friends in government thought – and no matter how hard Isaac Crompton tried to prevent her. There were days when she wished that Thomas had committed a worse crime. If he'd been a lifer she would have been with him by now, instead of struggling here alone.

Annie had been upset by the exchange as well, so Molly poured her some milk to drink to soothe her. Then she took the child down to the cellar and settled her on the blanket from the bed, hoping that she would play or sleep for a while. She was determined to get on with the latest quilt so that she could get the payment for it.

She'd intended to ask Nancy if she could lend her the money for this week's rent, but it had been forgotten in the throes of the falling-out and now she was too vexed with her sister to want to see her again – for a while at least. But Molly was worried about what would happen when Isaac came again on Friday evening. Although she could pay him what he'd loaned her for the week before, another two and six would be due and she was concerned that if she couldn't pay again, he might make good his threat to turn her out of the cottage. If he did, she wouldn't be able to do her work and it would be impossible to save any money. Perhaps she should go to speak to Mr Ainsworth, she thought and ask him if he would give her an advance on the price of the quilt she was weaving.

Molly didn't want to beg, but without any other option she decided she would go to the warehouse the next day and take Annie with her.

'Tha's never finished already!' joked Mr Ainsworth when he saw her. 'What's to do?' he asked, seeing her serious face.

'I've had all my money stolen,' she explained. 'I were wondering if tha could lend me a bit for rent and take it off the next quilt.'

'Stolen! That's a rotten thing t' 'appen,' he said. 'Did tha lose a lot?'

'A bit,' she admitted.

'Hast tha been to t' constable?'

'There's no point,' said Molly. 'I've no proof who did it. But I'm short for the rent money and a bit of food for the child.'

Mr Ainsworth frowned and Molly feared that he was going to refuse.

'I shouldn't really,' he said, 'but I knows as I can trust thee to pay it back. Say nowt, mind,' he added in a low voice. 'I'll be in trouble if anyone finds out. But I can gi' thee ten bob. Is that enough?'

'I'm that grateful,' she told him as he counted the money into her hand. It would tide her over until the quilt was done if she was frugal and worked hard.

Isaac was whistling again when he knocked on her door on the Friday evening. Molly went to answer it with the money in her hand so that he had no excuse to come inside.

'Two and six for last week and two and six for this week,' she said as she counted five shillings into his hand. 'Now we're straight and I owe thee nowt.'

'Where's tha got this from?' he asked.

'I have friends,' she told him and saw him frown. It was obvious he hadn't expected her to be able to pay him. 'And I've spoken to the constable,' she added. 'He's to enquire into who might have stolen my money from me.'

It was true that she'd been to see Mr Holt at Mr Ainsworth's urging, but the man hadn't seemed so much concerned about the theft, as interested in how she'd had so much money in her possession in the first place. He'd questioned her so closely and expressed such doubt when she'd told him that she was weaving and selling quilts that she'd begun to feel she was the suspect and had come home feeling thoroughly despondent.

'Dost tha know who it might 'ave been that took thy money, then?' Isaac challenged her. She met his eyes and was tempted to accuse him, but she was afraid of making him angry. He would deny it anyway and put the blame on her. There was nothing to be gained from it.

'No,' she said at last. 'I don't know who could have done such a terrible thing.'

'Aye,' he said, looking uncomfortable. 'But tha doesn't need to go borrowin' from other folk,' he told her when he'd had a moment to collect himself. 'I'll not see thee starve. Hast tha got enough to feed thyself?'

'I'll manage,' she replied. 'Good night to thee.' She shut the door firmly and turned the key in the lock with a trembling hand although she knew that it wouldn't be the end of it.

She heard Isaac walk slowly away and she stood behind the door until his footsteps had gone. Every time she thought she'd got the better of him he thought up some other way to spoil her plans and she dreaded what he would do next.

—

Molly worked on her quilts every hour that she could. The nights were drawing in very early as the year drew to a close and the dawn came later with every day that passed, meaning that she needed candles to see her work and they were an added expense. But slowly she paid off her debt and began to put a little aside again each week.

It was so cold in the cellar though and she wore layer upon layer of clothing and fingerless mittens to keep her hands warm so that she could work. It was too cold for Annie to be with her, so when Ellen wasn't minding her, she tucked the child up in bed and hoped that she would be safe there. It was too risky to leave her alone in the parlour with the fire lit.

She avoided her sister. What Nancy had said still stung her and when she looked around at the bare cottage she knew that there was some truth in it. It wasn't much of a home for her daughter. And although when she'd first sold all the furniture she'd thought it would only be a few weeks, or months at most, before she left to go to New South Wales, she knew now that it would take her much longer to raise her fare. Suddenly, the hopelessness of the

241

task overwhelmed her and she wept as she tried to work, wiping her eyes and nose again and again as she struggled to focus on the intricate patterns and not spoil the cloth with her tears.

–

One morning in December, she took her latest quilt to the warehouse. She pushed open the door and looked around for Mr Ainsworth, but when he saw her he didn't come over to greet her with his usual smile. She saw him hesitate and it was several minutes before he approached her with a reluctant and worried expression.

'Mrs Holden.' He greeted her solemnly and Molly could see that something was wrong.

'I've finished the quilt,' she said, holding it out to him.

He didn't reach out for it or ask her to spread it on the table and Molly's mood plummeted to her wet boots as she realised he was about to give her bad news.

'I'm sorry,' he said, 'but I can't buy from thee any more.'

'Why not? Tha's not even looked at it,' she protested, thrusting the quilt towards him. 'There's nowt wrong with it!'

He shook his head. 'I'm sure it's perfect,' he told her. 'Tha's a good worker, but…' He hesitated again and fixed his gaze on the stone-flagged floor.

'What's wrong?' she asked.

'No one wants the handmade quilts any more,' he told her. 'They're too expensive.'

Molly stared at him. She could see that he was finding it hard to refuse her. 'Tha never said that afore!' she accused him. 'I've worked for over a week on it,' she said, wondering if he was going to refuse to take quilts from her father-in-law as well and if so, how they would manage to survive without any work.

Mr Ainsworth took a step back from her, shaking his head. 'I'm sorry,' he repeated as he walked away.

'Is this Isaac Crompton's doing?' Molly called after him as it suddenly occurred to her that he might well be at the bottom of it.

Mr Ainsworth hesitated. 'Times aren't good,' he told her. 'I can't buy from thee any more. I'm sorry,' he said again.

Molly didn't believe what he was telling her. She was sure that other weavers were still taking their work to him.

'I saw a weaver taking bobbins away,' she challenged him.

'Aye. I can sell thee bobbins,' he agreed. 'I just can't buy back t' finished goods. Happen tha could sell them elsewhere,' he suggested. He pushed back his cap to scratch his scalp and glanced around before settling it more firmly back on his head. 'I shouldn't say,' he whispered, 'but I'll recommend thy work if anyone comes askin' about a commission. They pay well,' he told her.

'What about this one?' she asked.

He glanced at the folded bundle. 'I'm sure it's well done,' he said, 'but I can't buy it from thee.'

'Isaac Crompton,' she said again. He didn't reply but the merest inclination of his head was enough to confirm her suspicions.

She'd known that Isaac would come up with some other way to thwart her. She'd seen how angry and frustrated he'd become as the weeks had passed and every Friday she'd carefully counted out two shillings and sixpence into his outstretched hand. Each time he'd asked if she could afford it, if she was sure she didn't want to owe him a week. And every time she'd shaken her head, his face had darkened. But she knew that without work it wouldn't be long before she had to admit that there was no money for the rent.

She walked back to the fold with heavy steps, the quilt still in her arms, wondering what she could do next. She felt like an animal trapped underground in its tunnels. Every time she thought she saw the light of an escape route it was blocked.

Molly went to John and Ellen's house to collect Annie and give them the news.

'He's said nowt to me about not buyin' from me,' said John when he heard her voice and came up the steps from his workshop.

'I think it's just me he won't buy from,' said Molly. 'I think Isaac Crompton has threatened him.'

'Dost tha want me to 'ave a word with 'im?' John asked her. Molly shook her head.

'It'll do no good. Everyone's afraid of Isaac. Now he's rent collector he can turf folk out of their homes on a whim. He'll put me out straight away if I can't pay the rent. I'm sure of it.'

Molly despaired at the thought of it. How could Isaac ever think that she would go back to him when he treated her so cruelly?

'Tha'll 'ave to come 'ere,' said Ellen. 'We'll make room for thee and t' child.'

'Tha knows I'm grateful for that,' said Molly, 'but there's no room for another loom.'

'Loom's no good to thee if tha can't sell t' quilts,' pointed out John.

'Just because I can't sell to the warehouse doesn't mean I can't sell to folk who want one for a wedding or new baby. Mr Ainsworth said he'd recommend me if anyone enquired about a commission.'

'Does he think tha's up to it?' asked John. He seemed doubtful, even though he'd seen her work. 'Summat like that's not easy. There's no set pattern to follow if folk want summat special like their initials woven into it for a wedding gift – and if it weren't right they wouldn't pay.'

'But what else can I do?'

'Tha'd best come 'ere,' suggested John. 'Tha can't keep livin' in that empty cottage. It's not fair on Annie,' he added. Molly said nothing. She'd already fallen out with Nancy for saying the same thing, and she knew she mustn't fall out with John and Ellen as well. She needed them.

'But I wouldn't be earnin' owt. I couldn't save for a ticket.'

She saw Ellen and John glance at one another. It was obvious they'd talked about it when she wasn't there.

'It might be best to wait,' said Ellen. 'There's a year and a half gone already and tha's no nearer gettin' t' money. Maybe tha should wait it out. He might come back.'

Molly could hear the hope in her mother-in-law's voice, but she knew the truth was that if she couldn't raise money for her passage to New South Wales there was little chance of Thomas getting the money to pay for his fare back even if he did receive a pardon.

'No,' she told them. 'I'll not give up.'

–

Back in her own cottage, Molly counted her money. She had managed to save another four pounds and eight shillings, and she'd moved the leather bag from its hiding place in the kitchen to beneath a loose board under her bed upstairs. She kept a stinking chamber pot that she put on top of it whenever she went out. The smell was vile and she hoped it would put any thief off investigating too closely.

She needed to buy potatoes and flour from the market, as well as candles and she would need more bobbins if she was to continue to work. She'd told Ellen and John that she wouldn't give up, but as she sat on the upturned box by her small fire and watched her daughter playing at her feet, Molly knew that she was running out of options. If she could sell the quilt that she'd woven she could manage for a while, but after that she would be back in the same situation.

The knock on her door made her jump, and when she went to open it she wasn't surprised to find Isaac Crompton there. She was aware that he was always watching her and would know that she'd been to the warehouse.

'What dost tha want?' she asked him. 'It's not rent day.'

'I saw thee bringin' a quilt back from t' warehouse,' he said.

'What's it to do with thee?'

'I wondered if owt were wrong?'

He looked so concerned for her that Molly found it hard to believe that his inquiry wasn't genuine. She was tempted to tell him that he knew full well what was wrong, but she knew he would only deny it.

'There's nowt wrong,' she told him.

'I just wondered if Ainsworth had turned thee away.'

'Why would he do that?' she asked. 'He always praises my work. He's always given me a good price for it.'

'But not today?'

'No,' she conceded but didn't say more. She was determined not to give him the satisfaction of seeing that she was upset.

'There's no market for handwoven quilts now that t' mill can turn 'em out in a day,' he said. Molly didn't argue, even though she knew the mill couldn't produce the fancy quilts that she was making by hand. 'Tha knows my offer still stands,' he told her. 'I hate to see thee livin' like this in a bare cottage when there's no need for it.'

'I don't need any help from thee,' she told him, reaching to close the door. But as she did so, he reached out a hand to stop it.

'I'm only concerned for thee, Molly,' he told her, and if she hadn't known him better she would have believed that he really meant it.

'If tha were concerned for me tha wouldn't have given evidence against Thomas,' she snapped at him.

'But he were at that meetin'.'

'Aye, and so were thee,' Molly reminded him. 'Difference is, he were fightin' for the workin' man, aye and for the workin' woman too. Tha were there spyin' for Fletcher!'

'Molly, I'm an honest man,' he protested. 'I've never set a foot wrong. And now I've a good job with a decent wage, and I'm offerin' thee a home, a proper home, if only tha'd stop bein' so stubborn and take it.'

'I'll not give up on Thomas. And I'll go nowhere without my child,' said Molly.

'Tha'll think different when tha's no money,' he warned her and she felt a frisson of fear at the threat.

'I can manage,' she said, even though she wasn't sure that it was true. 'There's no need for thee to keep comin' around.'

'Well, I'll be round on Friday, for t' rent money,' he reminded her.

'And I'll pay thee,' she said as she finally managed to close the door on him.

Molly went into the back kitchen to see what food she had to make some dinner. Her stocks were low and she'd planned to go to the market after she'd been paid, but she'd been so upset about the quilt that she'd forgotten and come straight back. There was some oatmeal left and she made it up into a porridge. She would go to the market tomorrow.

—

The next morning, Molly left Annie with Ellen and took the quilt with her down to the market place. It had occurred to her when she woke from a dream in the early hours of the morning that even if Mr Ainsworth wouldn't buy it from her, she might be able to sell it herself.

The market was busy, with the stallholders doing a brisk trade. There was nowhere for Molly to spread the quilt out for inspection so she decided to walk around the stalls with it over her arm to ask if anyone was interested in buying it. One or two of the women paused to take a look, and they all said that although it was a beautiful quilt they had no use for it and couldn't afford to buy it anyway. Molly was in tears by the time she'd finished. It had been a silly idea and when the market overlooker came across and warned her that she could be taken before the magistrate for hawking her wares without a licence, she folded the quilt away, hurriedly bought some potatoes and more oatmeal and walked disconsolately back home, wondering what to do next.

'Could tha sell it for me? Pass it off as thine?' she suggested to John when she got back. He looked doubtful.

'Mr Ainsworth would know,' he said. 'He'd be suspicious.'

'Would it matter?' asked Molly.

'I could try,' he said. 'I could say as I've taken on an apprentice. He'll not believe me though. He'll know it's thy work.'

'But he wouldn't be buyin' from me. And that's what he's afraid of doin'.'

'I never thought Isaac Crompton would be so mean,' said Ellen. 'We've never done a thing to hurt 'im or 'is family.'

'No, but I have,' said Molly. 'He were hurt when I left him for Thomas. I knew it at the time, but I never thought it would make him so revengeful as this. He'll not rest until he's got me back,' she said. 'I'm beginnin' to wonder if I shouldn't just give in to what's inevitable.'

'But tha's wed to Thomas!'

'Aye, if he still lives,' said Molly. 'We've heard nowt.' She was starting to wonder if Thomas would ever write. There were so many things that could have gone wrong. She knew he'd been ill. She'd been told that many didn't survive the voyage, and she'd heard talk about ships lost at sea. She'd taken no notice of the doom-mongers at first, but as every day passed with no word, she began to think that maybe they were right. Maybe she was a widow and free to wed again.

'I'm sure he's alive,' said Ellen, breaking the silence after a few moments. 'I'd know if he wasn't. Mothers know,' she told Molly. Molly desperately wanted to believe her, but until she had proof she knew that she would never be free from the worry that she might never see her husband again.

Chapter Thirty-One

Thomas found himself dozing as he waited for the Allans to come out of the ball. It was two in the morning on New Year's Day and the heat was still oppressive. He'd been up since before six and he'd be expected to be up as early again the next morning. He thought he'd never been so tired in his entire life – not even when little Annie had kept him and Molly awake all night crying with the colic.

At last, word came that his master and mistress were ready to leave and he hauled himself onto the back step of the carriage as they drove round to the front of the governor's house. He jumped down to open the door and lower the step as they came out, laughing and talking. Mr Allan ignored him, but Mrs Allan paused, waiting for him to offer his hand to help her up.

'Thank you, Thomas,' she whispered as she climbed past him in a cloud of perfume, silk and rum. He stood back as Mr Allan got in, then closed the door, took his seat and shut his eyes for a few moments as they drove home.

Back at the residence, with the carriage and horses put in the stables, Thomas peeled off his uniform and stood for a moment, allowing his body to cool before lying down on the bed and falling asleep. It seemed he'd only been asleep for moments before he heard the bell that woke the staff in the outbuildings. Reluctantly, he rolled from the mattress. Mr Allan did not allow tardiness in his staff and his discipline, learned in the army, could be brutal.

Thomas washed and shaved and dressed in a clean shirt. It was important to look good. It was what the Allans kept him for. At home in Lancashire, Thomas had never considered himself as handsome. It wasn't something that was talked about and, for a handloom weaver, it was of no importance. There, it had been his skill with his hands that had made his living. But here things were different. He'd learned from talking to others whilst they waited around the back of various big houses that there was competition amongst the ladies to have the most desirable young men as their footman. And he'd seen the appreciative glances from other ladies as he'd escorted Mrs Allan around the town, following at a discreet distance, carrying her parcels. He supposed it ought to flatter him, but it didn't. It made him feel even more of a slave, a commodity, something to be used and possibly cast off when he'd outlived his usefulness.

Thomas went into the main house and laid the table before returning to the kitchen to collect Mrs Allan's breakfast tray. He hated this job. He knew that Mrs Allan should have her lady's maid take her tray upstairs, but she fussed and said it was too heavy for Betsy and that Thomas should bring it instead. He knew that when he set it down and tapped on her door she would call to him to bring it in – and when he did she would be sitting at her dressing table, wearing her nightgown and brushing her hair. It wasn't seemly and the other staff raised an eyebrow, but there was nothing he could do. A refusal would mean a complaint about him to her husband and he knew that would not end well.

'Thomas,' she greeted him as he put down the tray on a side table. 'I hope we didn't keep you up too late last night. It was quite an occasion.' She turned to look at him directly rather than through her mirror. 'Pour my coffee, will you.'

'Yes, ma'am.' He lifted the pot and watched the dark brown liquid steam into the cup. It was a drink he'd never encountered until he'd come here. They'd always drunk tea at home – strong and sweet from the big brown pot Molly kept on the hearth.

He handed Mrs Allan the cup.

'Thank you,' she said as she picked up the little silver spoon to stir it. Thomas sometimes wondered where all these fine things came from. By sea, he supposed. There was nowhere here that manufactured them.

'There's a ship come in,' she told him. 'I'm expecting some packages so I'll need you to come down with me.'

'Yes, ma'am.' He made a nod of his head, hating himself for being forced to show subservience. At home he'd been his own man, answerable to no one.

'I'll send for you when I'm ready,' she told him.

A ship, thought Thomas, as he ran back down the stairs to the kitchens. And it must have come from England. Perhaps there would be a letter for him from Molly. His letter that told his family he'd arrived safely had been sent long ago, but no word had come back from his wife and he was starting to worry that she might have forgotten him or worse, taken up with Isaac Crompton again. He seethed at the thought of the man who had done him so much wrong.

In the kitchen he sat at the table and ate his own late breakfast and drank the dregs of the strong coffee that he'd cleared away from the morning room, where Mr Allan took his breakfast alone. It was bitter, but he was growing used to the taste of it and he'd discovered that it helped him to feel less tired. At least there was no ball tonight, he thought. He hoped to get to his bed at a reasonable time and feel better the next day.

That afternoon, as he escorted Mrs Allan from her carriage to the wharf, he stared at the ships that were anchored in the bay, trying to see which was newly arrived. It was the *Wansted*. The sails were furled after her long voyage and the cargo she'd brought was being loaded onto boats to be rowed ashore. Might it be possible, he wondered, to pay a ferryman to take him out to the ship and then hide somewhere onboard on the return voyage to England? He'd spent so long on the *Fortune* that he was aware of all the little nooks and crannies where a man might conceal himself.

'Thomas!' He looked around as Mrs Allan called his name. 'You were lost in a dream,' she told him.

'Aye. Yes, ma'am. I'm sorry.'

'Carry these boxes to the carriage,' she told him. 'I'm waiting to enquire if there are any letters.'

Please let there be a letter from Molly, prayed Thomas as he stowed the boxes away and returned to his mistress.

'Is there anything for me?' he dared to ask when he found her glancing through the post she'd been handed by the captain.

'No. Were you expecting something?' she asked.

'I'm waiting for a letter from my wife,' he whispered.

'Perhaps there'll be one next time,' said Mrs Allan. 'Come along. We'll go back now.'

Thomas followed her disconsolately back to the carriage and handed her in. It was breaking his heart that neither Molly nor his parents had written to him.

'What's to do?' asked Sarah, the cook, when he arrived back in the kitchen. 'Tha's not in bother wi' Allan, is tha?'

'No.' Thomas sat down at the table. 'I were hoping to hear from my wife,' he said. 'But there were no letter. I think she's forgot me.'

'Don't say that,' said Sarah. 'Letters can take a long time to arrive.'

'Aye. But I were hopin' as she might write to let me know she were comin',' he said gloomily.

'That wouldn't suit Mrs Allan,' observed Sarah. 'She wouldn't want t' competition.'

Thomas felt his cheeks burn. Sarah found it amusing that the mistress seemed sweet on him and Thomas wished she didn't. He hated it, and he knew it meant that Mrs Allan was keen not to lose him.

He'd thought at first that he was lucky to be employed by the Allans, but now he wasn't so sure. His life was one of servitude and although he was paid a wage of sorts, it was meagre and barely enough to provide the essentials. He knew that he could earn more, much more, if he were a free man. He'd been told that when he'd been in New South Wales for a few years he would be entitled to a ticket of leave, which would mean he could leave the Allans' household and find his own work. But he would need to be recommended by the master and mistress for his good conduct and although he did his best to please them, he suspected that Mrs Allan might find some reason not to let him go. He just hoped that his petition for an absolute pardon would be successful so that he would be completely free and able to leave New South Wales to go home.

Chapter Thirty-Two

Christmas 1813 had been a miserable one for Molly. She'd been so sure that she would be able to celebrate it with Thomas, but once again she'd sat at the hearth of her parents-in-law's cottage and wondered where her husband was.

John had taken the quilt she'd woven to Mr Ainsworth but as he'd predicted, the warehouseman had recognised it as her work and told John that he was afraid to buy it. He hadn't named Isaac Crompton, but John had come back convinced that Molly was right when she said that Isaac had a hold over Mr Ainsworth.

Molly had taken the quilt home, and not knowing what else to do with it, she'd fetched it up to the bedroom on Christmas Eve and laid it over the bed to keep her and Annie warm.

As the weeks passed she'd had to dip into her savings again and again to pay the rent. She was determined not to give Isaac the satisfaction of putting her out and she knew there would be no chance of parish relief until every last penny was spent. John and Ellen begged her to give up the cottage and move in with them before all her money was gone, and Nancy told her she was a fool, but still Molly clung to Thomas's loom and the hope that someone might ask her to weave them a quilt.

She dreaded every Friday evening when Isaac came to collect her rent. Sometimes she even considered locking up and hiding in the cellar when he knocked, but she knew that it would do no good. He knew that she was there and on the occasions she'd been slow to answer the door he'd kept on hammering on it until she'd responded.

One Friday, at the end of January, it had snowed hard in the morning. Molly hoped it might keep Isaac away, but around four o' clock in the afternoon, just as it was growing dark, she heard his footsteps crunching over the frozen ground outside. The lantern he was carrying threw shadows across her walls and made Annie cry with fright. Molly shushed her as she went to open the door.

'Hast tha got enough to pay this week?' asked Isaac, standing on her doorstep with the lantern at his feet, trying to peer into her purse as she fished the coins out – threepenny bits, ha'pennies and farthings which she carefully counted out until he had two shillings in his palm.

'I needs another sixpence,' he said.

'I thought I had enough.' Molly stared into the empty purse in bewilderment. She'd been sure there'd been more in it – then she remembered that she'd bought potatoes and some milk earlier in the week. She'd meant to ask John to lend her sixpence. 'I'll have to run across t' fold and borrow it,' she told him. But he blocked her way.

'Tha can't go on like this, Molly,' he said, and the note of concern in his voice almost made her believe that his care was genuine.

'If I could have gone on selling my quilts I would have had plenty to pay thee!' she burst out in a rare show of anger.

'No one'll pay for handwoven any more,' he replied, echoing Mr Ainsworth's words. 'It's all factory weaving now, at half the price.'

Molly didn't argue. It would be pointless, but she knew that the special quilts that she wove were still popular as wedding and baptismal gifts.

'Let me past and I'll get thee thy sixpence,' she insisted.

'And what will tha do next Friday?' he asked. 'Tha'll not be able to stay on 'ere if tha can't pay t' rent,' he warned her again.

'Tha'd not put me out, would tha?' she challenged him.

'It's not up to me, Molly,' he told her. 'Tha knows I'd do nowt to harm thee, but I daren't go back to Fletcher and tell him that I'm short. I'll lose my job if I do that.'

He sounded so plausible that Molly almost believed him.

'Let me past and I'll fetch thee sixpence,' she said again.

'I'll tell thee what,' he replied. 'I'll put sixpence of my own money in – as a gift.' He made it sound as if it was a fortune, but she knew by looking at his fancy clothes and polished boots that he could well afford it.

'There's no need,' she said. 'John'll lend it to me.' She didn't want to be indebted to Isaac again, but he ignored her and continued to block her doorway.

'I'll 'ave to gi' thee notice to leave if tha can't pay next week though,' he said. He sounded regretful, but there was a gleam in his eye that he couldn't disguise. 'And tha'd 'ave to get yon loom out from t' cellar,' he reminded her as he leaned towards the light of his lantern to enter her payment in his ledger.

–

Molly knew that the only thing left for her to do, if she wanted to keep her home, was to go back to the Reverend Brocklehurst and beg once more for parish relief. She decided to take Annie with her. The sight of her daughter might help her case – after all, it wasn't her fault that she'd been left to bring up the child alone without the wages of her father.

She called in at the Golden Lion as she passed, although she had little hope of there being a letter from Thomas and that small hope was crushed when Uncle Richard shook his head.

'Nothing,' he told her.

'I'm beginning to wonder if we'll ever hear,' Molly told him. She reckoned that it was well over a year now since Thomas's ship had sailed. Surely a letter would have come by now if he was alive and able to write to her. She refused to contemplate the alternative. He couldn't have died. He just couldn't. Not her Thomas.

'Don't give up hope,' Uncle Richard told her as he poured her a drink. 'Keep thy chin up.'

'Aye.' It was easy for him to say, she thought, wondering if he would lend her money for the rent. But he was Thomas's uncle and not hers, and she didn't like to ask.

She drained the cup, hoping that the vicar wouldn't notice the smell of it on her breath, and went on her way to the church. It was icy cold inside and her breath misted on the air. In the vestry, she found the vicar wrapped in an overcoat and wearing gloves even though he had a small fire burning in the grate.

'Mrs Holden,' he greeted her. 'I've not seen thee for a while.' Molly knew it was an admonition for her irregular attendance at worship and she felt guilty and worried that her request would fall on less than receptive ears because she wasn't a regular churchgoer.

'I'm sorry,' she said. 'I've been workin'.'

'Not on the Sabbath day, I hope?'

'No, no. Of course not,' she replied quickly, even though the truth was that she'd slipped down to the cellar at every hour she could spare whilst Annie was sleeping and had often woven on a Sunday. 'But it's a long walk from Hag End and they have prayers in the schoolroom.'

He nodded. 'I'm pleased to hear you are not neglecting your prayers,' he said.

'I'm praying more than ever,' she told him. 'For Thomas.'

'Of course. You've heard nothing?'

'No. I've just enquired about a letter this morning. But none's come. I'm beginning to fear the worst,' she confessed.

'God's will be done,' the vicar reminded her. Molly didn't reply. She thought that if it was God's will that Thomas should die and she should be left alone with little choice but to throw herself on the mercy of the likes of Isaac Crompton, then she'd be better off weaving every hour of a Sunday rather than wasting her time on her knees.

'So, what can I do for you today?' he asked as he threw another cob of coal on the fire. It smoked and flamed blue around the edges as the fire took hold of it and Molly coughed as the smoke rose, covering her mouth with a handkerchief to hide any tell-tale aroma of the ale.

'I was hopin' I could get some help with my rent,' she said.

'But you said you were working?'

'Aye. I've been weavin' quilts,' she told him and watched as he raised an eyebrow in surprise. 'But the warehouse won't take them any more.'

'Well, it's not women's work, is it?' he said. 'You should be caring for your child,' he reminded her with a glance at Annie who sat on her lap, sucking a thumb. 'I hope she's not been neglected whilst you've been doing this weaving.'

'Of course not!' Molly's indignation flared at the suggestion. 'She's well cared for. But I needed to earn some money.'

'And what about your savings?' asked the vicar. 'You told me last time you came that you had savings.'

'It were all stolen,' she replied.

'That was unfortunate.'

'Thing is,' she went on, 'I'm threatened with bein' turned out of my cottage if I can't pay the rent and I've nowt. Look!' She opened her purse to show him that it was empty. 'I've nowt left to feed myself and the child.'

The vicar stared into her purse. 'You honestly have nothing?' he asked her.

'I owe sixpence to the rent collector.'

'And how much is the rent?'

'Two and sixpence.'

He nodded and went across to a cupboard, found the key and unlocked it. Molly watched as he drew out a cash tin and opened it. 'Two and six?' he repeated as he counted out a florin and a sixpence.

'Thank you,' she said as the vicar handed her the coins.

'I'll have to speak to the parish guardians about regular payments,' he said. 'The problem is that they might refuse to pay your rent when you could go elsewhere, with there only being the two of you,' he added.

Molly nodded. She understood his dilemma. Mothers like Hannah Fisher, who had several children, were less likely to find a place with a relative, but John and Ellen had offered her a home and the parish would think it a waste of their money to pay the rent on her cottage.

'It's just that there wouldn't be room for the loom if I moved in with Thomas's parents,' she explained.

'But if the warehouse won't take your quilts then you have no use for the loom,' replied the vicar echoing what John had already told her. 'Best sell it, I think.'

Molly didn't try to explain about Mr Ainsworth's promise to try to find her some commissions. She knew it would sound a hollow excuse. She had enough for her rent for one more week and she was grateful for that.

It had grown warmer in the vestry and the vicar had unbuttoned his coat. She would have liked to stay longer to warm herself by the fire, but she knew she was dismissed, so she hoisted Annie onto her hip and went back out into the perishing cold to walk home to Hag End where she had just a bit of slack left for her fire and half a bag of oatmeal in her kitchen.

–

That afternoon, after she'd tucked Annie into bed to keep her warm, Molly came downstairs to find Isaac Crompton at her door.

'Molly!' he called when he heard her footsteps. 'I wasn't sure if tha were here,' he said, pushing open the door a crack. 'Can I come in?'

'Aye,' she said, knowing it would be futile to refuse. She was pleased that at least he'd asked. 'What dost tha want?' she asked. 'Hast tha come for thy sixpence? I'll fetch my purse.'

Isaac shook his head. 'It doesn't matter,' he said. 'I've brought thee summat,' he went on, drawing a brown paper parcel out from under his coat and looking around for somewhere to lay it down.

'What is it?' she asked suspiciously as he put it down on her upturned box.

'Just a bit o' summat to help thee out,' he said.

Molly pulled back the wrappings and found two skinned rabbits. She wanted to refuse them but the temptation of something good to eat was too much.

'I'm worried about thee, Molly,' said Isaac. 'Tha looks poorly.'

'I'm fine,' she told him, taking the meat into the back kitchen. She'd put some in the pot later with the oatmeal.

'How long can tha go on bein' stubborn?' he asked when she came back. 'Is that all tha has for thy fire? I should 'ave fetched a bucket o' coal an all.'

'I can get some,' she told him. 'And I can pay my rent come Friday. Tha's no need to fret about me.'

'But look at thyself, Molly,' he replied. 'Tha's makin' thyself ill when there's no need.'

'I'm all right,' she told him.

'Tha's not,' he replied. 'And I'd take thee 'ome wi' me this minute if tha'd come. Tha could sit in a comfy chair by a roaring fire and fill thy belly wi' whatever took thy fancy.' He paused until she looked directly at him. 'Say tha'll come,' he said.

She could hear the pleading, wheedling tone in his voice and just for a moment she was tempted. She knew that he could be kind when he set his mind to it, so long as she didn't cross him. But she shook her head. She wouldn't give in to him.

'Hast heard owt from Thomas?' he asked, trying a different line of persuasion. 'Jack Fisher's wife's heard nowt. I wouldn't be surprised if t' ship went down.'

'Don't say that!'

'Well, there'd have been word by now, surely? How long's it been?'

Molly knew he was well aware of how long it had been; over a year since the *Fortune* sailed.

'Yon government would have written if the ship had been lost,' she said.

'Would they?' asked Isaac. Molly wasn't sure. It was a hope she was clinging to.

'Tha can't go on like this,' Isaac told her again, sweeping a gesture around her empty room, at the paltry fire in the grate and the ice clouding the inside of her window. 'How long is tha goin' to be stubborn afore tha admits that he'll never come back? Tha can't spend t' rest o' thy life livin' like this. See sense. Let me take care o' thee.'

'I'll not be parted from my child,' she said, feeling herself weaken at the thought of an easier life.

'Tha can see t' child. I'll not stop tha seein' 'er.'

'But tha'll not take her in.' She saw him hesitate and saw that she had a slight upper hand. But would she agree if he said he'd take Annie as well? She wasn't sure.

'Would tha come if I said aye?' he asked, echoing her own inner question.

'Happen,' she said, wondering if he would make the concession, and whether she could trust him to treat her daughter well.

'Well, that's progress,' he said, looking pleased with himself, although he didn't agree to it. 'I'd best get on,' he told her. 'But th' offer's there. Tha knows where to find me. Tha's only to knock on my door.'

He gave her a nod of his head and went on his way, whistling as he walked. Molly sank down onto the box and wondered what to do. What if he was right? What if she never heard from Thomas again? Could she really spend the rest of her life waiting for him?

Chapter Thirty-Three

The *Emu* had dropped anchor in Sydney Cove the previous evening and Thomas was on his way to the collecting office to enquire if any letters had arrived for Mr Allan. As he stood in the queue he prayed that there would be one for him as well.

'Name?' he was asked as he approached the counter.

'Mr David Allan,' he said and watched as the man retrieved a bundle addressed to his master. 'Anything sent care of Mr Allan?' he enquired.

'Just this one.'

Thomas reached out for it eagerly, sure that it would be from Molly. But his moment of excitement faded as he saw that it was not for him, but addressed to Sarah Cavanagh, the cook.

'Is tha sure that's all?' he asked, hoping that a letter for him might lie forgotten somewhere at the bottom of a sack.

'Just that one. And it needs to be paid for,' the man told him as he began to turn away to disguise his tears of disappointment. Thomas reached into his pocket and handed over one of the small coins known as a dump, then hurried away before its value was questioned. Many people were suspicious of the new currency, and although it was useful for small payments, Thomas knew that it was rum that held the real value in exchanges and transactions.

A bottle could readily be exchanged for the worth of a five-pound note.

'There's a letter for thee,' he told Sarah when he got back to the kitchen, relieved to be out of the hot sun. 'I paid the postage,' he told her as she dried her hands on a towel and reached for it, the delight clear on her face making his own disappointment even worse.

He watched as she turned it over in her hands, peering at the writing and then sat down at the table where she brushed away some spilt flour to make a place to spread it out to read it.

'From thy family?' he asked her.

'Aye.'

Thomas watched as she bent her head over it, her lips moving to form the words as she marked her place under each with a forefinger. He knew that she was thinking about her family and imagining them kissing the letter before they sent it to her. Thomas turned away with tears in his eyes. He longed to hold a letter of his own, one that had been kissed by Molly.

'Was there nowt for thee?' asked Sarah when she eventually looked up and folded the letter to put it carefully in her pocket. Thomas shook his head. 'I'm sorry,' she told him as she fetched her purse to pay him back the cost of the postage.

'I wish I could get home,' he told her. 'I've a mind to look out for a ship to slip on board.'

'Tha can't do that!' she warned him.

'I could,' he insisted. 'I could hide away somewhere.'

'Don't talk daft,' she said as she returned to her pans that were simmering on the hob. 'Even if tha got on a ship and went back before th' expiration of thy time, they'd catch thee and send thee back – probably for life and then tha'd have no chance of a pardon. Best serve thy time and hope for a pardon. But why go back?' she asked as she lifted a lid off a pan to stir its contents. 'There's lots o' folk makin' a life for themselves here.'

'I have a wife and child.' His voice trembled at the thought of Molly and he worried again about why she hadn't written to him. 'But there were this other chap,' he explained and told her about Isaac Crompton and what he'd done, and how worried he was that he would pursue Molly.

'Perhaps it'd be better to put her from thy mind and think about making a fresh start here,' suggested Sarah when he'd finished the tale. 'Once tha gets thy ticket of leave tha could make a life for thyself – happen find someone else.'

She was looking at him intently and he guessed her meaning. She was a bonny lass and he liked her, but he wasn't ready to give up hope that Molly might come to him. Maybe she was already on a ship, he told himself, and that was why she hadn't written. Maybe, before long, he would go down to the harbour and he would see her, being rowed ashore, come to surprise him.

Chapter Thirty-Four

Molly went down to the cellar. The chill that struck up through the stone flags made her legs hurt and her hand was numb as she ran it along the edge of the empty loom. No wonder Thomas had always come up every so often in the wintertime to rub his hands together in front of the fire and warm himself for five minutes, she thought. How hard it must have been for him to raise the delicate knops when his hands were so numbed that they could barely move.

Reluctantly, she'd agreed that John should come and take the loom apart. He was going to carry it across the fold and see if it would fit into his workshop, propped against the wall. If not, then it would have to be be burned because it was clear that no one would buy it.

For weeks Molly had struggled on, begging her rent from the parish, taking charity and handouts and refusing to give up hope that she would weave on it again. But the last time she'd gone to the Reverend Brocklehurst he'd told her that the parish couldn't pay her rent any longer. There were families in more need of help. She must move in with her parents-in-law.

Molly felt defeated. It meant that she would no longer have any chance of saving up the money to join Thomas. She'd looked for other work, but everywhere she went she was turned away. She knew Isaac Crompton was behind it. He continued to pursue her. He would never give up, not even if she was living with John and Ellen and she wondered how long she could keep up her resistance when there was no word from Thomas. Then, with tears in her eyes, she told herself that she must not begin to imagine that something bad had happened to him. A letter would come soon to say that he was safe. She must hold on to that thought and no other.

Molly was disturbed by a knock at her door and her heart raced. It could only be Isaac Crompton, come to press his suit once more.

She went up the steps with trepidation and opened the door a crack. But the man who stood there was a stranger to her.

'Molly Holden?'

'Who's askin'?' She eyed him apprehensively, wondering what he wanted. He looked too prosperous to be a weaver, but surely Isaac hadn't sent a bailiff? She didn't owe any more rent until Friday.

'I'm Walter Flitcroft,' he told her. 'Mr Ainsworth at t' warehouse told me to come. I were askin' about a quilt for a weddin', and he said that tha could make one.' The man looked at her dubiously, as if he thought he'd been sent on some wild goose chase. 'I didn't think women could do weavin',' he said with a note of disbelief.

'Come in,' said Molly, her hopes soaring. She opened the door wider. 'Come in and I'll show thee.'

She ran up the stairs and lifted the quilt from her sleeping daughter without disturbing her. 'Here,' she said, as she held it up by the corners, still standing on the bottom step so as not to let it trail on the floor. 'Look at this one.'

She couldn't see the man's face as she held up the quilt and for a moment he said nothing. Molly was sure that he was going to say he'd changed his mind, but after a moment he spoke. 'Can tha make one with a date and initials on it?' he asked.

'Aye, of course I can,' said Molly, hoping that she sounded more confident than she felt. She'd never done one like that before, but she was sure that she would manage it with a bit of help from John. 'I'd need a payment up front,' she warned the man as she lowered her aching arms and folded the quilt. 'I've bobbins to buy.'

'How much?'

'Half,' she said, not sure how such negotiations were done. The man began to nod. He seemed as unsure as she was.

'What would that be?' he asked.

Molly quickly calculated what Mr Ainsworth would have paid her, taking into account the time it would take to weave something complex. 'Two pounds now, and the same when it's finished,' she said. 'And tha can choose whatever pattern tha wants,' she added.

'Can tha do roses?'

'Aye I can do that,' she said, relieved that the man wasn't asking for anything too difficult.

'With *R* and *W* and *April 1814* in't middle with flowers round and a border with leaves?'

'Aye. Tha can look at my patterns and choose what tha wants,' she said.

'All right.' The man nodded. 'I'll have to fetch thee t' money later,' he said. 'I haven't got it on me.'

'Tha'll have to bring it afore Friday, or I'll not be able to do it,' she warned him, knowing that if she couldn't pay the rent on time then this one chance would be lost to her forever.

'Aye.' He nodded. She closed the door behind him after he'd gone and then watched from the window as he walked away. She wasn't sure if he would return with the money. She knew it was a lot to ask and even if Mr Ainsworth had recommended her work, there was no reason for this man to trust that she could weave the quilt she'd promised him. But the visit had raised a flicker of hope in her. Perhaps if she did weave this quilt then others would come. Perhaps if she could make a living she could stay in the cottage after all.

'Don't get thy hopes up,' warned John when she went across to tell him and Ellen that she might not have to move in with them after all. 'Weavin' one quilt isn't goin' to make thee a fortune.'

'But it's a start,' she said.

'Aye. If yon chap comes back. Tha's asked him for a lot o' money wi' nowt to show for it,' warned John. 'It were all right to ask for summat to buy bobbins, but I've never heard o' folk payin' for summat before it's made.'

Molly knew that he was probably right. She thought she'd most likely never see Mr Flitcroft again, so she was surprised when there was another knock at her door that same afternoon and he handed over the money to her.

'Mr Ainsworth said I can trust thee,' he told her. 'He told me to say he'll have bobbins ready for thee – best quality thread.'

'I'll not let thee down,' promised Molly as she took the money. 'I'll start on it right away. It'll be done within a couple of weeks.'

'Can I come for it a week on Monday?' he asked.

'Aye. It'll be ready then,' she agreed, knowing that she was going to have to work hard and long to get it finished.

–

Molly hurried down to the warehouse to collect the bobbins straight away. Mr Ainsworth greeted her with a wide grin and handed her the thread.

'I'm grateful to thee for recommendin' me,' Molly told him.

'Aye. Well, it's t' least I could do. But don't go tellin' folk,' he warned her and Molly understood that he was afraid that Isaac Crompton would hear about it.

'I'll say nowt,' she promised, wondering if she would need to revert to keeping her work secret from Isaac.

She hurried home through the sleet and after warming her hands at the fire for a few minutes, she went down to the cellar and began to beam up the thread on the loom before the light failed. Even though she was so cold, she was glad to be doing her work again. She enjoyed weaving and even though she knew that making this quilt was going to be a challenge, she was looking forward to it.

Next day, when the warp was fixed, she applied the size and whilst it was drying she took her basket and walked down to the market to buy some much needed food and the candles that she would have to burn through the dark nights and early mornings to get the quilt finished on time.

Before Molly went for the supplies, she called in at the Golden Lion. Every time she pushed open the door she clung to the hope that today there would be a letter. But as soon as she caught Uncle Richard's eye she knew that she was to be disappointed again.

Afterwards, she went round the market stalls and made her purchases. She knew that she should have felt more optimistic than she did, but although she was pleased to have work, the continued absence of word from Thomas was beginning to concern her. She couldn't understand why he hadn't written to her. Surely he hadn't forgotten her and the child, and his parents? But the alternative, the nagging worry that something bad had befallen him and he hadn't arrived safely in New South Wales was too awful to contemplate.

It had begun to snow again and the flakes thickened as she trudged back home. Her boots had a split on the sole and her feet were sodden by the time she arrived. She fetched Annie and then hung up her shawl, still covered in a layer of melting snow and put her boots by the fire to dry. It would be too cold to work in the cellar barefoot, so after dinner she put Annie in bed, under the quilt, and found some old rags to wrap around her feet to try to keep them warm. Then she sat at the loom and sent the shuttle flying, battened down the cloth and after a few rows, she picked up the hook to begin to raise the pattern.

–

Molly worked on the quilt every moment that she could, relying on Ellen to mind Annie as much as possible. The cold in the cellar seemed to fade as she concentrated on her weaving, and row by careful row, the quilt began to form.

On the Friday evening, she was careful to finish early, and even though she was tempted over and again to complete just one more row, by five o' clock she'd blown out the candles and gone up to the parlour to wait for Isaac.

The snow had stopped but it was thick on the ground. Footsteps were muffled and she jumped at his knock on her door. When she answered it, he stood there, well wrapped against the weather, with his lantern and his ledger, and a smug smile on his face.

'I've come for t' rent,' Isaac said with a look of satisfaction and Molly could see that he was certain she was going to tell him that she couldn't pay.

'Just a moment,' she replied, trying to keep her own face straight. 'I'll just fetch my purse.'

As she turned away she caught the look of bewilderment on his face. Molly allowed herself a small smile as she counted out two shillings and sixpence and offered it to him.

'Where's that come from?' He almost growled with suppressed anger. She knew that he hated to be bested.

'Is it not good enough for thee?' she asked.

'Where's tha got it from?' he repeated. 'I knows tha's not on t' list for parish relief any more. I thought tha were leavin' and movin in wi' John and Ellen.'

Molly shook her head. 'I've decided to stay on a bit longer.'

'Hast got a lodger or summat?' he asked, peering past her into the parlour. 'Tha knows it's not allowed.'

'No. It's just me and the child.'

'Then how come tha can afford t' rent all of a sudden?' he asked. 'Where's it come from?'

'Dost tha want it or not?' asked Molly, continuing to hold out the coins.

'Aye.' Isaac took the payment and slipped the money into his leather bag.

'Best enter it on thy ledger,' urged Molly. 'Then tha knows I owe nowt.'

'One more week'll make no difference,' Isaac warned her. 'I know tha can't keep payin'. Why not give notice now and be out by next Friday?'

'I don't need to give notice,' she told him. 'And tha's no need to worry. So long as I pays thee every Friday then tha need have no concerns.'

'What's tha up to now, Molly?' he asked. 'I know tha's up to summat. It'll do thee no good to be thievin',' he warned her.

'I've stolen nowt!' She wanted to tell him that he was the one who knew something about taking what wasn't his, but she held back. She could see how close he was to losing his temper in his utter frustration.

Isaac slammed the ledger closed and bent to pick up his lantern. 'I'll see thee next week,' he said. It sounded like a threat.

'Aye. I'll have t' rent ready for thee,' Molly assured him and closed her door with a thudding heart.

–

'Isaac Crompton were very suspicious,' John told Molly the next day when he came across to offer his advice on the weaving of the initials into the quilt. 'Kept on askin' why tha wasn't movin' in with us.'

'What did tha tell him?' she asked.

'Said as tha'd changed thy mind and that tha'd decided to stay on 'ere. He asked if it meant tha'd changed thy mind about goin' to New South Wales.'

'That would please him,' remarked Molly.

'Aye.' John hesitated. 'But tha wouldn't take up with 'im again, would tha?' he asked.

'Of course not! I'm Thomas's wife.'

'Aye, but… we've heard nowt,' he said and Molly could see from his pained face that he too was beginning to wonder why Thomas hadn't written. 'If Thomas doesn't come back,' he began, obviously finding it difficult to even consider such a possibility, 'well, tha's young. Tha wouldn't want to spend t' rest o' thy life alone.'

Molly sank down onto the bench with her back to the loom and met John's eye. It was something she didn't want to think about either, although she'd acknowledged, in her darkest moments, that it was a possibility.

'It's a bit soon to be talkin' like that,' she told John. 'Trouble is, I don't think Isaac Crompton'll ever let me alone.'

'But tha wouldn't take up with 'im?' persisted John.

'No.' Molly shook her head. 'Not him.' But she knew it wasn't that simple. It would be hard to keep away from Isaac. She knew that he was convinced he could wear her down eventually. He refused to believe that she didn't still like him, and he thought it was only stubbornness that made her keep refusing him. The trouble was, as time passed and she saw how hard her life was without Thomas, she sometimes caught herself thinking about a warm fireside and comfy chair.

Chapter Thirty-Five

Thomas stood outside Mr Allan's study and racked his brains for any way in which he might have displeased the man. It was the first time he had been summoned to see him here and he was afraid. As he waited, his imagination ran riot as he pictured himself with Mrs Allan. She continued to insist on an intimacy that he was uncomfortable with, yet he was shrewd enough to know that it would not be her who would take the blame if her husband discovered what had been going on.

After a moment or two, the door was opened and Mr Allan called him in.

'Mr Holden,' began his master, 'I wanted to have a word with you.'

'Sir?' he replied, trying to gauge the man's mood.

'My wife has been speaking to me about you.'

'Sir,' he responded again as his stomach lurched to his well-polished boots.

'Mrs Allan has a high opinion of you,' went on Mr Allan. Thomas didn't reply. He was afraid of incriminating himself in some way. 'She's very pleased with the way you carry out your duties.'

'Thank you, sir.'

'She tells me that you are hoping to receive a full pardon.'

At last, thought Thomas, Mrs Allan appeared to have kept her promise to petition her husband on his behalf.

'Yes, sir,' said Thomas hopefully, although he knew that if he was freed it wouldn't be the end of his problems. He would somehow need to raise the money for his passage back to England.

'It's much too soon for me to recommend you for an unconditional pardon,' said Mr Allan, dashing Thomas's hopes as quickly as they'd been raised. 'But I have decided to promote you to the job of steward.'

'Steward?' repeated Thomas in surprise.

'Yes. Mr Henderson is to leave us soon. He has his ticket of leave and I believe a pardon will follow for him. He's to become a farmer, up at Parramatta. I think you could take on the job. You know the household and I know that you can read and write – and I've seen that you're trustworthy.'

'Yes, sir. Thank you, sir.'

'And in time,' said Mr Allan. 'I will consider the matter of your recommendation for a pardon.' He paused. 'What would you do?' he asked. 'I know you're a weaver by trade.'

'I was hoping to go home, sir.'

'What? Back to England? You would need an absolute pardon to do that.'

'I have family there.'

'A wife?'

'Yes, sir, and a daughter.'

'Would they not join you here?'

'It's a matter of money for the voyage, sir,' explained Thomas.

'Of course.' Mr Allan nodded and Thomas saw that he'd never been in the position of not being able to do something for lack of money. 'Well,' he went on, 'let's see what sort of steward you are. Mr Henderson will show you what's what before he goes.'

'Yes, sir.' Thomas realised the interview was over and backed out of the study and closed the door gently behind him. He turned around to see Mrs Allan in the doorway to the sitting room.

'Did he tell you?' she asked.

'Yes, ma'am.'

'I told you I'd do something for you,' she said, coming to him and stroking his cheek with the palm of her hand. 'I hope you'll be grateful,' she whispered.

'I am grateful, ma'am. Thank you,' he said, wondering what she would demand of him next.

Chapter Thirty-Six

Molly finished the quilt for Mr Flitcroft in good time and had it ready for him when he called. She took him down to the cellar where it was spread across the loom so that he could examine it.

She waited, hardly daring to breathe whilst he looked at it.

'Is it all right?' she asked at last, unable to endure his silence for a moment longer.

'Aye.' He turned to look at her. 'Aye, it is.' He sounded surprised, thought Molly, as if he'd prepared himself for disappointment. 'Folk told me I were fool,' he admitted, 'to let a woman weave it, but it looks faultless to me.'

Molly moved forward with a smile to fold and wrap the quilt for him. She was glowing with pleasure as she handed it to him. 'If tha knows anyone else who's looking to commission one, will tha mention me?' she asked.

'Aye, I will,' he agreed as he paid her the two pounds that he owed. 'I will,' he repeated as she showed him to the door and watched him walk away. A satisfied customer, she thought and went to add some money to her purse and to hide the rest away upstairs.

After dinner, she went down to the market and called in at the Golden Lion on her way. As soon as she saw Uncle Richard's face she knew that there was news. He waved the flimsy, grubby letter above his head as if it were a trophy.

'It's come!' he called across the bar. 'He must have arrived safely! I were goin' to send thee a message.'

Molly ran forward to grasp the letter and simply held it against her as the tears flowed freely down her face. He was alive. He'd written, and he had held this letter.

'Open it then,' encouraged Uncle Richard. 'Let's see what he has to say.'

Molly would have preferred to read it when she was alone, in case it contained bad news, but Uncle Richard was waiting and the other patrons had fallen silent, their ears straining as they tried to hear what it said. They were all friends of Thomas's and she wasn't afraid of them hearing what he'd written, so she sat down on a bench and carefully opened the letter.

> *Sydney, Port Jackson, New South Wales.*
> *June 24th 1813*
>
> *Dear Wife, I hope this will find you and my dear child in good health as it leaves me. I take the opportunity of writing to let you know that I am safely arrived. The voyage was very uncomfortable and I was very sick for much of the time, but feeling better now. I have to inform you that I have been taken into the employ of a man called Mr David Allan and he travelled with us on the* Fortune. *I am employed as a footman, but it is very hard to do as I am kept up late and made to rise early leaving me very tired. Please to write to me with all haste and let me know if there is any chance of you procuring my pardon, and if not if you are*

282

able to come here as I cannot bear to be parted from you. Your ever loving husband, Thomas Holden.

Write to me at: Thomas Holden, Commissary Allan Esquire, Sidney Cove, New South Wales.

To be left at the Golden Lion, Churchgate, Bolton for Molly Holden, Hag End, near Bolton-le-Moors.

Molly ran most of the way back to the fold with the letter clutched against her heart, only stopping to walk a few paces to regain her breath before running again.

'Whatever's the matter?' cried Ellen as she burst in through the door, panting. Alarm was clear on her face.

'There's a letter!' Molly told her. 'From Thomas!'

'Let me see!'

Ellen grasped the paper and it shook in her trembling hands as she tried to read the words through her tears. 'He's alive! I told thee he were alive!'

'Who's this Mr Allan?' asked John when he'd read it too. 'He sounds like he might be an important gentleman. We must make enquiries. Thomas has done well if he's been taken into th' house of a gentleman!'

'It sounds like he's having to work long hours though,' said Molly, worrying that Thomas might become over-tired and fall ill again. 'He's always needed his sleep.'

'Aye. But he could be worse off. This Mr Allan must think him worthy of a place, and footman to a gentleman's a good job.'

'He might be able to help Thomas get a pardon,' suggested Ellen hopefully. 'He might be able to help him come home.'

'We must write back straight away,' said Molly, although she knew that not all her news would be good.

All their pleas for clemency and her petitions had come to nothing, and much as she longed to join Thomas, she was beginning to realise that it was going to be much harder than she'd ever thought to raise enough money.

'I'll fetch paper and pen,' said John. 'Dost tha want me to write it?'

'Aye. But I'll tell thee what to say,' Molly told him.

Hag End Fold, Bolton-le-Moors.
March 4th 1814

Dear Husband, Your letter came safe and welcomely to hand by which I am very glad that you was in good health at that time. This leaves me and the child in good health, together with your father and mother who send their love to you. It is some consolation that you should fortunately meet with such kind reception, for, from the tenor of your letter, we are led to believe that the man you are living with is a gentleman. We beg you to say to him we are very thankful that he hath condescended to take you into his service. We are glad you have found a residence that promises fair for your comfort even in those remote regions called New South Wales.

Dear Thomas, you ask if I am able to come to you. It certainly would be the greatest pleasure to me in this life to be with you in whatever part of the world you may be but the answer to my petition was that nothing could be done. If I can find any way that is legal to come to you I will and you should have no doubt that if it were possible I would have been with you before now.

Your affectionate and loving wife until death,
Molly Holden.

Once the letter was done, Molly kissed it and folded it. John wrote the address: Commissary Allan Esq., Sidney Cove, New South Wales. Then Molly walked back into Bolton straight away and went to the post office. She took one shilling and eightpence from her purse to send it postage paid to be sure that Thomas could receive it if he had no money of his own.

As she walked around the market, hoping that there was enough left to make her forgotten purchases before the stallholders packed up for the day, she felt happier than she had since before Thomas was taken away from her. He was alive! He was safe and he was working for a man who sounded as if he were of some importance. She would have been even happier if she could have gone to him and it saddened her when she thought of him hoping that she might do that. She knew that he would be disappointed when he received her letter, but she hoped that he would understand and wouldn't think that she didn't want to go.

–

'I had a letter from Thomas,' Molly told Isaac Crompton when he came for her rent that Friday. She watched as the disappointment flickered across his face. 'He's working for an important man named Mr Allan and he's keen for me to join him.'

'And will tha go?' he asked.

'Aye. Of course I will!'

'When tha's thirty-five pounds. Because I don't suppose he sent money to pay thy fare,' replied Isaac.

'What makes tha say that?'

'Tha would have been packed and gone if he had,' he replied and Molly knew that he was right. 'Why not admit it's not possible?' asked Isaac.

'I'll not give up hope,' she told him. 'Even if I can't go to New South Wales, I'll wait for Thomas to come home. I'll not leave him.'

Isaac shook his head. 'How can he come back?' he asked. 'How can he raise money for his fare? Besides,' he added. 'He might not be allowed.'

'What dost tha mean?' asked Molly, wondering what sly trick he was up to now.

'I were askin' Colonel Fletcher,' he told her. 'He said that only them that's granted an absolute pardon can come home. Aye, some gets a pardon, but they still has to stay in New South Wales.' He looked triumphant and Molly didn't know how to reply. She wasn't even sure he was telling the truth.

Isaac grinned. 'It's not such good news as tha thought,' he told her, looking pleased with himself. 'Hast got t' rent money?'

Molly took two and six from her purse and placed it in his outstretched hand. Isaac frowned over it.

'Where's this money comin' from?' he asked as he glanced around her bare parlour. 'Who's payin' thee – and what for?' he demanded as jealousy surged across his features at the thought of what it was she might be selling.

'What dost take me for?' she demanded. 'I'm doin' honest work.'

Isaac's eyes lighted on the basket of bobbins at the top of the cellar steps and Molly followed his gaze, cursing herself for having left them there.

'Tha's never weavin' again?' he asked. 'I thought they weren't buyin from thee at the warehouse?'

Molly saw the flash of anger in his eyes as he thought that Mr Ainsworth might have duped him in some way.

'I'm workin' directly for customers now,' she told him, realising that it was pointless trying to keep it a secret from him. Besides, she didn't want to bring his wrath down on Mr Ainsworth after the warehouseman had been good enough to help her.

'Who?' demanded Isaac.

'Walter Flitcroft.' She watched as Isaac tried to place the man, probably wondering if he could make some threat against him.

'Where does he live?'

'I don't know,' she replied truthfully. 'He came here. I wove him a quilt for a weddin'.'

'And who's tha weavin' for now?' asked Isaac, pointing to the bobbins.

'I'm weavin' one for myself,' she told him.

'So tha's no more customers?' He sounded satisfied and Molly was worried that he had good reason. The money she'd earned would soon run out and if there were no more commissions then she would be no better off than when Mr Ainsworth had stopped taking her work.

After Isaac had gone, Molly wondered if she'd become too optimistic. John was right when he'd said that one quilt wouldn't make her fortune and she knew that within a couple of weeks she'd be unable to pay her rent again unless she got another commission. But she found it hard not to work, and after a restless weekend she went down to the cellar on the Monday morning and set to beaming up the loom for a quilt. She knew that she couldn't make one with initials but she could weave the year into it and someone might be prepared to buy it from her.

The letter from Thomas had lifted her spirits, and despite what Isaac had told her, she held on to the belief that they would eventually find a way to be together again.

She worked with determination, thinking about the letter she'd sent. Had it reached Portsmouth? Had it been put on a ship? Was it sailing somewhere out on the seas? It would be months before it reached Thomas, she knew, but with every row that was woven she urged the ship onwards to carry it to him with all speed.

Chapter Thirty-Seven

Molly finished her latest quilt, folded it carefully and took it upstairs to put it in the chest in the back bedroom that had once held Thomas's things. The flannel shirts had been sold now and the ruined trousers she'd worn down the pit thrown away for rags. All she had left of Thomas's clothes were a few of his undergarments. Sometimes she took them out of the drawer to check that the moths hadn't got in amongst them. At first she'd held them to her face, breathing in the scent of him that lingered there, but as time passed the smell faded and she sometimes wondered if he would ever wear them again.

She'd been so happy when his letter came, but there had been no more. She worried that he might not write again. He was so far away and he might not be allowed to come back after all. That's what Isaac Crompton said, anyway. He was certain that Thomas would never return and he told her that sooner or later she would realise that he right, and that when she did, he would be waiting for her.

Molly placed the quilt carefully in the chest. She had no buyer for it yet, but she'd had two more commissions. She was earning enough to keep herself and had even bought a chair to sit by the fire in the evenings. She would have liked to get back the things of her mother's that had gone to the pawnbroker but when she went to enquire, the man said her ticket was out of date and they'd been sold long since.

She went back downstairs and opened the front door to take some water out for the vegetables she'd planted in the little garden beside the cottage. The summer sun was high in the sky and it was warm on her back as she bent to tend to her crop.

'Mama!' She looked up and saw Annie toddling towards her across the fold, followed by Ellen. She was growing so fast – a little lass now and no longer a baby, but so like her father that it made Molly's heart ache.

'Thy mam's busy,' Ellen told the child as she caught up with her.

'I'm finished for now,' said Molly. 'She can come home.'

'Who's this?' said Ellen as they saw a stranger turn into the fold and glance about. The man saw them and came over.

'I'm lookin' for a weaver by t' name o' Molly Holden,' he said.

'Aye, that's me,' Molly told him, liking the way he described her as a weaver.

'They say as tha can make quilts.'

Molly smiled at the tone of incredulity in his voice. They always sounded the same, these folk who came asking about her work. They never quite believed she was capable of producing the work their friends had shown them.

'Aye. I can weave thee a quilt,' she said. 'Or I've one for sale that's finished if tha'd prefer.'

'I wanted summat special,' said the man. 'For a baptismal gift.'

'Come on in and tell me what it is tha'd like then,' she said as Ellen nodded and took Annie by the hand to mind her for a little while longer.

The man followed her inside, obviously puzzled by the bareness of her cottage and Molly fetched a pen and paper to put down the names and dates he wanted on the quilt. She asked him for his part payment and told him to come back in two weeks. He didn't seem hesitant to part with so much money and it pleased her. She knew that it meant her reputation was growing by word of mouth, and because she dealt with someone new each time, Isaac Crompton had found it impossible to prevent her working by issuing threats.

When the man had gone, she took the two pounds and added it to her hidden savings. She had fifteen pounds now. In another year she might have thirty. Perhaps if Thomas did have to stay in New South Wales she would still be able to join him when she'd saved enough. She refused to give up hoping that she would see him again, but they were hopes that she kept to herself. She knew that Ellen and John would be upset if she hinted at leaving again. All they talked of now was Thomas coming home – and even though she'd made up her quarrel with her sister Nancy and saw her regularly, Molly knew that she too would try to dissuade her from travelling so far, alone, with a child. So for now she did her work and continued to save what she could.

–

The months passed and soon the autumn came again. The leaves on the trees turned to glorious shades of orange and fluttered down to make a carpet that crunched under

Molly's feet as she walked to the market. Every week she called at the Golden Lion, but no more letters came from Thomas.

Molly had become used to her new routine. Now that Annie was growing older, she needed more attention and she'd begun to leave her with Nancy most days, where she played happily with her little cousin Billy. Alone in the cottage, Molly worked on her loom, either weaving a quilt that had been commissioned or making a plainer one that took less time, but that she was not so sure of being paid for.

She enjoyed her work, but she had to admit to herself that she was lonely. She missed having someone about the house, especially in the evenings when Annie had been put to bed and she sat alone by the fireside. She saw Nancy every day, but there was little time to chat when her work was calling her back to her own cottage, and although Ellen and John were kind it wasn't the same as having a husband to keep her company.

At first she'd dreaded Isaac Crompton's visits on Friday evenings, but as time passed she found that she was looking forward to seeing him. He'd come to accept that he couldn't prevent her weaving and that she was capable of making her own living and needed no help from him. But he never stopped reminding her that he knew no one who had returned from New South Wales. She knew that he still hoped she would call herself a widow and agree to marry him, and although there were plenty of lasses who set their caps at him Isaac seemed only interested in her.

'Hast heard owt?' he asked when he came for the rent one dismal Friday evening. He asked the same question every week as she counted the two and six into his hand.

Molly wished that she could say aye, but she shook her head. 'How long is it now?' he asked.

'There was the letter in March,' she said.

'Seven months ago,' he reminded her, 'and there's a ship sails every three months.'

Molly had made the same calculations, and a hundred excuses as to why there'd been no replies to the letters she'd sent. 'Happen it can't be relied upon,' she said, 'comin' all that way.'

'I wouldn't be surprised if he's found someone else,' remarked Isaac as he put the rent money away.

'Thomas wouldn't do that.'

'Why not?' asked Isaac. 'Tha can't expect him to be alone for t' rest of 'is life.'

'He'll come home,' she insisted.

'He's not even written to thee,' Isaac pointed out. 'I don't know why tha's bein' so obstinate. I'll not wait for ever,' he warned her.

'Then why not marry some other lass?' she asked. 'There's plenty that'd have thee.'

'I want thee, Molly,' he told her. 'I always have. Tha knows that.'

'Aye,' she said. She knew that it was true. From the first time he'd seen her, Isaac had made it clear that he wanted her for his wife.

'Will tha think on it, Molly?' he asked.

She knew that he wouldn't go until she agreed and so she nodded her head. It seemed to satisfy him, for the time being at least, but after he'd gone Molly sat down on her chair and stared into the flames of the fire. He would wear her down, she thought. If no letter came from Thomas then he would wear her down. Even Nancy thought she should give him another chance.

'He's changed,' her sister had said. 'He's a bit older now and he's goin' up in the world. Tha could do worse.'

He'd have to agree to take Annie, thought Molly. Ellen wasn't well enough to care for her and it would break her heart to send her to Nancy permanently, even though her sister had said she would be willing to take her on. 'Tha can't keep pinin' after Thomas,' her sister said. 'He's gone. Make a life for thyself instead of strugglin'.'

It was tempting, thought Molly. Isaac had a nice house. She'd walked past it to see what it was like and it was a cut above the cottages on Hag End Fold. She'd peeped in at the window and seen the fireside chairs, the table, the cupboards and the rug on the floor.

But she would have to give up her weaving. There was no place for a loom in Isaac's house and she knew that he wouldn't allow her to work. And she enjoyed her work. It occupied her mind and she found it soothing. It was just that in the night time she felt so lonely, and as Annie grew, she craved another baby to rock in her arms.

She just wished that Thomas would write, so that she could be reassured that he hadn't forgotten her, that he hadn't found someone new, because whilst she heard nothing she couldn't quite quell the nagging voice that told her that Isaac might be right.

Chapter Thirty-Eight

'I never knew how expensive things were here,' said Thomas to Sarah as he sat at the kitchen table and added up what needed to be spent on their supplies. He was enjoying his role as steward and wanted to prove his trustworthiness and competence to Mr Allan. He knew that the man had it in his power to recommend him to the governor for an absolute pardon and he was determined to do everything he could to persuade him that he deserved it. 'Sugar at three shillings a pound and butter at seven shillings a pound.' He shook his head at the thought of it.

The cost of fabric was especially high, he'd realised. Mrs Allan had wanted some muslin for a new dress and she'd had to pay twelve shillings a yard for it. The muslin weavers back in Bolton would only have received a fraction of that for weaving such cloth.

Thomas put down his pen and took a drink from the cup of coffee that Sarah had set down beside him. 'I've had an idea,' he told her.

'I hope it's a good un,' she replied as she kneaded dough at the other end of the table.

'That length of cloth that the mistress sent for. I wouldn't be surprised if it came from somewhere in Lancashire. But it cost a lot for what it was. Somebody must be takin' a profit from it.'

'Well, it would of cost summat to send it out 'ere,' reasoned Sarah.

'Aye, but not such a mark-up as that,' said Thomas.

'So what's this big idea?' asked Sarah as she formed the dough into loaves for the oven.

'I were thinkin' of writin' home and askin' them to send me a box full of stuff that I could sell on. The profit would help pay for my passage back.'

'Tha's not still thinkin' of goin' back?' asked Sarah. He could see the disappointment in her eyes in the moment before she turned to open the oven door and a blast of heat swept across the kitchen. 'They've not even written to thee,' she reminded him. 'What makes thee think they'd go to all the trouble of sendin' out stuff?'

It was true. Three ships had been and gone and still there'd been no word. Each time one had anchored, Thomas had found an excuse to go down to the harbour to watch the passengers come ashore. Whenever he'd seen women in the boat with the free passengers his hopes had risen as he'd desperately scanned their faces, hoping to see Molly. But every time they had been other men's wives who'd clambered up onto the wharf with wide-eyed children clinging to their skirts. Sometimes he'd even seen them run into the arms of their husbands and cling to them, weeping with relief to see them again. And he'd been forced to walk away, alone, without even a letter to console him.

In his darkest moments, Thomas believed that he'd been forgotten and was tempted to take Sarah to his bed. He knew it was what she wanted, but his loyalty to Molly was too strong. She would write. He was sure of it.

'Besides,' went on Sarah, as she wiped her hands, 'don't tha think tha's getting' a bit ahead of thyself? Tha's not got thy ticket of leave yet, never mind a pardon.'

'I know, but there's no harm in making plans,' he said.

It was making plans that helped him to keep his spirits up as he worked through the day and dreamt through the night. In his dreams he was often back in Bolton, either drinking ale in the Golden Lion or working on his loom in the cellar of the cottage at Hag End Fold. Sometimes, in that moment between sleeping and waking, he thought he was in bed at home, but when he reached out for Molly and found himself alone in the room above the stables the loneliness and despair threatened to overwhelm him. It was only by thinking of ways to make it real again that he had the courage to face another day.

–

It was the middle of October when the *Somersetshire* dropped anchor in the cove. As it was a Sunday and Thomas had an hour or two to himself, he walked down to the wharf and sat on a pile of old ropes to watch the passengers come ashore. By the time he had to return to his work, he knew that Molly still hadn't come and the only hope left to him was that there might be a letter. But that would have to wait until the next morning when the collecting office opened.

The following day, as Thomas stood in the queue for the post he tried to school himself not to be disappointed if no word had come from his family.

'Mr David Allan,' he told the clerk and a bundle was pushed towards him.

'And this!' called the man as Thomas began to turn away. He recognised the postmark immediately and his mood soared. At last! A letter from home.

He wanted to open it immediately, but he was anxious about his master's letters so he tucked it inside his shirt and walked back to the Allans' house with a determined stride. He delivered the mail to Mr Allan then hurried down to the privy to read his own letter in private.

He scanned it quickly to see if there was any word about his pardon or a message to say that Molly and the child were on their way. His mood sank as quickly as it had soared. The news about both was bad. But they had written, he reminded himself. Molly had sent her love.

'Mistress is lookin for thee,' said Sarah when he went back to the kitchen. 'Tha's been gone a while. Tha's not poorly, is tha?' She looked concerned. Illness was a constant worry and people fell sick with diseases that were unheard of back in England.

'No, I'm fine,' he reassured her. 'I got a letter!' he told her.

'From thy wife?' Thomas could see she was trying not to show her disappointment. 'Is she comin'?'

'She's still tryin' to save up enough money.'

He could see that his reply pleased Sarah, although she refrained from saying what she was probably thinking – that saving so much money when Molly had no husband to support her was probably impossible. But she'd written, Thomas reminded himself. She hadn't forgotten him and she'd sent her love; *from your ever loving and affectionate wife*, she'd put. So she couldn't possibly have taken up with Isaac Crompton.

'Best go and see what t' mistress wants,' Sarah reminded him.

'Aye.' He ran a hand through his hair and straightened his shirt sleeves before he went to find Mrs Allan. He needed to keep her sweet so that he could ask her to keep reminding her husband about recommending him for an absolute pardon. A ticket of leave or a conditional pardon was no use to him, although other men and women were pleased to get them. It was only an absolute pardon that would allow him to go home.

Chapter Thirty-Nine

'What's tha doin' on Christmas Day?' Isaac asked Molly as he entered her rent payment in his ledger.

He was sitting on the chair by her hearth and she was pouring him a cup of tea. He'd been caked in snow when he'd arrived at the door and his lantern had been flickering and on the verge of going out. He'd looked so cold and wet that she'd asked him to step inside and then, because his coat had been dripping melting ice across her floor and threatening to reach the rug that she'd bought to prevent Annie catching a chill from the stone floor, she'd told him to take it off and she'd hung it near the hearth to dry.

'I'll probably be goin' over to John and Ellen's,' she said. 'And I'll go to see our Nancy in the afternoon if the weather's fit.' She glanced up as the wind blew another flurry of snow against her window and the door shook. She pulled her shawl more tightly around herself and handed him the cup.

Isaac stirred in the sugar and took a sip. 'I were wonderin' if tha'd like to visit me for thy tea,' he said.

'I thought tha would have been goin' to thy own family,' she replied, reaching for the little stool that was Annie's and crouching down in front of the flames to warm her hands.

'I am. But I'll not stay all day. My mother'll send me home wi' half a turkey and a Christmas puddin'. It'll be too much for me t' eat on my own. I'd like to share it wi' thee.' He watched her, waiting for an answer as she hesitated. 'Bring t' child an all,' he conceded after a moment.

He'd warmed towards Annie, thought Molly as she poked at the fire to encourage a blaze. Her daughter would be three years old on St Stephen's Day and had grown into a sweet little lass who seemed to have the gift of charming all those she met. If she was still up when Isaac called on Friday evenings she would bombard him with all sorts of questions about what he was doing and why. *What's rent? Why are you writing in that book? Why did you put our money in your bag?* Her questions were endless and at first Molly had shushed her, not wanting Isaac to be irritated by her, but he'd smiled and showed her the figures in the ledger and asked her if she was big enough to go to the school and learn to read.

'Say tha'll come,' went on Isaac.

'I'll think on it,' promised Molly.

She was tempted. Even though she was managing to earn enough to keep herself and Annie, it was hard work as she had to weave every hour that she could to make enough to put some aside as well. And her savings hadn't grown as fast as she'd hoped. There was always something that needed to be bought, and not all her quilts had been sold. She still had several, folded into the chest upstairs. Her dream of joining Thomas in New South Wales seemed as far off as ever and she'd heard nothing more from him.

Isaac drank down his tea. 'I'd best get on,' he said. 'I wouldn't have turned out tonight if it hadn't been for t' prospect o' seein' thee,' he told her. He handed her the empty cup and she watched as he put on his wet coat. He turned to her and reached for the gloves she was holding out, that had been warming by the fire. She thought he was going to say more, but he didn't. He'd stopped asking her outright to go to live with him, but he reminded her, now and again, that his offer was still there – and the lasses who had set their caps at him had married other men and told their friends that Isaac Crompton had eyes for no one but Molly Holden.

She opened the door for him and peeped out. It was still snowing hard.

'I hope tha gets home safe,' she said. Just for a moment she considered suggesting that he should stay, but she knew that if she did, her decision would be made for her. Folk would talk and her reputation would be ruined.

'I'll be waitin' for thee – come Christmas,' he said as he stepped out into the storm. 'Please come, Molly.'

She watched as he walked into the night and the light of his lantern disappeared as he turned the corner, out of the fold. She shut and locked the door and went back to her fireside. Perhaps she would go for her Christmas tea, she thought. It would make a change from the drudgery.

–

The snow cleared away to the east, leaving bright blue skies behind it and Christmas morning dawned sunny with a sharp frost that made the world sparkle. Molly wrapped Annie up in warm clothes and they walked across the fold to see John and Ellen. Annie was excited. It was the first Christmas that she'd understood what the holiday was about and she was looking forward to singing carols with the neighbours and then tucking into a special dinner. Molly watched her indulgently as she jumped about in the snow, leaving trails of footprints. How Thomas would have loved her, she thought.

She sometimes talked to Annie about her father and how he had been forced away to the other side of the world. She wanted the child to understand that he hadn't left them by choice, but she knew that when Annie saw other children with their fathers it made her feel different. John did his best and played with her whenever he could, and her brother-in-law William was kind to the child, but Molly had found it hard the day her daughter asked her why she didn't have a daddy like her cousin Billy did.

Ellen had made a new doll for her granddaughter and Annie hugged it in delight and insisted it sat at the table with them to eat their dinner. Afterwards, the neighbours gathered in the fold to sing and then Molly walked over to see Nancy and take the small gift of some toy soldiers that she'd bought for Billy.

The children played with them on the rug in front of the fire and as the afternoon began to cloud over, Molly wondered whether she should go straight home or accept Isaac's invitation to tea. She knew that he would be waiting for her as it approached five o' clock. She also knew that it was better to keep on the right side of Isaac Crompton. And what harm could it do? It was only for an hour or so and she could make the excuse that it looked like snow again if she didn't want to stay long.

'What's up?' asked Nancy as she saw her becoming restless.

'Isaac Crompton invited me to have some tea with him,' confessed Molly.

'Will tha go?' Nancy seemed excited at the idea.

'I don't know. I'm not sure what to do. It's not like anything could ever come of it,' she said. 'No matter what he says, I can't be wed to him, and I'll not live in sin.'

'No. But tha's heard nowt more from Thomas,' Nancy reminded her.

'It doesn't make me a widow!' she snapped at her sister. 'I'm sorry,' she added after a moment. She didn't want there to be a falling-out, especially not at Christmas. 'It's only for tea,' she added, more in an effort to convince herself than anything. 'And I'll not stay long. Annie'll be tired.'

—

Molly hesitated at Isaac's door, but he must have been watching out for her because he opened it with a huge smile and stood aside to welcome her in. The parlour was warm with a huge fire blazing. Molly guessed that Colonel Fletcher kept him well supplied with coal.

'Let me take tha coat,' he said, helping her out of it. 'Sit thee down. T' kettle's on to boil.'

Molly sat on a chair to the side of the fire. It was soft and comfortable and Isaac had brought a little stool for Annie.

'What's tha got there?' he asked the child.

'It's a new dolly, from my grandma.'

'And very nice it is too,' he said. 'I think I've a little summat for thee an all,' he told her with a conspiratorial wink. Molly watched as he took a paper bag from the table and handed it to Annie. Her daughter peeped inside and gasped in delight.

'Look!' She held out the bag towards her mother and Molly saw that it was filled with little sugar mice with string for their tails. 'Can I eat them?' she begged.

'Maybe just one, after tea,' said Molly. Annie's face crumpled in disappointment and Molly hoped that she wasn't going to cry.

'Let 'er eat one now,' advised Isaac. 'It is Christmas Day.'

'All right,' conceded Molly and watched as Isaac winked at the child again and Annie beamed and began to suck at one of the sweets.

'And what would tha like?' he asked her as Molly gazed at the bread and butter and cold meat that he had set on his table, along with cake and mince pies. It was quite a feast and he began to fill a plate for her with much more than she could ever eat.

'I'm right glad tha came,' he told her as he handed her the food. 'Tha knows I want to take care o' thee. Aye, and I'll take care o' child an all,' he agreed. 'Say nowt,' he added as Molly began to protest. 'Say nowt today, but just think on that tha could be warm and fed like this every day instead o' workin' in yon freezin' cellar from morn to night.'

Molly accepted the plate of food and only spoke to thank him. He poured tea and they sat by the fire and ate, watching Annie as she pretended to give her new dolly a taste of her sweet. It could be like this every day, thought Molly as she stretched her damp boots towards the warmth of the fire to dry them. She would have everything she needed, and maybe Nancy was right when she said that Isaac had changed.

Chapter Forty

After the new year had come and January brought more snow, Molly found herself thinking more and more about Isaac. It was icy cold down in the cellar and she had to pause in her work every few minutes to rub some warmth into her fingers. Even though she was wearing the mittens that had been Thomas's, the tips of her fingers turned white as she held the hook to make the knops on her latest quilt. And as she worked, she found herself craving the comfort of the ample fire in Isaac's cottage, his comfortable furniture and well-laid table.

But could she ever marry him? He'd told her that there was no reason not to. He'd said that by being found guilty of a crime and being sent away Thomas had deserted her, so the marriage was null and void. He'd sounded convincing, but Molly was unsure whether or not to believe him.

She knew that she couldn't ask John about it. He and Ellen would be heartbroken if she even hinted that she was thinking of not waiting for Thomas. They had convinced themselves that he would come home. But Isaac maintained that it was a one-way ticket, and Molly was beginning to think that he was right. And even if Thomas was free to come back, how would he raise the money for his passage? She'd worked all hours these past years to try to save enough to join him and it seemed impossible, so how much harder would it be for him?

What work would he be able to do that would raise thirty-five pounds?

When the cold in the cellar became too much for her to bear, she went upstairs to try to warm herself at her hearth. Whilst she was sitting, staring into the flames, Molly decided that she would go to see the Reverend Brocklehurst again to ask him. Annie was safe with Nancy for the time being, so after having a meagre bite to eat, Molly wrapped herself in her warmest clothes, and slipped out of her cottage, hoping not to be seen. She walked down to Churchgate with flurries of snow blowing in her face, some from the dark sky overhead and some from the drifts that lined the path, which was only passable where other boots had trodden a way through. The impacted snow had turned to ice and she slipped and slid much of the way, cursing herself for having been so foolish as to set off, but reluctant to turn around until she had an answer to the question that was plaguing her.

Molly found the vicar hunched over his fire in the vestry. He looked up in surprise when he saw her.

'Come to get warm,' he said, moving to one side and pulling forward the wooden chair so that it was nearer to the blaze. 'What brings you out on a day like this? Is something wrong?'

Molly lifted her shawl from her head and snowflakes fell to the floor where they melted, leaving pools of water. Her feet were wet inside her boots and her nose was dripping. She reached into her sleeve for a handkerchief to wipe it.

'I need to ask you something,' she said.

'It must be important,' he coaxed, putting aside the bible he'd been reading.

'I wanted to ask about gettin' wed again,' Molly blurted out.

'Getting married?' The vicar sounded surprised. 'Who to? I thought you were set on joining Thomas?'

'I was,' she told him. 'But he's not written again. I haven't heard from him since the letter I got last March. And Isaac Crompton says he's probably found somebody else by now. John and Ellen Holden think Thomas will come home, but Isaac says no one comes back. Do you know anyone who's come back?' she asked the vicar.

He shook his head. 'No, I don't. But I thought you were saving to go to New South Wales?'

'What if I save enough and I go all that way and he's got someone else?' she asked. 'Isaac says that they persuade convicts to marry one another so that there'll be children—'

'Is it Isaac Crompton you're wanting to marry?' interrupted the vicar. 'I thought you blamed him for Thomas being sent away?'

'I did. I do,' she admitted. 'But he's been kind to me – and he's offered me a home. He's said he'll take Annie too. And I'm beginnin' to wonder if it would be for the best.'

'What's changed your mind?' asked the vicar.

'I'm tired,' admitted Molly. 'I'm tired of workin', tired of strugglin'. And I'm still nowhere near that thirty-five pounds. I think it were always an impossible dream. If he'd written,' she said, 'if I knew he hadn't forgot me it might be different, but...' She hoped that the vicar would understand how she felt.

'It must be hard,' he sympathised. 'But you've done so well. I've heard that your quilts are good work and you haven't asked for parish relief again like so many have been forced to do.'

Molly glanced up and met his eyes. 'I'm lonely,' she admitted. 'It's been nearly three years that I've been alone.'

The Reverend Brocklehurst nodded and put his hand on hers for a moment. 'Yes,' he said. 'You're young. Too young to be alone. But it's not as if you're a widow,' he reminded her.

'So I can't get married again?' she asked.

'Not yet,' he said. 'If you were to hear nothing from your husband for seven years then you could apply to have the marriage annulled. It would count as abandonment. But as you said, it's only been three years – and if you received a letter from him in March then I'm not sure how that would change things.'

So Isaac had spun her a tale once again, she thought. She wondered what his plan had been. Maybe he'd thought some other priest, who didn't know her, would have married them without asking questions.

'I'm sorry to dash your hopes,' said the Reverend Brocklehurst. 'In time, if you hear no more, it will be possible, but not yet.' He paused. 'What will you do?' he asked. 'It would be a sin to live with a man as his wife when you know your husband lives.'

'If he lives.'

'You would surely have heard if he didn't.'

'I don't know.' Molly wiped her nose again as tears threatened to overwhelm her. 'Hannah Fisher has heard nothing of her husband. Can you be certain that word would have come if he was…?' She couldn't bring herself to say the word out loud – the word that haunted her dreams.

'I can't be certain, no,' admitted the vicar. 'But don't do anything hasty,' he advised. 'Wait a while longer.'

Molly thanked him for his kindness and left him to his reading. He was right. She was sure he was. But she knew that when she told Isaac what the vicar had said, he would persuade her that the Reverend Brocklehurst was mistaken and she wouldn't know who to believe.

She shut the heavy church door behind her and began to walk back down Churchgate, stepping into the footprints she'd made on her way up. It seemed she was the only person to have approached the building that day. Lost in thought, she didn't hear her name being called the first time.

'Molly!'

She looked up to see Uncle Richard in the doorway of the Golden Lion beckoning to her. 'A letter! There's a letter!' he called.

She made her way across to the doorway, snow spilling over the tops of her boots. She knew she should be relieved, but she couldn't brush aside the thought that it might be bad news.

'Come inside,' said Uncle Richard. 'Come to the fire. I didn't expect thee to come down today. I were goin' to send a lad up with it tomorrow if t' weather cleared.'

He handed the letter to her and she recognised Thomas's own handwriting.

The few patrons who were in the Golden Lion moved aside for her to sit down on a stool and Molly opened the letter with her numbed fingers. Something bright green floated gently down and settled on the floor. She bent to retrieve it. It was a feather, but not from any bird that she could imagine. She twisted it in her fingers for a moment, then turned her attention to the letter, not knowing what to expect.

Sydney. June 30th 1814

My Dear Wife,

I take this opportunity of writing to you, hoping to find you and my dear child in good health as this leaves me. I am very unhappy to think that you have forgot me so soon. For my part I know that I am shut up in one corner of the world, but I hope that you won't forget to write to me every three months as there is a ship sails from Portsmouth and nothing will give me more happiness than to hear from you. There is never a ship comes to this country but I goes to know whether there is any letter for me or no. And when there is no letter I think you have quite forgot me.

Let me know how the trade is and whether I can get an honest living or not. There is a strong report of me getting my pardon.

In this country things is very dear. Men's hats is two pound, two shillings and stockings ten shillings per pair, and shoes sixteen shillings per pair. Cotton prints twelve shillings per yard, velveteen one pound per yard, 40 reed muslin is twelve shillings per yard and everything accordingly. My wages is twenty pounds per year in currency — about twelve pounds in English coin.

Could you send me a few things — some of them prinilled bed covers I was making at home, some stockings, and bolts of the best cotton prints that you can get, and fine linen for shirts, the best you can get, and blue ribbon and some fine pocket handkerchiefs.

Dear Father, direct them to Mr Heath, Sherby Street, Halton Gardens, London. And please send a letter to William Heath to send them to New South Wales along with the Allan things and I shall be sure to get them safe. Put Mr Allan's name on the box and nail it down fast. Send as much as you can in goods, and sell my loom and all my clothes, and send as much as you can because it would be a great thing to have my passage to England as it is a long way for me to come home.

I have sent you a parrot feather. And so, no more from your loving husband till death, Thomas Holden.

'It's not bad news, is it?' asked Uncle Richard in a concerned voice as Molly mopped the tears from her face.

'No. He's well,' she sobbed, 'but he says he never got any of the letters I sent him.'

Molly felt so guilty. All this time she'd been thinking that Thomas had forgotten her, and he had thought she was the one who didn't care. Why hadn't her letters arrived? She'd addressed them carefully and handed them in at the post office. It made no sense.

'I'd best get home and tell John and Ellen,' she said as she put the letter and the feather carefully into her pocket and gathered her shawl.

Outside, the sky, like her hopes, had brightened and there was a hint of sunlight through the scattering clouds. Her interview with the Reverend Brocklehurst forgotten, she hurried to the fold to give the good news to Thomas's parents.

'We must get what he asks for and send it straight away!' cried Ellen. 'He might be waiting for it so he can come home. See,' she said, turning to Molly, 'I told thee he'd come back.'

'It'll cost a fair bit to get everything he asks for,' reasoned John. 'His clothes have already been sold and no one wants t' loom.'

'I'm not parting with the loom,' said Molly. 'He'll need it when it gets back.'

'Then how are we to afford all this cloth he's askin' for?'

'It's all right,' said Molly. 'I've some money set aside.'

'Set aside? I thought tha'd given up the notion of savin'?'

Molly shook her head. 'I kept on savin' a bit,' she told him. 'I've enough to fill a box – a big box,' she added, smiling.

Chapter Forty-One

Molly lifted the quilts that she'd been unable to sell out of the chest in the back bedroom and carried them downstairs to add to the box that John had asked the carpenter to make.

At first, Molly had doubted whether she could afford to fill it despite her insistence that it needed to hold plenty, but she'd taken her money from its hiding place under the floorboards in the bedroom and gone down to the warehouse to see Mr Ainsworth.

'Bobbins?' he'd asked when he saw her.

'Not today,' she'd said. 'I need cotton prints and fine linen.'

He'd stared at her as if she was mad.

'It's to send to Thomas,' she'd explained. 'To pay his way home.'

'So tha's heard from him?'

'Aye.' Molly hadn't been able to keep the smile from her face. 'He's says he's to get a pardon.'

'That is good news,' Mr Ainsworth had replied. 'I'll be right glad to see him back. I'm sure everyone will.'

Molly had nodded but she knew that not everyone would be glad to see Thomas back. Isaac Crompton wouldn't. She was sure of that.

She folded the quilts carefully and packed them into the box on top of the bolts of cotton print and linen that she and John had carried home from the warehouse. There were stockings and handkerchiefs and blue ribbon packed into all the spaces around the cloth – she'd bought as much as was available on the market at Bolton. Altogether, there was just short of twenty pounds' worth of goods apart from the quilts. Surely that would be enough to get her husband home?

'Is that it?' asked John as Molly glanced out of the window and saw the cart was backing into the fold.

'Aye. We just need to get the lid on,' she said as she leaned her weight onto the last quilt.

John fetched the lid from where it was propped up against the wall and Molly pushed in the stray corners of the quilt as he pressed it down. When everything was finally in, Molly held it firm whilst he picked up a hammer to drive in the nails.

The address was written clearly on the lid and they'd sent a letter to William Heath as Thomas had instructed to tell him to expect the box to send on to New South Wales. Molly just hoped that it would arrive safely, because she knew that things were lost, like many of the letters she'd sent, and she knew that ships disappeared at sea. There were no guarantees, but she had to believe that it would reach Thomas.

Mr Bailey, the carter, came to the door and between them he and John manoeuvred the box out and began to lift it onto the back of the cart.

''Ere! Give us a lift wi' this!' Mr Bailey called to someone and Molly was horrified to see that it was Isaac Crompton who had just come into the fold.

'What's all this?' he asked, looking from Molly to John and back. 'Is tha movin' somewhere?' he demanded.

'No, of course not,' she told him.

'Then what is it?' he asked again as he watched John and Mr Bailey struggle to lift the heavy box. 'Where's it goin'?'

'It's goin' to our Thomas,' said John when the box was eventually on the cart and Mr Bailey began to rope it down.

Isaac didn't answer John. He was staring at Molly.

'Hast tha heard from 'im? Tha never told me,' he accused her.

'I've not seen thee since. He said he's to get his pardon.'

'What's tha sendin' 'im?'

'It's cloth for him to sell, to raise his passage home.'

Isaac stared at the box on the cart. 'Is that what 'e told thee?' he asked after a moment, with a sneer in his voice. 'I'd say as tha's wasted thy money on it.'

'It's not wasted!' she told him, feeling her anger rise. 'Thomas says as prices are high in New South Wales. He can turn a profit.'

'Aye. 'E'll turn a profit,' said Isaac. 'But how does tha know 'e'll spend it on comin' back 'ere? Why would he do that when trade's as bad as it is? And from what I've heard men are doin' well out there. Tha's a fool, Molly,' he told her. 'Thomas'll not come back. He'll use thy money to buy himself a farm or summat. That's what men are doin'.'

'He'll come home all right,' interrupted John. 'He should never have been sent away in t' first place,' he added, glaring at Isaac. 'Perhaps it's time tha stopped pesterin' our Molly,' he told him. 'She's a married woman.'

Isaac grew a dangerous shade of puce as he squared up to John and Molly was afraid that he would start a fight. She doubted that her father-in-law would land as lucky a punch as her husband had so she stepped between them, her arms outstretched to keep them apart.

'John's right,' she told Isaac. 'I can't see thee again, not now that I've heard from Thomas. And he is comin' home. I'm grateful for any help tha's given me,' she added in an effort to calm him, 'but John's right. I'm Thomas's wife.'

Isaac balled his hands into fists and then let them relax. He stared at her and she was terrified by the hatred that she saw there.

'Well, don't think tha can come cryin' to me when it all goes wrong!' he shouted at her. 'I've done my best for thee. Tha knows I 'ave. And this is all t' thanks I get? To be tossed aside again as soon as Thomas Holden whistles for thee! He'll not come back!' he repeated, glaring at both her and John. He spat on the floor. 'Tha's not worth t' trouble,' he muttered. 'But don't say as I didn't warn thee.'

He stalked away from them and Molly found that she was trembling with emotion.

'Let's go in out o' the cold,' said John as Mr Bailey climbed up into his seat and picked up the reins.

Molly was still shaking when she sat down in the chair by the fire. 'I hope he doesn't come back,' she said, glancing anxiously towards the window for any sign of Isaac.

'He'll not come back,' John reassured her. 'Tha's set 'im straight now. I didn't know he were still botherin' thee,' he added.

'He's never stopped botherin' me,' she admitted, wishing now that she'd never encouraged him. She'd thought that Thomas would never write again, and now she felt guilty for having doubted her husband and for nearly giving in to Isaac. She hoped he would stay away now, but what he'd said had sowed a doubt – a doubt that she knew she mustn't allow to grow. Because she knew that she'd never be truly free from him until Thomas was safely home. And there was so much that could go wrong.

–

After John had gone, Molly swept the floor in the parlour and tidied the back bedroom. Thomas would need new clothes when he came home, she thought and she regretted sending all the linen. She should have kept some back to sew him a couple of shirts. Still, she thought, there would be time to buy more. The box would take six months to reach him. Then he would have to sell the contents, and then six months to come home. Time seemed to stretch before her in an endless uncertainty and she worried that Isaac would continue to pester her once his temper had died down.

She dreaded the coming Friday when he would call for the rent money. She didn't want to face him and she tried to rehearse the words she would say to him, not sure whether he would be angry or persuasive. Neither would be easy to resist.

She left Annie with Nancy on the Friday afternoon, asking if she could stay overnight.

'I don't want her to be in the cottage if there's to be a scene,' she told her sister.

'Well, tha can hardly blame Isaac,' her sister reminded her. 'Tha's been leadin' him on all these months – practically agreein' to be wed to him in time. He's bound to be upset when tha suddenly changes thy mind again.'

Molly didn't reply. Her sister seemed to have been charmed by Isaac lately. It was a pity she couldn't marry him herself, thought Molly. She almost said as much but she held her tongue. It would only make matters worse if she fell out with her sister again.

Back in her own home, Molly put a florin and sixpence on the side of the hearth so that she could pick them up quickly and have the money to pay Isaac at the door. She wouldn't let him come in, she'd decided. If he wanted to shout at her, he'd have to do it on the doorstep where everyone could hear him.

She fidgeted about, sitting down and then standing up and peeping out of the window to see if she could see him coming. Time seemed to move slowly and still there was no sign of him. Perhaps he wouldn't come at all? She was clinging to that hope when she heard footsteps approaching. Her heart began to race. She picked up the money and hesitated behind the door, waiting for his knock.

Even though she was expecting it, the rap on the door made her jump when it came and she took a deep breath to steady herself before she lifted the latch and cautiously opened it.

'Rent,' said the man who was standing on her step.

Molly stared at him. She didn't know him. He was young, dressed in a dark coat and a cap.

'Rent money,' he repeated. He studied the ledger in his hand. 'Two and six,' he added.

Molly gave him the money and watched as he made the entry. 'Where's Mr Crompton tonight?' she asked.

The man shrugged. 'I don't know,' he told her. 'Everyone keeps askin' me. All I know is Mr Fletcher set me on to rent collectin' a couple of days ago.'

He put the money in his bag, touched his cap and said good evening. Molly watched as he went across to John and Ellen's house and then she shut the door. She'd been reprieved, for now at least.

—

'Hast tha heard about Isaac Crompton?' Mr Ainsworth couldn't keep the grin from his face when she went down to the warehouse for bobbins a few days later.

'I know he didn't come for the rent money on Friday,' she said, wondering what had happened to make Mr Ainsworth look so pleased.

'He's been arrested!'

'What? Isaac has?' Molly felt bewildered by the revelation. 'What for?'

'Fiddlin' t' books apparently. That's what I heard, at any rate. Seems he's been takin' advantage of his rent-collectin' duties to help himself to a few bob. Old Fletcher's apoplectic by all accounts.' Mr Ainsworth laughed again. 'Folk say Fletcher only has himself to blame. That's what happens when tha puts thy trust in a crook.' He passed Molly the bobbins she'd asked for. 'I thought tha would have known,' he said.

'No.' She shook her head. 'I had no idea.'

'I hope tha's not upset,' said Mr Ainsworth, his face suddenly serious. 'I know tha'd got a bit friendly with him, despite t' trouble he'd caused.'

'He kept pesterin' me,' she replied.

'Aye, well, he'll not pester thee no more,' said Mr Ainsworth with satisfaction as Molly paid him. He hesitated again. 'I might be in a position to start buyin' from thee again now,' he told her. 'If tha's time to do a quilt or so between t' commissions...'

He seemed slightly embarrassed. And with good reason, thought Molly. It was plain that it had only been his fear of Isaac that had stopped him buying from her in the first place. Still, she thought, a sale was a sale and she was in no position to turn him down. With all her savings gone on the cloth for Thomas, she needed to start putting some money on one side again. The cottage needed putting to rights. She didn't want Thomas coming back to an empty home.

'What'll happen to him? To Isaac?' she asked.

Mr Ainsworth shrugged. 'A spell in t' prison if he's lucky. But I wouldn't be surprised if Colonel Fletcher gets him transported.'

As she walked home, Molly thought about what she'd been told. She hoped Isaac would be sent as a convict. It would serve him right. But she'd had a lucky escape, she mused. All the comfort of the home that he'd offered her – the cushioned chairs, the polished table and the roaring fire – had all been paid for with stolen money. If she'd agreed to be married to him, she would have probably lost it all. And she'd have been no better off than when she started – a convict's wife.

Chapter Forty-Two

'Mr Holden!' said the master as he caught sight of Thomas coming in from the yard where he'd been checking the stores. 'A word, if you please.'

Thomas followed Mr Allan inside, hoping that the summons didn't mean more trouble. There'd been a misunderstanding over a bottle of rum a few weeks before and he'd spent two nights in a prison cell before a court had cleared him of any wrongdoing. The experience had disappointed Thomas. He'd worked hard for the Allans and always been honest. The sudden accusation had shocked and surprised him – and disappointed him too because he'd thought they had some respect for him. And now, as Mr Allan waved him into his study, Thomas couldn't help but feel a frisson of fear that he'd come up with another accusation.

'I have some good news for you,' said Mr Allan. He held up an official-looking paper. 'It's relating to your petition. You're to receive an absolute pardon on the first Monday of next month. You'll be free to go anywhere you choose. I'll be sorry to let you go,' he went on. Then he paused. 'You could stay of course – as an employee.'

'Thank you for the offer, sir,' said Thomas, 'but I'd thought to seek more lucrative employment elsewhere.'

'Farming?'

'No. I just need to earn some money so that I can go home.'

Mr Allan frowned. 'So you're still determined to go back to England? There are good opportunities here,' he added, 'and trade is not that good at home.'

'I'm still determined,' Thomas told him. 'I need to get back to my wife and child.'

'Why not send them the fare to join you?'

Thomas shook his head. 'No, sir,' he said. 'Once I have the money I'll be on my way.'

'A pity,' remarked Mr Allan. 'New South Wales needs young men. And I thought that you and Sarah…?'

'We're friends. That's all,' Thomas told him.

Mr Allan nodded. 'I'll be sorry to lose you,' he said and then turned to his other letters, dismissing Thomas with a gesture of his hand.

Mrs Allan was outside as he gently closed the door. She looked worried.

'Is everything all right, Thomas?' she asked.

'Aye.' He smiled. 'I'm to get an absolute pardon,' he told her. 'I'm grateful if you had a hand in it.'

She didn't reply and he could see from the disappointed look on her face that she had known nothing of it and that it wasn't what she'd hoped for. A dismal thought struck him and he wondered if it had been Mrs Allan who had concocted the story about the rum being stolen in an attempt to keep him from going away.

'I'll miss you,' she said, putting her hand on his arm.

He nodded and moved away from her. He knew that she wanted him to say he'd miss her too, but he knew the words would choke him if he tried. They wouldn't be true. He would be glad to get away from her and not be compelled to give in to her every whim and demand.

'Excuse me. I've to get on,' he muttered.

–

The following day, word came that the *Alexander* had dropped anchor. Thomas told one of the boys to hitch up a horse to the cart and they went down to the quayside to collect the boxes of supplies for the Allans. It was a chilly morning and the weather was growing colder. The winter would soon begin and it still seemed odd to Thomas because he thought of June and July as being summer months. But here everything was topsy-turvy.

He watched as the cargo was hauled ashore, looking for the boxes that were directed for Mr Allan so that they could be loaded onto the cart to carry them up the house. It was a year since he'd sent the letter home asking for goods to sell and although he was hoping that his family had received the letter and responded, he was preparing himself for disappointment.

It wasn't until the box that had been marked *from Bolton* was open that he allowed himself to feel pleasure. It had been well nailed down. He'd struggled to lever the lid free, and it wasn't until the wood split with a crack that the nails came loose and he was able to lift it off. He caught the familiar scent of his home – cotton. He breathed it in with his eyes closed, trying to picture the parlour at Hag End Fold in his mind's eye. The image was hazy but the aromas of cotton and grease, tallow and coal were vivid.

He lifted the top quilt out and allowed it to unfold. It was good work, he thought, as he examined it, wondering if it had been woven by his father.

'That's bonny,' said Sarah coming up behind him. She reached out to feel it. 'It'll fetch a good price at market.'

She watched as Thomas lifted out the other goods, exclaiming in delight at the patterned cloth and the ribbons. There was more than Thomas had hoped for. He was sure that the sale of it would provide him with the money he needed.

'Tha could raise a gradely homestead on some land wi' t' money from this lot,' observed Sarah.

'I'm goin' home,' he told her. He'd told her often enough but he knew that she'd never really believed him before. She'd always thought it was a dream of his and that he'd change his mind when he received his pardon and was offered a parcel of land to farm. He knew that she clung to the hope that he'd eventually ask her to be his wife.

'Convicts can wed again after seven years,' she'd told him and he'd seen the desire in her eyes.

Feeling guilty, Thomas held out a pair of stockings. 'These are for thee,' he told Sarah. 'But don't go gettin' any ideas,' he added. 'Tha knows tha's been a good friend to me, but I'm a married man and it can never be more than that.'

Sarah took the stockings and ran them through her fingers.

'Don't look so sad,' Thomas told her. 'I can't go yet. But I will go.'

She turned away from him and he felt guilty that he'd made her weep, but it could never be. He was certain now that Molly wanted him home. She would never have sent the box otherwise and its contents must have cost her dearly.

He must write and thank her, he thought. He could send a letter on the *Alexander*, on its return journey. And next time a ship came, it would be the one that would take him home.

Chapter Forty-Three

The letter from Thomas had arrived as Christmas was approaching once again.

Sydney, New South Wales. May 30th 1815

I take this opportunity by the ship Alexander with pleasure to inform you that Mr Allan has procured a promise from the Governor of Emancipation for me which I am to receive the first Monday of next month. I expect to leave Mr Allan in hopes of getting into some more lucrative employment and in time I will have the inexpressible happiness of being with you once more.

From your loving husband, Thomas Holden.

It was the best Christmas gift that Molly could have asked for, apart from him being there with her, but she hoped that by the time the next Christmas came around they would be together again.

Although she had no idea how long it would take him to come home, once six months had passed and the summer nights were drawing in, Molly began to light a candle in the window in the evenings. She had no idea what time Thomas would arrive, but she thought that it would be late and he would be gladdened by the sight of the candle in his window, guiding him back, as it should have guided him home all those years ago when he went to the meeting on the moor.

'Is that for my daddy?' asked Annie as she watched Molly set the candle on the sill as usual.

'Aye. It's to bring him home to us,' said Molly. 'He'll be here soon.' What would he think of his daughter? She wondered. Would he even recognise her? The baby he'd nursed on his shoulder was long gone and now a pretty little lass with a halo of dark curls stood in the parlour and watched out for the return of a man she didn't remember.

–

Thomas hurried out onto the deck of the ship when he heard the cry.

'England!' grinned one of the sailors and sure enough, Thomas could make out the swell of land in the distance. 'We'll reach the channel afore sundown and the pilot'll come aboard to guide us in,' the man told him.

Thomas could only nod. He didn't want to cry in front of the sailor but he couldn't prevent the tears of pleasure and relief that he felt. He was home in his own country and before long, he would hold his family in his arms again. He ached for them. It had been so long, and so many times he had lost hope, but now it was within his grasp.

When Thomas stepped down from the coach on Churchgate he felt as if he'd just woken from a dream. Everything looked the same as the images he'd cherished in his memory over the years. He glanced across to the Golden Lion. The door was open and he was tempted to go in, but his desire to get home was greater and, with his bag in his hand, he took the road towards Hag End Fold with eager steps.

Molly had just lit the candle and placed it on the sill when she saw a figure turn the corner into the fold. The man, with a bag grasped in his hand, seemed familiar as he walked towards the cottage.

'Thomas?' She spoke quietly, to herself, questioning her senses. Then she cried it louder. 'Thomas!' She wrenched open the door and began to run towards him.

'Molly!' He dropped the bag and when she reached him, his arms closed around her in a fierce embrace. He felt solid. He was real.

'Tha's home,' she sobbed as she clung to him.

'Aye, I'm home,' he said as the doors began to open and his parents and friends and neighbours all came running out to welcome him. 'And I promise as nowt'll ever part me from thee again.'

Author's Note

The idea for *The Convict's Wife* originated in the question – what happened to the wives of the men who were transported to New South Wales? At the time I wasn't entirely sure, but when my research uncovered the story of the convict Thomas Holden, from Bolton and the letters he exchanged with his family, I knew here was a story that I wanted to tell.

Thomas Holden was a real person. He was convicted at the Lancaster Assizes on 1st June 1812 for swearing an illegal oath, found guilty on the evidence of a man named Isaac Crompton. It's probable that Crompton was a spy, but nothing more is known about him and his relationship with Thomas's wife is entirely invented by me.

Many of the letters that Thomas wrote to his family have survived and are currently held in the Lancashire Record Office at Preston. They reveal the thoughts of a frightened young man, worried that he will never see his family again, and at times they reduced me to tears as I read them for the first time. I decided to use as many of Thomas's own words as I could to tell this story and although the letters have been edited for clarity and continuity, I've tried to keep them as authentic as possible. However, one letter is entirely fictional. I wonder if you can guess which one?

There were other letters and a diary that Thomas Holden kept, but these are missing, although a booklet that came into my possession, *The Letters of a Lancashire Luddite Transported to Australia* by V.I. Tomlinson, records a few extracts from them, including a diary entry for 16th February 1818, which reads: *We made the land of ould Ingland, and the pilot came hon board and told that we was hofe the coust of Plimoth and he nou pilotous hop to the chanel.* How happy Thomas must have been to see England again!

Thomas Holden came home to Lancashire and was reunited with his family. The census of 1841 shows Thomas Holden and his wife Mary living at Hag End Fold. He is 50 years old and a cotton weaver. Also living with them are four more children: Ellen 21, John 19, Thomas 14, and Margaret 8. I wonder what stories he told them about his years in New South Wales?

Such a homecoming was unusual. Most men and women sent as convicts never came back. After completing part of their sentence, most convicts received a ticket of leave. This was similar to parole. A ticket of leave allowed a convict to work for themselves provided they remained in a specified area, reported regularly to the authorities and attended church every Sunday. They were not allowed to leave the colony. After their sentence was completed they were issued with a certificate of freedom, which meant they could go anywhere, including back to their home, although they were required to pay their own way. Those who received a life sentence could receive a conditional pardon. This allowed them the freedom of the colony, but they were not at liberty to return home. An absolute pardon allowed a convict to leave before the end of their original sentence, but didn't solve the problem of paying their fare home. In Thomas's case, his request for goods to be sent so that he could sell them seems to be the method he used to raise the money.

Some of the other characters in the story are also based on real people. One of these is John Fisher, or Jack as I've called him to prevent confusion with Thomas's father. I will go on to tell the story of his wife, Hannah, in the next book in the series.

Caddow Quilts

Caddow quilts are a speciality of the Bolton area. They are cotton quilts that were produced on a broadloom with raised 'knops' on the weft thread to create a pattern. After the mechanisation of weaving they continued to be made by hand and were often woven to commemorate events such as marriages.

Wakes Holiday

The Wakes holiday that is mentioned in the book is a northern tradition that has its roots in the celebration of the saints day of the local church. It's also linked to rushbearing as this was often the day that the old rushes were swept up from the floor of the church and fresh ones put down. It also heralded the arrival of a fair. In most towns by the 19th century it was simply a local holiday that lasted for a week or two, and when mill owners found that none of their workers turned up they simply shut down production. The Wakes Weeks continued until quite recently. Each town had its own dates and here in Blackburn it began on the third Saturday in July when the schools broke up, all the shops closed and everyone went on holiday, usually catching the train to Blackpool!

Acknowledgements

Thanks to my editor, Emily Bedford, and all the team at Canelo for their enthusiastic input whilst bringing this first book in my new series to publication. You've been a pleasure to work with.

Also, huge thanks to my agent, Felicity Trew, and everyone at the Caroline Sheldon Literary Agency, for all the support, advice and hard work.